Not the least of Crane's worries were a drunken bull-dog, a stolen corpse, and a taxi dancer.

"Crammed full of the most disconcerting performances ever assembled in less than 300 pages."

— Mortimer Quick
Chicago Daily Tribune
1936

"Latimer's masterpiece...as funny and bizarre as a Marx Brothers comedy and...a cleverly contrived mystery at the same time."

— Robert A. Baker & Michael T. Neitzel
Private Eyes: 101 Knights
1985

"Moves like a body snatcher berserk upon a skateboard."

— William Ruehlmann
from his new introduction

JONATHAN LATIMER

THE LADY IN
THE MORGUE

INTERNATIONAL POLYGONICS, LTD.
NEW YORK CITY

*This story is fiction,
and the characters and incidents have no relation to actual facts.
Any similarity of name or circumstance is purely coincidental.*

THE LADY IN THE MORGUE

Copyright © 1936 by Jonathan Latimer, renewed 1964.
Cover: Copyright © 1988 by International Polygonics, Ltd.
Library of Congress Card Catalog No. 88-80760
ISBN 0-930330-79-X

Printed and manufactured in the United States of America
First IPL printing May 1988.
10 9 8 7 6 5 4 3 2 1

INTRODUCTION

Screwball.

It's a term best applied to those antic, side-of-the-mouth, quintessentially American motion pictures of the Depression era and after that blew one big, lubricious, democratic razzberry at conventional behavior. With civilized society at home and abroad coming spectacularly and emphatically apart, only two responses seemed remotely appropriate — laughter or tears; and the sassier cinematic artists, refusing to cry in their beer, dropped an egg in it instead. Director Howard Hawks comes immediately to mind, with insouciant offerings like *Twentieth Century* (1934) and *Bringing Up Baby* (1938), fast, flip and steeped in sexual innuendo.

So does writer Dashiell Hammett, whose 1934 detective novel *The Thin Man* became pretext for a scapegrace series of five screen exploits through 1947 of cocktail-bibbing Nick and Nora Charles, whom audiences pronounced outrageous but their creator deemed only smug.

And, perhaps less instantly though every bit as visibly, former journalist Jonathan Latimer (1906–1983), whose tongue remained at once tough-tart and poked firmly in his cheek, not only in bestselling hard and paperback murder tales but a number of slick screenplays as well, one of which became the top treatment of Hammett's *The Glass Key* with Alan Ladd in 1942.

Screwball.

That's Latimer's hand in *Topper Returns*, the Roland Young–Joan Blondell 1941 romp featuring disappearing bodies, cops locked in an ice box and an assortment of secret passages. At one juncture, after a stabbing, a shooting and the dropping of hapless Eddie "Rochester" Anderson through a trap door into the subterranean soup, Topper thinks to use the telephone for assistance. The cord, of course, has been cut.

Young: "This thing is dead."

Blondell: "It's epidemic!"

Latimer had nothing to do with the shooting script for his own *The Lady in the Morgue,* which by consequence became a routine programmer for Preston Foster in 1938. But, with others, he did write lively action and dialogue for crisp features like *Nocturne* (1946) with George Raft, *The Big Clock* (1947) with Charles Laughton and *Alias Nick Beal* (1949) with Ray Milland. Notes critic Leonard Maltin of Latimer's 1939 *Lone Wolf Spy Hunt* with Warren William, Ida Lupino and Rita Hayworth: "an excellent, chic, entertaining film by any standards."

Which is to say that funny as he was, the inventor of hard-boiled and half-boiled private eye Bill Crane was a steady professional with a pervasive, film-influence emphasis on patter and pace. He may not have taken his subjects seriously, sniping away persistently at starlets, police officers and the fourth estate, but Latimer was quite serious about his craft. Not, one can safely add, about himself.

He clearly was responsible for the authorial jacket blurb that appeared beneath his squinty, cigarette-sucking photo on *Black is the Fashion for Dying* (Random House, 1959). This reads: "Jonathan Latimer was born in Chicago, the setting for his early successful novels. He now lives in California, where he writes movies and an occasional brilliant novel."

Screwball.

The author graduated from Knox College, Galesburg, Ill., magna cum laude and Phi Beta Kappa. His first job was with the City News Bureau as a police reporter for the Chicago *Herald-Examiner* in 1929, where he remained until 1935. He dude-ranched in Montana, did movie stunt work and provided publicity for former Secretary of the Interior Harold Ickes, moving on to screenwriting at Paramount and Metro-Goldwyn-Mayer.

During World War II Latimer was executive officer on a destroyer escort doing convoy duty in the Atlantic.

He had two marriages, one daughter and two sons. From 1960 to 1965 Latimer wrote for the *Perry Mason* television series, adapting 50 of Erle Stanley Gardner's books for the show and providing 45 original scripts of his own. He died of lung cancer June 23, 1983, in La Jolla, California.

Latimer's mystery fiction begins black and darkens. *Murder in the Madhouse* (1934) starts in an asylum, *Headed for a Hearse* (1935) in a death-house cell and *The Lady in the Morgue* (1936) in the Cook County slabworks, punctuated by the laughter of an insane woman in the nearby Psychopathic Hospital. The protagonist of these high-spirited grotesques (and star of two subsequent, *The Dead Don't Care* and *Red Gardenias*) is New York agency operative William Crane, who likes women and whiskey and whiskey, and not necessarily in that order. Latimer quotes his hero: " 'Never drink when I'm on a job,' he lied..."

Morgue moves like a body snatcher berserk upon a skateboard. In and out, over and down the dance hall dives, penthouses and even creaky-door crypts of Depression Chicago heat stalks Crane, customarily oiled, and gum-shoe cohorts Doc Williams and Tom O'Malley, wrapped in the sound of Louis Armstrong and the scent of Guerlain's Shalimar. The book is very much of a place and time. At moments, Latimer's blinkless regard captures photographic scraps of the past, as in this tight snapshot of the contents to a murdered girl's medicine chest:

> Tall silver-labeled jars stood next to squat white jars; three
> Dr. West toothbrushes were sprouting from a red, flower-
> potlike container; a round cardboard box was half-filled
> with pale orange dusting powder; loose platinum-shaded
> Hump hairpins were scattered along one shelf; on another
> lay a tube of Ipana toothpase, a metal-sheathed lipstick . . .

Pages from a curling and discarded calendar. Too, the lens can move, recording without comment. Witness this Gatsbyesque party vignette:

> A girl was dancing on the terrace in an orange-colored
> chemise. Somebody was smashing crockery in the kitchen.
> Two men were being dissuaded from fighting. A baby-faced
> blonde borrowed a dollar from Crane for cab fare home. A
> couple were necking on one of the davenports. Three men
> were bitterly arguing politics on the other.
>
> A man in shirt sleeves asked O'Malley if he was having
> a good time.
>
> O'Malley asked him what the hell business it was of
> his . . .

In these segments, some of the laughter stops. But it is never very far away, nor is there much opportunity to muse over matters of heavy import. O'Malley has occasion to recap the breakneck progress of the cockeyed threesome three-quarters of the way through the book. He grumps:

> "In two days we start a fight in a taxi-dance joint, find a
> murdered guy and don't tell the police, crash in on Braymer
> and his dope mob, bust in on a party, kidnap a gal and rob
> a graveyard."

And we haven't even made off with the dead woman's restless remains — yet.

Private eye fiction has traditionally been the literature of exhaustion as readers follow a succession of sleepless knights to their undaunted if fagged-out finishes. Latimer has his fun with this convention. Crane, whom we first encounter flat on his back on morgue bench, head pillowed by a folded flannel coat, spends a good deal of his time prone or comatose, even to ending up under an operating table in Chapter 22; between these bookend respites are sundry other snoozes, a session in the sack, an interview on a davenport, and assorted interludes upon the leather seat of a Packard, a bathtub and a rolling morgue gurney.

It's all that exertion, of course.

Or perhaps the consequence of a relentless inbibition of scotches and soda, single and double martinis, champagne, Planter's punch, Seagram's V.O., stout, Mumm's, Martell's, Bushmill's, Gilbey's, Liebfraumilch, Bass ale and Pilsner.

Crane does disdain the formaldehyde, however.

Too stiff.

William Ruehlmann
Norfolk, Virginia
September, 1987

William Ruehlmann, Ph.D., is an award-winning feature writer for *The Virginian-Pilot* and *The Ledger-Star* and author of *Saint with a Gun: The Unlawful American Private Eye*.

Chapter One

THE MORGUE attendant jerked the receiver from the telephone, choked off the bell in the middle of a jangling ring. "Hello," he said. Then impatiently: "Hello! Hello! Hello!" Wan electric light, escaping like Holstein cream from a green-shaded student desk lamp, made the sweat glisten on his lemon-yellow face. His lips, against the telephone mouthpiece, twitched. "You want Daisy? Daisy! Daisy who?"

Elbows leaning hard on the golden-oak rail dividing the morgue office from the waiting room, two newspaper reporters idly stared at the attendant's white coat. Their shirts were open at the collar; their arms were bare; their ties, knots loosened, hung limply around their necks; their faces were moist in the heat. On the wall beside them a clock with a cracked glass indicated it was seventeen minutes of three.

"Oh, y' want Miss Daisy Stiff," said the morgue attendant. "She told ya to call her here, did she?" He screwed up one eye at the others. "Well, she can't come to the phone. She's downstairs with th' other girls."

Ballooning dingy curtains, waves of hot night air rolled in through the west windows, rasped the reporters' faces, made their lungs hurt.

The morgue attendant said, "I don't care if y' did have a date with her; she can't come to the phone." He chuckled harshly. "She's stretched out."

The reporter from the *Herald and Examiner* was named Herbert Greening; he was twenty-two years old and he still thought newspaper work fascinating. He was pudgy and when he laughed his plum-purple cheeks quivered.

The morgue attendant held a palm over the telephone mouthpiece. "He says he's worried because some dame he met last night didn't show up for a midnight date." His laughter ended in a fit of coughing. He put his lips to the instrument. "Buddy, do ya' know who you're talking to?" He coughed again, spat blood-streaked rheum on the marble floor. "This is the Cook County Morgue, and if your Daisy's here you'll hafta come down an' get her." He flipped the receiver onto the hook.

Fat Reporter Greening was trembling all over now in mirth. "I'd like to see that guy's face," he said between gasps. "Yes, sir, I'd like to see it." His hand plopped against the golden-oak rail.

The morgue attendant swung back in his swivel chair, smiled dourly. "I bet I get twenty calls like that a day." Coughing made his face drip with sweat. "The gals trim some sucker, then give him this number to call 'em. Tell him t' ask for Joan Stiff, or Daisy Still or somethin' like that. We keep changin' the number, but it don't seem to do no good."

The reporter from the *City Press* was named Jerry Johnson. His face had an unhealthy pallor; his black eyes were set deep in discolored sockets; he was drinking himself to death as fast as he could on a salary of twenty-six dollars a week. He said: "Aw, you wanta keep all them babes down there for yourself." He lifted his elbows from the oak rail, straightened his back, balanced himself with difficulty, as though the floor were pitching under his feet.

"I'm a married man, and I don't like your accusations, Mister Johnson," said the morgue attendant with pretended indignation. "You know I wouldn't touch one of 'em except in the way of business."

Johnson said, "Not much, you wouldn't." He faced Greening. "That's what the coroner says, too. But I notice he finds some business down here every time they get hold of a pretty girl's body."

The attendant giggled. Mister Johnson was right. Mister Johnson certainly knew the chief. "She don't even have to be especially pretty," he added.

Greening watched them with circular blue eyes. His mouth had dropped open and he was breathing through it.

"It's a wonder he hasn't been down to see that little honey they brought in this afternoon," said Johnson. "She must have had plenty on the ball."

"Plenty!" The attendant rubbed the back of his hand across his face. "She's the best I seen since that nightclub singer was carved up by her Mexican boy friend." He wiped the sweat from his hand to his white coat. "I don't understand why nobody has been able to identify her."

The curtains ballooned again in the hot air. In the distance a woman began to utter clear, high-pitched peals of mirthless laughter, unhysterical and unhurried, like one of those laughing phonograph records, except in her case there was not even an intent to be funny. She laughed, caught her breath in gasps, laughed again.

The morgue attendant paid no attention to the noise. "They carried a front-page story about her in every paper in town," he continued. "You'd think somebody that knew her would have seen it."

"Lots of times, when they commit suicide, they go as far away from home as they can," said Johnson. "They don't want to disgrace their families."

Greening pursed his thick lips. "That's probably what she did. My editor says that Alice Ross is an assumed name. Too short. That's why he wants me to get the name of everybody who asks to see her. Maybe we can trace her that way, he says, even if somebody who knows her decides not to identify her."

"Editors always tell you that," said Johnson.

The attendant said, "It's goddamn funny, anyway. That girl had class, yet she was living in that honky-tonk hotel."

"Maybe she was trying to hide herself," said Johnson. He pulled an unlabeled pint whiskey bottle half filled with pearl-cloudy liquid from his hip pocket. "Maybe she was going to have a baby or something."

Eyes on the bottle, the attendant said, "When they posted the body they found she didn't have no baby."

Johnson uncorked the bottle, wiped the mouth on the seat of his blue serge pants and drank, ignoring the attendant.

"She was broke and couldn't get a job," said Greening. "They only found four dollars in her room."

The woman was laughing again, louder this time and higher-pitched and jangling, as though she were being tortured by having her feet tickled. The sound was off key and chalk-on-blackboard shrill.

A man's head appeared above the back of a bench at the rear of the morgue office. "Holy Kar-rist!" he said. "What in hell's that?" His name was William Crane, and he was a private detective; he had been sleeping on the bench for three hours, his gray flannel coat under his head.

The morgue attendant said over his shoulder, "It's a crazy dame in the psychopathic hospital. She's been there three days and she laughs all the time. They gotta dope her up to keep her quiet."

Johnson supplemented, "They pulled her out of a Wilson Avenue cat house."

Crane sat up on the bench. "I wish they'd slip her a shot," he said. His shirt, where he had been lying on it, clung to his chest, and his regimental striped tie was twisted around so that it hung over his back. "She gives me the creeps." His face was clear-skinned and young and tan: he rubbed his eyes vigorously. He looked about thirty, and was thirty-four.

Sliding over the rail dividing the office from the waiting room, Johnson offered Crane the bottle. Crane accepted it with interest, lifted it to the light, smelled it, then quickly handed it back. "Never drink when I'm on a job," he lied, and asked, "What's in it, any-way?"

"Alky and water. I don't fool around with sissy drinks like whiskey and gin."

Crane pursed his mouth, blew air softly through it.

Greening joined them. "Are you the detective who broke the Westland case?" he asked. His stare was curious, unoffensive.

Johnson said, "This is Greening of the *Herald-Examiner*. He relieved the fellow who was here when you came." He put the bottle back in his hip pocket. "His uncle's an attorney for Hearst."

"An attorney for Hearst," repeated Crane, impressed. "That's pretty important."

"My uncle didn't have anything to do with my getting this job," Greening said to Johnson, "And anyway, what if he did?"

"Nothing. Nothing at all."

The clock with the cracked face struck three times.

Crane said, "I've been asleep since twelve."

The morgue attendant said, "And how! I was just getting ready to move you downstairs to the cold-storage room."

"I read all about the Westland mystery in the papers," said Greening. "What do you attribute your breaking the case to?"

Crane said, "I ate two heaping dishes of Post Toasties for breakfast every morning."

Johnson said, "I'd a hell of a lot rather be in that cold-storage room downstairs than up here. It must be ninety."

The attendant looked at a table thermometer set in ivory-painted celluloid. "It's ninety-one."

"Why don't they cool the whole morgue, instead of just the down-stairs?" Crane asked.

"The stiffs stink," said Johnson; "while we just suffer without doing anything objectionable."

"It stinks up here," said the attendant; "with the wind coming right over the stockyards."

The madwoman was laughing again.

"I've got an idea," said Johnson. "It's a game I used to play when I was first on this West beat."

Crane said, "Anything to keep from hearing that dame."

"But how did you find the pistol in the Westland case?" Greening persisted. He edged around in front of Crane, peered into his face. "The papers said you did it with a stop watch."

Crane said, "A little bird told me."

"The idea is this," said Johnson. "We go down into the vaults where they keep the stiffs and start at one end. One guy takes white

14

men, one takes buck niggers, and the other gets both white and black women. There's a dime on each vault. That is, if Crane here had the white men, and it was a white man, the other two would owe him a dime. Sort of like golf syndicates."

"I'll take women," said Crane. "I like women."

The attendant flicked the sweat off his yellow forehead. "I remember that game. I lost plenty of dimes at it."

"Yeah," said Johnson indignantly. "You did until you went and shifted all the bodies around one night and won every syndicate."

The attendant giggled reminiscently.

"We'll keep him out of it," Johnson said to the others. "He's a professional." He started to pull out the whiskey bottle, overcame the impulse. "Just us three'll play."

"I don't know," said Greening. "I . . ."

"Aw, come on." Johnson slid over the rail. "Augie, here, will let us know if anything happens."

Crane and Greening followed his thin back across the marble-floored waiting room, past mahogany-colored benches, a sign reading MEN, a drinking fountain, and down a narrow flight of metal stairs. The heavy air became moist as they neared the bottom, and there was a musty odor of decomposition, as in the basement of a deserted house. Johnson pushed a row of electric-light buttons on the cement wall, unlatched and swung open a heavy steel door, motioned them inside.

Brilliant white light from a long row of bulbs on the ceiling of the room made their eyes blink. Their nostrils sucked in the sweet, sharp, sickeningly antiseptic smell of formaldehyde. Icy air caused their shirts to stick clammily to their flesh. The steel door shut with a muffled thud, and all three of them momentarily experienced a feeling of being trapped.

"Creepy place, ain't it?" observed Johnson.

The plaster walls of the room had been painted oyster white, and there was in front of them a corridor between two long rows of black metal cabinets, something like those in the locker room of a golf club.

"Usually forty or fifty dead ones down here," said Johnson. "They hold 'em for a month before they let the county bury them."

"That means a guy could lose four or five bucks at this game," said Crane.

"It generally balances up pretty close," said Johnson. "There are more white people killed than niggers, but more people come to claim the white ones, too."

The sound of their voices seemed to circle the room, echoing from several places, as though searching for a way to escape.

15

"How about it, Greenie?" asked Johnson. "Shall we flip to see who gets what?"

Greening had to swallow twice before he was able to speak, and then his voice came out falsetto. "Sure," he said.

Crane was odd man and he selected women. Greening took white men and that left Johnson with the buck niggers.

"Let's begin here," he said, "and work down this side. That's the way the numbers run." He started to pull out the drawer marked with a brass 1 on the upper part of the first cabinet to the right.

"Wait a minute," said Crane. "How about Mexicans? Do they count as white or black?"

"I'm taking money out of my pocket," said Johnson, tugging on the drawer, "but they count as white."

In the drawer, which slid out quite easily on roller bearings, was a middle-aged white man. They could tell he was white, even though his skin was a dirty blue and his face was covered with half-inch stubble. His cheeks were hollow, and his lower lip hung down, showing blackened teeth. He had been blind in one eye.

"A bum," Johnson said, closing the drawer. "Probably got hold of some wood alcohol. That's one for Greenie."

Number 2 drawer in the bottom part of the same cabinet was empty, and Johnson hurriedly closed Number 3 when it revealed a man's bloated face. "Drowning," he said. "Two up for Greenie."

Number 4 was interesting. It was a large white man who had either been stabbed or shot in the left eye. He must have been a sailor because there were tattoo marks all over his chest. Johnson pulled the sheet down so they could see better. Near the neck was a pink-and-blue mermaid, under which was written in black letters, Jeanne; while across the chest, in order, were an American flag, two naked women dancing, a kewpie doll, and a setting sun. But the masterpiece was on the stomach: the battleship Maine being blown up under Morro Castle in Havana harbor. The flames from the explosion were done in vermilion and they soared magnificently up the lower part of the man's chest, almost scorching the feet of the dancing women. There could be no doubt the work was intended to represent the Maine disaster, because below it was printed: "Remember the Maine."

Crane said admiringly: "They ought to stuff him and hang him in the Art Institute."

Johnson said, "That makes Greenie three up."

After that there was more variety in color. Negro men alternated with white men, and finally Crane recouped most of his losses with a dazzling run of four women: two middle-aged black ones, a very old and very withered white one, and a young one, either Mexican or

16

Italian. Then Johnson won a syndicate with the largest Negro Crane had ever seen; he must have weighed 350 pounds, which Crane thought was unusual for a black man; and then they came to Number 27.

"I guess this is mine without looking," said Crane.

Johnson said, "Miss Alice Ross."

Greening pressed forward. "Oh, this is the lady we're waiting for them to identify." He had recovered some of his spirit. "I'd like to see her."

"Open it up, then," Johnson said.

Alice Ross had hair the color of a country road after a long dry spell. It was too pale to be called gold and too rich to be compared with honey. Her eyelids were a delicate violet, and she had that tragic look some women have when they close their eyes. Her lips were gentle, and there was a dark line about her neck where the rope had bruised the skin.

Johnson jerked the sheet off her body. "Nice, eh?"

She was slender, not with the stringy slenderness of a boy, but firmly rounded, and her skin was like cellophane which had been tinted the color of a cherry stone clam. It had luster and depth, and its texture was fine.

Greening touched her shoulder with his finger tips, drew them away. "Cold!" he said. "Cold." His voice was surprised.

They stared at her in silence until the morgue attendant came downstairs and called:

"There's a guy up at the desk wants to see you, Johnson."

"Me?"

"He said the reporters."

"I guess that means you, too, Greenie." Johnson winked at Crane. "Don't let me scoop you." He led the way along the corridor, out the door, Greening following at his heels.

The attendant was looking at the girl's body. "I wonder how long a guy would live if he had a wife as swell as that?" He ran a yellow hand over her smooth hip.

"You'd get used to her after a while," said Crane.

"I'd like to try." The attendant's sharp yellow face was wistful. "I'd be willing to trade my wife in if I could get a model like this. I suppose it 'd take a lot of money to keep her in clothes, though."

"Plenty."

"Yeah, I guess so."

Crane said, "I think I'll go up and see what that fellow wants with the reporters. He didn't say, did he?"

The attendant's face was oblivious. The bright light thinned the wispy gray hair on his head, showed a vivid purple scar across the top. He paid no attention as Crane moved away.

The stairway, taken alone, was a dark trap through which poured air, heavy and hot like an animal's breath. Something seemed to move in a doorway back of the stairs, and Crane's heart went thump-thump, thump-thump, thump-thump. He went up the stairs and into the room marked MEN. Then he had a drink from the fountain and finally walked over to where the two reporters were in conversation with a stocky Italian.

"I'm willin' to play ball wid youse guys, if you'll play ball wid me," the Italian was saying. "It's just that the big . . . the guy I rep'esent don't want this dame I'm tellin' you about to know he's worried about her." He had on a violet shirt which sweat had turned to purple. "If it's her down there, O.K. The papers can have the whole story. But if it ain't her he don't want no story, because this dame I'm telling you about will find out he's worried about her. D'ya see?"

Greening said, "But how are we going to know if it is the right girl? There's nothing to prevent the man you represent from walking in here, looking at the girl, recognizing her and saying, 'No, that's not the right one.'"

"If it's her he'll identify her, all right." The Italian caught sight of Crane, scowled fiercely at him. "Who's this mug?"

"He's all right," said Johnson. "He's the *Associated Press* man." He gave Greening a warning glance.

"Well, how about it, then?" asked the Italian, still looking at Crane.

"I've seen you somewhere before," said Johnson to the Italian.

"Naw, you haven't." Rivulets of perspiration flowed crookedly through the forest of black hair on his arms. "You never seen me before."

"All right. I never saw you before."

The Italian nodded to Johnson, said, "You got tha idea." He repeated, "How about it, then?"

"Sure. Go get the fellow you represent."

The Italian went out the wide corridor to the front door. "What's the idea?" asked Greening. "We can't protect his boss, can we?"

"We aren't going to." Johnson leaned against the oak rail, rested his elbows on it. "We can't lose anything by having the guy come in to look at the body. If he identifies it then we got a story. If he doesn't then we're no worse off than we were."

"He'll have to give his name to the attendant, anyway," said Crane. "That'll give you something to work on."

18

Johnson grinned, showing strong, irregular teeth. "He don't have to give his right name."

The Italian came back. His face was puzzled. "I don't know whas th' matta," he said. "He's gone. He musta drove around th' block." He looked at Johnson. "I think I take a look at her myself."

"I've seen you somewhere before," said Johnson.

"Naw," said the Italian. "Not me." He turned to Crane. "Which way you go?"

Crane led them down the stairs. The big steel door was ajar and a stream of cold air poured out of the storage room. The lights were still on, but the attendant wasn't there. None of the vaults were open. They halted and Johnson called:

"Hi, Augie."

The words beat back on their eardrums.

"Where they got her?" asked the Italian.

"Over there," said Johnson. He called again: "Augie . . . Oh, Augie-ee."

There was no answer.

"That's funny," said Johnson. "Where the hell could he have gone?" He shouted, "Augie!"

They paused in front of Vault Number 27. The silence was threaded with the faint, shrill laughter of the insane woman in the Psychopathic Hospital, feverish and excited and mocking.

"Well, here she is," said Johnson. He grasped the handle of the vault, swung his shoulder in a half pivot to the right.

Up at them, from the depth of the steel box, stared a man. He had on a white coat and there was a smear of heavy blood on his yellow forehead. It was Augie, the morgue attendant, and there was no need to touch him to know that he was dead.

"What the hell!" Johnson stepped back two paces.

The Italian asked, "Whassa matta? Where's the dame?"

Johnson pulled open the bottom vault, but it was empty. The huge Negro was still in the one to the right, and there was an old woman in the one to the left. "She's gone!" Frantically, he began opening other vaults. "Somebody got her."

The Italian exclaimed, "That sonabitch Frankie French!" He turned and ran clumsily down the corridor and up the stairs.

"Hey!" yelled Johnson. "Wait a minute!"

The Italian's footsteps sounded above their heads. He was still running. "For Christ's sake, let's get the police," said Johnson.

Chapter Two

SIREN SCREAMING, the squad car detailed to rove in the neighborhood of the morgue arrived first, poured out men with revolvers, sawed-off shotguns. Then came the homicide squad from police headquarters, the official police photographer, two special investigators from the coroner's office, an assistant state's attorney, photographers from all the newspapers, and four *Tribune* reporters. Everyone was occupied in getting in everyone else's way until Captain Grady, night chief of detectives, arrived in a Lincoln sedan with a uniformed chauffeur.

"Now, first of all," he demanded; "who found the body?"

Crane said he and the two reporters had found it. He explained they had been looking at the woman's body when the morgue attendant had told them a man wanted to see them, and he related how they had taken the Italian down to view the body, but he didn't say anything about the game they had been playing.

"I think I've seen that Dago somewhere before," Johnson added.

Captain Grady stared at him with pale blue eyes. "We'll take a look at the body," he said. He was within two years of the retirement age and his hair was cotton white, but he rated ninety-three in the annual police physical examination. His face was crimson from years of John Jameson's Irish whiskey and Lake Michigan's wind, and his cheeks were filigreed with tiny blue veins.

The policeman guarding the storage room was glad to see them. He said, " 'Tis a hell of a place, Captain."

"Keep them other reporters and photographers out of here for a while, Officer," said Captain Grady. "I'll talk to them in a minute." He walked over and looked into the open drawer. "It was obliging of the murderer to lay him away like that."

The police photographer was packing his bag. "Looks like somebody grabbed his wrists, Captain." He pointed his tripod at the body.

There were 'maroon bruises about both the morgue attendant's wrists. Bending closer, Crane saw that there was hair between the thumb and forefinger of the left hand. He pointed it out to the Captain.

"It's red," said Johnson. "The murderer must have been red-haired."

Captain Grady grunted, plucked an envelope from his inside coat pocket and carefully put the hair in it.

Crane said, "One of the assailants must have tried to hold his wrists. That's how the bruises got there."

Captain Grady looked at him. "The assailants?"

"There must have been two. You can't hold on to somebody's wrists with both hands and also sock him over the head."

"Some sock, too, Captain," said the police photographer. "Whole top of his skull is bashed in."

The captain looked and saw that this was so.

"The proverbial blunt instrument," said Johnson.

"I don't think they meant to kill him," Crane said. "He had a nasty scar on his head that might have weakened his skull. They might have been trying to knock him out."

"You seem to know a devil of a lot about this business," said Captain Grady.

"I noticed the scar earlier in the evening."

The officer at the door said, "Here's the assistant state's attorney, Captain."

"Hello, Burman," said the Captain. "Made out anything?"

The assistant state's attorney was a small, dark, alert man with glasses. "Not a thing," he said. He was a graduate of the University of Chicago Law School and his family had wanted him to be a rabbi. He was troubled with indigestion.

The captain repeated what Crane had told him and added, "This fellow seems to be pretty smart. Maybe he can tell us who the girl was."

"I don't know any more about her than you do, Captain," Crane said. "Not that I would've minded knowing her before——"

"Smart guy, eh?" said Burman. "Maybe you can tell us just how you happen to be here." His voice sounded as though he wouldn't believe the explanation, whatever it was.

William Crane looked at him in quiet surprise, then down at the corpse again. "Sure, I'll tell you. I like it here because it's cool."

Greening had edged around by the open vault. "He says he's a private detective."

Captain Grady said, "Where's your permit?" Crane showed it to him. "All right," said the captain. "But that doesn't mean you can't answer a civil question."

"I'll be glad to answer a civil question."

"Well, how do you happen to be here?"

"I work for Colonel Black in New York. I happened to be in Chicago last night, and I got this wire from him."

Crane pulled a Western Union telegram from his coat pocket, unfolded it, handed it to Captain Grady. It read:

WILLIAM CRANE . . . SHERMAN HOTEL . . . CHICAGO . . . 6:34 P.M.
LEARN IDENTITY OF WOMAN SUICIDE PRINCESS HOTEL NOW AT MORGUE.
BLACK.

Crane continued, "It seemed to me the best thing was to come to the morgue and wait until somebody showed up and identified her, so I did. That's all I know about the lady."

"And you came right over to the morgue when you got that telegram?" asked the captain.

"He got over here a little before eight," said Johnson. "I was here then."

"I grabbed a bite to eat first," explained Crane.

Burman stroked his cheek with his hand. "How do we know you didn't get another wire telling you to remove the body to keep it from being identified?" His words tumbled from his mouth. "This second wire could have been to cover you up." Across his cheek his hand made a sandpaper noise.

Greening said, "He was down here alone with the attendant for some time while we were talking to the Italian."

"You fat son of a bitch," said Johnson.

"Sure, I murdered the attendant," said Crane, "and carried the girl out in my hip pocket." He slapped his hip. "I got her there now."

Burman whirled around and faced the captain. "He could have done it with an accomplice." His eyes were like horehound cough drops. "They could have murdered this poor fellow here, and the accomplice could have carried away the girl while Crane joined the others upstairs."

"Nothing ventured, nothing accompliced," said Crane.

"He might have," said the captain, "but it doesn't seem likely."

Burman's hand clung to his jawbone. "Why not?"

"Well, he wouldn't have stuck around like this."

"That's exactly what he would have done to throw suspicion from himself." The assistant state's attorney balled one hand, pounded it on the palm of the other. "I'm not saying he did kill this man——"

"Not much you're not," said Crane.

"I'm not saying he did, but he was on the scene; he had the chance to do it, and I'm telling you, Captain, I think you ought to lock him up."

Crane said, "Sure. Have the captain lock me up. It won't be you that'll have to take the rap for it."

Captain Grady glared at the police photographer. "What the devil are you hanging around for, man? Isn't your work done?" The photographer made a disorganized exit, his arms laden with partially packed plates, flashlight guns and a camera. Captain Grady continued: "I'll lock this fellow up if I feel like it, and I won't if I don't feel like it. Is that clear enough?"

"That's your prerogative, Captain," Burman said. "I was merely suggesting."

"Suggesting?" Crane asked.

"Let's get on with our business." Captain Grady jerked at the craggy, salt-and-pepper brow over his right eye. "Mister Crane, do you have any idea who the girl was?"

"Not the slightest."

Burman said, "Your boss must have had some idea, or he wouldn't have wired you to watch her."

"Why don't you ask him, then?"

"I'll do the questioning for a time, Mister Burman." Captain Grady's voice was brittle. "Your chance will come in the courtroom."

Crane said, "It won't do you much good to question me. I've told you everything I know."

"Have you an idea who the client your agency is representing is?"

"Not the slightest." Crane decided he was getting tired of this. "But even if I did I wouldn't tell you."

Captain Grady said, "So that's your attitude, is it?"

"Of course that's my attitude." Crane raised his voice. "You ought to know, Captain, that information about a private detective's client is confidential." He could see the reporters outside the metal door were listening. He raised his voice still more. "If you want to arrest me, go ahead, and I'll get hold of a lawyer. If you don't, let's get this over with."

"You seem bound and determined to be locked up," the captain said, "but I don't see why I should please you." He turned to the door, bellowed: "O'Connor!" The big sergeant of the homicide squad pushed through the crowd of reporters and cameramen by the storage-room door, said: "Yes, sir." The captain said, "Take this man's name, and call the Hotel Sherman and find if he's registered there. If he is, let him go." To Crane he added, "You'll have to come to the inquest."

The sergeant crooked a finger at Crane. "Come on." There was a button off the coat of his Oxford gray suit and the pants reflected the light shinily, as though they had been varnished.

Crane said, "So long" to Johnson. The captain roared, "Where 're them reporters?" Eyes narrowed, Burman watched Crane leave.

Sergeant O'Connor telephoned the Sherman from a booth in the upstairs waiting room, found that Crane was registered there, said reluctantly, "I guess you can go."

"Thanks." Crane started to walk away, then paused. "Say, aren't you a friend of Lieutenant Strom?"

"I used to work on the same squad with him."

"I worked on the Westland case with him myself. Next time you see him ask him if he remembers me, or Doc Williams."

"I was wonderin' if I hadn't heard him speak about you. He still thinks you planted the gun in that case." The sergeant thrust out a huge hand, grinned sociably. "I'm pleased t' meet you, though."

Crane winced under his grip. "I wonder if you could do me a favor?"

"I dunno. What is it?"

"I'd like to see the place where they carry the corpses in and out, and I'd like to ask somebody on the squad that got here first if they saw any strange cars about the time the attendant was killed."

Sergeant O'Connor's round face wrinkled as he pondered. "I guess it won't do no harm to let you prowl around a little." He added in reservation, "Not if I go with you."

They walked out the front door and around to the driveway leading to the morgue's side door. On it Crane knelt and lit a match, but he blew it out as soon as he saw the surface was of dark asphalt. "No tire marks," he said.

Further along a red light burned faintly over a double door. There was a cement runway, instead of steps, leading up to the door.

"This is where they haul 'em up," said the sergeant. He opened the double door. "Inside's the receiving room." With a click the lights came on.

Crane paused at the entrance, his hand resting on the inside knob of the right door. The room was chill and very clean, and at the other end were five white enameled hospital tables with sheet-covered bodies on them. Half-a-dozen empty tables were also in the room.

"Waiting to be posted this morning," explained the sergeant. "The coroner's doctors don't work at night unless it's something special."

"Where do they perform the post-mortems?" asked Crane. "In there?"

"Naw, they got a room back here." Sergeant O'Connor opened a door and revealed a room with a stationary operating table under a battery of overhead lights and two cases filled with stainless steel instruments. He closed the door, opened another and said, "This one goes to the storage room where they keep the mummies on file."

There was a man standing in the passageway. His arm was resting on the rail of a series of metal stairs which Crane recognized as those leading up to the waiting room. "Hi, Tom," the man said.

"Hello, Prystalski," Sergeant O'Connor replied, closing the door to the receiving room. "Just taking a look around."

"You won't find nothing. My squad was the first here and we cased the whole joint. We looked in every vault and even lifted the sheets off the stiffs in the receiving room. There's no doubt but somebody got away with the gal's body."

Crane asked, "Before you got the flash to come here did you see any cars parked around the morgue?"

Prystalski's black hair was oily. He scratched his head, then rubbed his fingers off on his shirt. "We did see a big sedan parked out front. We drove around the block so we could take another look at it, but it was gone when we come back."

The metal door to the storage vault opened and some people came out.

"You're sure it was a sedan and not a hearse?" Crane asked.

"I ought t'know the difference between a sedan and a hearse, oughten I?"

"The devil!" It was Captain Grady. "O'Connor, I thought I told you to get rid of this fellow." His face was turkey-gobbler red. "What d'you mean, allowin' him to be askin' my men questions?"

Confusion made O'Connor's face moronic. Crane said quickly: "The sergeant and I were waiting until you had finished with all these reporters, to see if you wanted me any more."

"An' so ye whiled away the time by askin' a few questions?"

From beside the captain a *Tribune* reporter asked, "Is this the man you were telling us about, Captain?" The reporter's name was Shadow Jones, and he was popularly believed to have worn his suit for seven years without ever having had it pressed. Some even asserted he hadn't taken it off for seven years.

"It's the same." Captain Grady was about to say something more when one of the homicide men appeared at the top of the stairs, called down, "Captain." Testily, the captain asked, "Well, what is it?" The homicide man said, "There's a man here says he can identify the body."

"Identify the body? Identify the body?" Up the scale rose the captain's voice. "Why should we be needin' anybody to identify the body? We all know it's poor Augie."

Patiently, the homicide man said, "The girl's body."

"Why didn't ye say so, man? Send him down."

Emerging into view, feet first, the man could be seen to possess twenty-two-dollar bench-made shoes, saddle-soaped the color of cinnamon toast; tan gabardine trousers and coat of the kind William Crane had always wanted to buy but never felt he could because of the comparative inexpensiveness of Palm Beach suits; a white shirt, a tie the shade of a mild havana, and no hat. There was a lot of style tailored into the gabardine, especially around the pleated and half-belted back, and until he saw the coat had been cut loose at the waist Crane thought possibly the man was a gangster, or at least someone who had a connection with race horses.

Pausing uncertainly on the bottom step, the man blinked in the channel of light from the storage room. "Is Captain Grady here?" He was a young man about twenty-seven years old, and his blond hair was wind-blown. He was not handsome, but he was the sort of man women, especially older women, would call nice-looking.

Brows lowered in an official scowl, the captain said, "I'm Grady."

"My name is Brown—A. N. Brown of San Diego—and I'd like to see the young lady who was brought here yesterday afternoon." He moved from the bottom step to the floor. "Alice Ross, I believe her name is."

"Do you know an Alice Ross?"

"No, I don't. But I'm afraid this woman may be my cousin . . . unless, of course, she's already been identified . . . ?"

"She hasn't been identified." The captain thrust his hands in his coat pockets. "What makes you think it may be your cousin?"

"My mother and I (I live with her in San Diego—Mission Hills) have been worried about Edna (that's my cousin) for the last month. We haven't heard a word from her, and we're afraid . . ."

The captain had a pipe in his right pocket. He took it out, clenched it between his teeth. "Well?"

"We're afraid she may have killed herself." Brown spoke hesitantly. "She hadn't been well . . . heart trouble . . . couldn't dance or play any games . . . made her very despondent."

"Didn't she have any family?"

"That's just the trouble. We were, are, the only family she has. Mother and father both dead. She lived with us . . . of course she had a small income, enough to travel on . . . and I'm afraid she was worried about being a burden to us." He was looking at the captain. "Can't I see her?"

Shadow Jones of the *Tribune* said, "What was your cousin's last name, Mister—" He consulted his notes on the back of an envelope—"Brown?"

Apprehension clouded Brown's face. "We're not going to have any newspaper publicity about this, are we?" he asked Captain Grady.

"Don't worry, Mister," said one of the other *Tribune* men. "We wouldn't think of putting this in the newspapers."

Captain Grady seized Crane's arm, spoke to Brown. "Do you know this man? Ever seen him before?"

Brown's eyes were intent on Crane for a second, then he shook his head. "I never saw him before in my life."

Crane's arm, released, dropped to his side. To him the captain said, "You can scram. You'd think you were a special observer for the crime commission, the way you've been hangin' around." To the reporters he said, "You guys, too. I want to talk to Mr. Brown alone."

Johnson and Shadow Jones walked up the stairs with Crane. "That son of a bitch, Greening," said Johnson. "He got you into all this trouble. Why couldn't he have kept his mouth shut?"

"I don't mind," said Crane. "I've been in trouble before."

Shadow Jones remarked, "Burman seems to have it in for you." He gave his trousers a hitch. "He thinks you had a hand in stealing the body. Thinks you were hired to do it and accidentally killed poor old Augie."

"What does he think I wanted the body for?"

"I'm damned if I know," Shadow Jones pulled at his pants again. "I don't think he does, either." The pants looked as though they had been made for somebody about four sizes bigger than he was. "I guess it's just a policeman's intuition."

"You'd be in a cell now if I hadn't told him you had some powerful connections in town," said Johnson.

Crane asked, "What makes you so sure I shouldn't be in a cell?"

"Well, it was me who suggested the game that brought you downstairs. You'd never have gone down if I hadn't."

"That's right," said Crane.

Shadow Jones asked, "What game?"

Johnson winked at Crane. "That's a secret among us girls."

Crane went into the phone booth and called a taxicab. "I better get out of here before the captain changes his mind," he said when he came out. He went out in front and waited on the curb for the cab.

Chapter Three

THE NIGHT was breathless now and clear, and the rays from the cab's headlights were the color of lemon juice on the pavement. Even so slight a movement as getting into the cab made William Crane sweat. He rubbed his forehead with a wadded handkerchief, said, "The Princess Hotel."

They got away smoothly. As they neared the first corner Crane saw that the grass between the street and the sidewalk was covered with sleeping people. Overhead, too, on fire escapes and porches other people were sleeping.

Conversationally, the driver said, "Well, is it hot enough for you, brother?"

Crane responded wearily, "Plenty hot." He decided he'd better get the whole weather phase over with right away. "But it's not the heat that gets you, it's the humidity," he added.

"That's what I always say," said the driver. He said it. "It ain't the heat, it's the humidity."

Another car, motor roaring, suddenly pulled up from behind, forced them to the curb. One of the four men in the car got out and opened the cab door. The automatic overhead light disclosed the Italian of the morgue.

"Listen, I got nothin' t' do with this guy," began the driver earnestly. "He's just a fare, see. I just . . ."

"Shut up." Leaning forward until his face was in front of Crane's, the Italian said, "What j'you tell the cops?"

"Nothing. I didn't know anything to tell them."

In the sedan the three men kept their faces turned away from the cab. They all had on Panama hats.

"You tell 'em about me?"

"Sure, but none of us knew who you were."

"You know me now?"

"Only as the man who came to the morgue."

"You know me next time?"

"Why, sure."

28

"No." The Italian patted himself under his left arm. "You don't know me."

"Maybe you're right." Crane could see a bulge where the holster was strapped on. "I never could remember faces."

The Italian looked at him seriously. "I'm right." He stepped backward, slammed the door, spoke to the driver, "On your way, lucky."

Crane's head hit the back window of the cab. Three blocks down the street the driver spoke. "Nice playmates you got." Crane rubbed his head, asked, "Know the guy?"

"After the way he talked," the driver said feelingly, "I wouldn't know him if he was my brother."

They turned right on Michigan Avenue and nine blocks south they stopped in front of the Princess Hotel. Crane gave the driver a dollar. "If anybody wants to know, you let me off at the Sherman."

"O.K., buddy."

The Princess Hotel was also known as the South Side Riding Academy. It was twelve stories high and it looked as though there would be red bricks under its outer coating of soot and dirt. There was a green rug in the lobby, and the illumination was furnished by pink-shaded lamps of the kind that go with ninety-three-dollar living room suites for newlyweds. In a corner of the lobby the rug had been thrown back, and two slick-haired young men were tap dancing on the tile floor. One of them clapped his hands and cried:

"You're better than Fred Astaire, Angie."

"Fred Upstairs," said the other in a shrill voice.

They both laughed delightedly.

A big-bosomed blonde in a yellow silk dress was talking to the night clerk. "If my strip act's good enough for Minsky, I told him," she was saying, "it's good enough for the Star and Garter." A cigarette dangled from her lips.

Without lifting his elbows from the counter, the night clerk said to Crane, "Yes, sir?" He was tall and thin, and one of his front teeth was mottled.

At the woman's feet lay a brown Pomeranian, his tongue out, his breath coming in quarter-second pants. Crane avoided him, registered as Edwin Johnson, of Galesburg, Illinois, paid in advance for a two-dollar room. He felt the woman staring at him as he got into the elevator with the sleepy-eyed bellboy.

Windows in the room opened, the bellboy paused in the doorway. "Anything else, sir?" His pale face was sullen.

Crane lifted a twenty-dollar bill from his pigskin wallet. "How'd you like to earn this?"

The bellboy said, "Anything short of murder, mister," and presently

29

it was arranged for Crane to examine 409, the room Miss Alice Ross had occupied. The bellboy went down to the lobby, told the clerk he was going out to eat and then came up to Crane's room by the back stairs.

"It'll be my job if they find out," he said, as he led Crane down two flights to the fourth floor. He added, "Not that I give a damn."

Quietly the door to 409 opened under the thin passkey. The bellboy switched on the lights. "Nothin's been moved since they found her," he said. "The coroner's office ordered us to leave everything until after the inquest." He swung the door shut behind them. "This is where she was hanging." He pointed to the varnished bathroom door, open halfway into the room. "She didn't have a stitch of clothin' on her." The door was white on the bathroom side, mahogany brown on the other.

"Naked!" said Crane, surprised.

"Not a stitch."

On the floor the heavy rug had once been crimson, was now magenta. The window drapes were purple; a violet spread covered the three-quarters bed; there were two imitation needle-point chairs by the windows. A spindly straight-backed chair stood by a writing desk.

Three feet from the bathroom door Crane halted. "Funny it opens into the room," he said, "and not into the bathroom."

The bellboy said, "The john's in the way. It has to open out." He pointed to a heavy steel rail, presumably for towels, on the white side of the door. "The rope was tied around this rod and then carried over the top of the door. She was hangin' from the other side, sort of facin' the wall."

"Did you see her?"

"Say, I wouldn't miss a thing like that. Not little ol' Edgar." Eyes glistening in memory, the bellboy continued. "I came to work early especially t' take a peep at her. She was the kind of dame it takes more than two bucks to see. Her legs——"

Crane cut him off. "Was she still hanging up then?"

The bellboy shook his head. "Naw, they cut her down right after they found her." He swung the varnished door around so the white enameled seat of the toilet was no longer visible. "The only thing left was her footmarks on the door."

There was a small, green bathroom scale back of the door. Crane squinted at it, then asked, "Footmarks? On the door? What was she, a human fly?" The scale was not new, and the arrow pointed at 5, even though there was nothing on the foot-square platform.

Kneeling now on the magenta carpet, his face close to the back of the door, the bellboy was saying, "You can still see the marks——"

pointing a finger at some smudges two feet above the floor—"where she beat her heels."

Crane bent over. "They're marks all right." His handkerchief was still damp. He rubbed one of the smudges; it disappeared. He straightened his back, rapped sharply on one of the higher panels with his fist. He examined the place closely, saw there was no mark, and prepared to strike the door again.

"For Krizakes, don't," said the bellboy. "You'll have the coppers up here lookin' for spooks if you make any more noise."

"I was trying to figure out what made those marks."

"Water."

"Water?"

"Yeah, water." Like a Cossack dancer, the bellboy swung around on bent knees, allowed the door to open again. "She took a bath before she strung herself up. See, the water's still in the tub."

Half a foot below the tub's edge, half an inch below the drain pipe, was placid pale-green water. On the porcelain flat between the wall and the back of the tub were a nail brush, an orange washrag. There was a pink blob on the bottom of the tub by the stopper. White sleeve thrust up above the elbow, Crane plunged his arm in the water, retrieved a soft, fatty cake of soap. It had a scent of carnation. He dropped it back in the water, sent ripples circling the tub.

"Soap must have been there ever since she took the bath," he observed.

Returning to the bedroom, he examined the smudges on the back of the door again. "I suppose the water ran down her body to the heels, then made the marks on the door where they touched the wood."

The bellboy said, "That's what the dicks figured."

Crane stood on the foot-high scale, saw it read 182, deducted five pounds for the error, three pounds for his clothes, said, "I better quit drinking beer." Then he asked, "Was this dame a hooker?"

"No sir, she was high class." The bellboy's voice was positive.

"Anybody visit her?"

"One guy."

"You see him?"

"Yeah."

Crane was balancing with one foot on the scales like the Greek statue of the discus thrower. "What did he look like?"

"He was a good-lookin' guy about the same——" The bellboy drew back a step. "Say, you better look out, or you'll break your neck." He went on, "The same age as you. About your size, too. He was real dark, though, and kind of woppish lookin', somethin' like George Raft in the movies."

31

"Know his name or what he did?"

"I got an idea he was in some band." He thought for a minute. "I think I seen him carrying some kind of a case for a musical instrument."

Crane stepped down off the scales. "An instrument?" He looked at the boy. "Are you sure he had a musical instrument in the case?"

"Jeez!" The bellboy's eyes widened. "Y' think maybe he was a mobster?"

"A instrument case is as good a place to carry a tommy-gun as any." Crane drew out a crumpled pack of Lucky Strikes. "Have one?" He lit the bellboy's, his own, tossed the match out the window. "Can you think of anything distinctive about this fellow? A scar, or a lame leg, or something?"

Scowling, the bellboy said, "He wore a black Fedora hat."

That was all he could remember, but he promised to tell Crane if he thought of anything else. He said, "I better be gettin' downstairs. Mister Glaub'll be wondering what's happened to me."

Crane held the twenty between his thumb and forefinger. "A couple more questions. Who was the first to find her?"

"Annie. She's the maid for this and the third floor."

"What's her last name?"

"I don't know." The bellboy's eyes were hungry on the twenty. "But I'll find out for you, mister."

"How long had this Miss Ross been here?"

"Just one night before she knocked herself off. She come in about three o'clock in the morning."

"All right. Now, where's the rope?" Eyes momentarily leaving the twenty-dollar bill to look at the bathroom door, the boy asked: "You mean the rope she used?" Crane said, "Yeah." The boy said, "The deputy coroner took it." His cigarette, stuck to the lower right-hand corner of his mouth, twitched when he spoke. "That and her pocket-book were the only things the cops took, though. They left everything else just as it was."

"O.K." Crane gave him the bill. "You've got an extra key to this room, haven't you?"

"A passkey."

"Well, leave it here with me. I want to look around some more. I'll lock the door when I'm through and give it back to you then."

In dubious, reluctant agreement, the bellboy said, "You better wait and give it to me tomorrow night." He took the key out of the door, handed it to Crane. He backed out into the hall. "For God's sake, don't let nobody catch you in here."

Crane closed the door behind him and locked it, leaving the key

32

in the hole. He went over to the bed and sat on the violet cover.

It was just about daybreak. Changing from navy to robin's-egg blue, the brightening sky made the lights in the room wan. In the next block a milkman was pounding up and down wooden back stairs, banging his heavy case on back porches, clashing empty glass bottles together. Automobiles were beginning to pass along Michigan Avenue, on the front side of the hotel.

Crane wished very much to lie down on the bed, which was springy, but instead he went into the bathroom and opened the medicine chest. A regiment of beauty aids, toilet articles, stood on the glass shelves like gaudy German toys in a display case. Tall silver-labeled jars stood next to squat white jars; three Dr. West toothbrushes were sprouting from a red, flower-potlike container; a round cardboard box was half filled with pale orange dusting powder; loose platinum-shaded Hump hairpins were scattered along one shelf; on another lay a tube of Ipana toothpaste, a metal-sheathed lipstick. The jars were filled with a variety of facial creams. There was also a bottle of Fitch's shampoo, a smaller one of Odorono, and a prescription bottle of eye drops. He took the number off this: 142366, and the name of the drugstore: Boyd's at Wabash and Twenty-second Street.

Next he went into the closet, which was large and had been converted into a dressing room. At least there was a small chest of drawers, tinted pink and decorated with blue fleur-de-lis, in the closet, and a round mirror. On the chest were a pair of nail scissors, an orangewood stick, a nail buffer, a brush and comb, a bottle of Shalimar perfume. He turned on the bulb hanging from the ceiling and pulled out, one after the other, the three drawers in the chest. They were all empty. He fingered the clothes on the wire hangers at the other end of the closet. There were two silk chemises, a faintly pink silk nightgown with delicate needlework around the neck and sleeves, a sky-blue silk slip, a darker blue dress and a tan camel's-hair polo coat. They all bore Marshall Field's label. From a wall hook hung a flesh-colored girdle with garters attached. From another hung some very sheer silk stockings. He looked around for a brassière, but, remembering the firm breasts on the corpse in the morgue, he was not surprised not to find one.

Then, almost frantically, he searched for shoes. He examined the closet floor, peered up on the shelves, felt under the chest of drawers, looked in the bathroom, under the bed, back of doors, even out the windows. He went over every inch of the bathroom, the closet, the bedroom. It didn't do any good. There weren't any shoes.

Bewildered, he stood in the center of the bedroom, mopped his dripping face and muttered, "What the hell!"

His eye caught some dark marks on the rug near the door connecting with the room at the right. The marks were long and thin and clean, as though somebody had been rubbing the rug with a washcloth. He tried the connecting door. It was locked.

He went back and inspected the clothes in the closet again. The dress felt quite new, but the stockings were worn. The chemises had been washed, all right, but they showed no signs of wear. There were no laundry marks on any of the garments. He was looking at the girdle when someone tried the knob of the hall door.

A voice said, "This is the room." There was the sound of a key being fitted into the hole.

Crane ran on tiptoes to the right-hand window, leaned over the sill. There was a roof about two floors below. It looked like a dangerous jump.

Another voice demanded querulously, "What's the matter?" It was the voice of Captain Grady.

The first voice said, "I can't get the key in." There was a clash of metal against metal.

The gray light of daybreak showed another window about three feet further along the wall to the right. Crane backed out of his window and stood up on the sill, his hands holding onto the bottom of the fully opened frame. He pushed his left hand along the wall, caught hold of the similarly opened frame on the other window.

The original voice in the hall said, "There seems to be another key in the door."

"A key!" Captain Grady's voice was deep. "You mean somebody's inside the room?"

"Looks that way."

His left foot firmly planted on the cement outer ledge of the other window, his left hand anchored to the frame, Crane shifted his weight, pulled himself away from Miss Ross's window. He heard the captain roar:

"Sergeant, break the door down."

He slid into the other room. Clothes were strewn in disorder about the floor, over chairs, a bureau, the double bed—a man's and a woman's clothes. Silk stockings, silk panties hung from a chair by the bed; wrinkled linen trousers and a Brewster green dress lay on the carpet; a shoe with a brown sock in it rested on the dresser; a pair of B.V.D.'s were draped over a brass light fixture on the wall. Under the bed, beside two green French-heeled slippers, were empty ginger-ale bottles; on the small table by the head of the bed were glasses, an imperial quart of Dewar's White Label Scotch whiskey.

A woman sat up suddenly on the near side of the bed, drew the

34

sheet up to her neck, took a gasping breath. He leaped, got one knee over her hip. Teeth bruised his hand, but he kept it in her mouth until he could get hold of the stockings hanging from the chair. She struggled, beat the mattress with her heels, squirmed, but he held her with his elbow, his knees; finally forced the wadded silk into her mouth, gagged her by tying the other stocking tightly around her head.

Beside her, on the other half of the bed, a man breathed heavily, painfully, in a drunken stupor.

The woman was naked. Crane rolled her over, tied her wrists behind her with his necktie. Then he tied her feet with the Brewster green dress and half covered her body with the sheet. "You'll be all right, if you behave," he said. She turned on her side and glared at him. She was young and dark, and her skin was fresh. She worked herself further under the sheet.

Next door there was a crash, a splintering of wood, a trampling of feet, loud talk.

Crane went to the door and opened it a crack. A fat policeman stood in the hall, swinging his club. He closed the door quickly, pondered a second, then crossed to the windows. He pulled down the green shades, came back to the bed and took hold of the man under his arms. There was black hair on the man's legs, on his chest. "Upsie daisy," he said, and dragged the man into the bathroom, where he put him in the tub and pulled the shower curtain around him. Some men ran by in the hall. He came back into the bedroom, took off his shirt and the top of his two-piece athletic underwear and mussed his hair with his hands.

The woman's dark eyes were luminous with impotent rage.

He jumped up on the bed, quickly unscrewed the 125 watt bulb in the ceiling socket, jumped down again. Glancing around the darkened room, he saw the whiskey bottle, lifted it to the light seeping around the down-pulled shades, observed that it was a fifth full, took a long drink. He put the bottle back on the stand. "Slide over, tutz," he said. He climbed into bed with the woman, adjusted the sheet so that it covered his shoes, his trousers.

"I'm sorry about the shoes," he said. "I don't generally wear 'em in bed, but I may have to do some running." After a moment he added, "I'm sorry about the trousers, too."

In back of the hotel there was the sound of men running, talking, shouting. Finally someone called, "There's nobody down here now, captain."

Captain Grady must have had his head out Miss Ross's window. He shouted back, "Look around some more."

Presently there was a knock at the door. In a thick voice Crane demanded, "Whoosh ere?" The door opened a crack. "It's the night clerk." The man put his head in the room, squinted in an effort to see through the gloom. Back of him in the lighted hall Crane could see Captain Grady. The clerk asked, "Have you had trouble with anybody passing through your room, Mister un-huh?"

"Go ri' head," said William Crane loudly and thickly. "Pass on through." He made a sweeping gesture with his bare arm. "No trouble 'tall. Glad t' be of co'venience, sir."

The clerk said patiently, "We don't want to go through your room." He pushed the button for the light, but nothing happened. "We'd like to know if you've seen anybody in your room."

Crane had one hand on the woman's throat. As she tried to sit up he tightened his fingers warningly. "If y' don' wanna go through thish room," he demanded logically, "whash idea of knockin' at my door?" He sat up in bed, exposing his bare chest. "Whash idea disturbin' sanktity priv' ci'zen? Hey?" He pretended he was going to get out of bed.

The clerk looked at Captain Grady. The captain shook his head. The clerk said, "Sorry," and started to close the door.

Crane waved an arm at him. "Wash Bunka Hill in vain?" he demanded. "How 'bout Bos'on Teapot?" The door closed, he continued, "Who took th' letta t' Garcia? Not you, I bet." He muttered to himself for a couple of minutes, then sighed heavily, sank back on the bed. He released the woman's neck.

Ten minutes later the police had gone, and he had finished the whiskey. He felt a great deal better and not so sleepy, and he climbed out of bed and put on his athletic top and his shirt. The woman's eyes, watching, brooded sudden death. He went into the bathroom, lifted the hairy man out of the tub and carried him back to the bed. He said to the woman, "I bet you could sell him to the zoo." He straightened his hair with his fingers, looked regretfully at the bottle on the stand, bowed gallantly to the woman. "I hope I'll see less of you sometime, madam."

He walked out into the hall, down the back stairs, through the lobby and out on the avenue. The sun was already well above the lake; sparrows on window ledges, in the gutters, were chirping. A man was sweeping the sidewalk. He glanced at Crane, said, "Looks like another scorcher, don't it?"

Crane said it did, indeed.

Chapter Four

FATLY, ANGRILY, recklessly, a blue-bottle fly circled the room, banged into the closed upper halves of windows, tickled the coroner's bald pate, caused the drowsy jury to break into fits of arm waving, head shaking. High in the sky the copper sun made the occasional breeze a torment to lungs. The air in the room felt as though it had been dusted with red pepper.

"Then, Mr. Greening, your testimony is practically identical to that of Mr. Johnson?"

Greening looked like a plump cherub. "Yes, sir." His cheeks were rosy, his small eyes blue.

"And you would estimate the time Mr. Crane stayed down in the storage room as . . . ?"

"At least ten minutes."

"Do you recall any earlier conversations Mr. Crane had with the deceased? Any efforts to secure permission to remove Miss Ross's body?"

"No, sir."

"Thank you very much, Mr. Greening." The coroner thumbed the untidy stack of papers on the desk in front of him. "Now, Captain Grady, you say you are unable to trace the man who asked to see the reporters just before the mur—ah—hem—tragedy?"

Women, mostly, filled the wooden benches in the narrow room where inquests were held at the County Morgue. There was a general leaning forward of bodies, a craning of necks. The newspapers had played up the mysterious Italian visitor.

From his seat between two of the homicide men the captain spoke in an aggrieved tone. "My men are doin' the best they can, Coronor, but it's a diff . . ."

"I am sure they are doing everything that can be expected, Captain Grady. Now I would like to call—" papers rustled on the coroner's desk "—Mrs. Liebman."

Captain Grady helped her to the stand, squeezed her arm. She was a large, shapeless woman with red hair and a brand-new black dress.

She gave Captain Grady a look in which there was more warmth than might have been expected from a widow of eight hours. She pulled her skirt around her ankles.

First glancing importantly at the newspaper men around the table opposite the jurors, the coroner leaned over his desk, said gravely, "Mrs. Liebman, I wish to assure you of the deepest, the very deepest sympathy of myself and of these jurors, and it will be my endeavor to shorten your painful appearance here as much as possible." He swung back in his chair, looked at the reporters for approval.

Three of the newspaper men were matching pennies. A small girl reporter from the *Tribune* was reading a Modern Library edition of *The Magic Mountain*. The *City Press* man, who was supposed to supply news to all the papers, was asleep.

Slightly depressed, the coroner continued, "Now, Mrs. Liebman, will you give me your full name?"

"Gertrude Finnegan Liebman." She cast a sly look at Captain Grady. "Me father was for many years a desk sergeant at the Warren Avenue Station." She rolled the r's in Warren.

"Your home address, Mrs. Liebman?"

"1311 North St. Louis Avenue."

"How long had you been married to Mr. Liebman?"

"Twenty-seven years this September."

"Have you any children?"

"No, sir. He . . . Augie . . . was all . . . I had."

"Now, Mrs. Liebman, try to be brave."

Mrs. Liebman tried. She mopped at her eyes with a piece of linen the size of a postcard, blew her nose vigorously. She smiled through her tears at Captain Grady. She smoothed her skirt.

The coroner looked at a piece of paper, asked, "Was your husband right- or left-handed, Mrs. Liebman?"

"Why, right-handed."

The coroner glanced at Crane, who nodded his thanks for the inquiry.

Further questioning brought out that Mr. Liebman had worked for the coroner's office as night morgue keeper for six years, that he was in no financial difficulties, that he had no enemies, that he was, in fact, the best-hearted man in the world, without exception.

The coroner asked, "Your husband was in no trouble of any sort?"

"No, sir!" Mrs. Liebman glared at the reporters matching coins. "Anybody that says that is a dirty liar."

"Then you have no ideas who was responsible for his death?"

"Yes, sir; I have."

The *Tribune* girl looked up from her book.

"You have! Who, Mrs. Liebman?" asked the coroner.

"The young fellow sittin' over there . . . that calls himself William Crane."

Conversation, like a breaking Atlantic roller, deluged the room. A woman in the audience said, "He doesn't look like a killer to me." One of the jurors awoke with a start, looked bewilderedly at his five companions, asked, "Is it time for lunch?" The reporters swung around from their table, stared at Crane. Captain Grady looked pleased. The coroner shouted:

"Order! Order! Please. Order! If we can't have order, I shall have to clear this room."

The blue-bottle fly was trying to force his way through one of the panes. His buzzing was loud in the sudden silence.

"Mrs. Liebman, you are making a very serious statement," the coroner stated. "Are you basing it on personal knowledge?"

Mrs. Liebman tossed her red head about like a high-spirited horse. "Well, the captain said he was the only one who could have done it."

"The captain?"

"Captain Grady, here, to be sure."

"And the captain's idea is the only basis for your statement?"

"Well, the captain said . . ."

"I am afraid, Mrs. Liebman, I shall have to ask the jury to disregard your statement."

Guided tenderly by Captain Grady, the widow passed William Crane on her way to a seat at the back of the room. "Murderer," she hissed, like the outraged mother in a pity-the-poor-working-girl melodrama. Crane, his nerves jangling from lack of sleep, wished for a minute he *had* killed her husband.

The coroner's physician, Dr. Bloomington, testified expertly, rapidly. Death was caused by concussion, the result of a blow on the skull. In his opinion the blow was of an unusually violent nature. No, he could not say positively what instrument was used. A guess, a pure and simple guess, would be the butt of a heavy automatic pistol.

Fingers rustling his papers, the coroner then asked Captain Grady, "Where is Mr. A. N. Brown, of San Diego?"

The pleased smile fled from Captain Grady's face. He compressed his lips, spoke. "The man has disappeared."

"This is highly irregular." The coroner's fingers beat a rapid tattoo on the desk. "Can't you keep track of your witnesses, captain?"

On his feet now, one hand resting on the back of his chair, Captain Grady said, "The man was not a material witness, anyhow, Mr. Coroner." He was addressing the reporters, his back to the jury, his side to the coroner. "We took the man to Miss Ross' hotel early this morning and showed him her clothes, which he could not identify."

The reporters were sliding back of the coroner, around the jury, through the audience, bound for telephones. In thirty minutes husky men in trucks would be throwing bundles of papers to news-stand operators in the Loop; banner lines reading "Heat Wave Kills Seven" would be replaced by "Witness Vanishes in Morgue Mystery."

Once more tumbling his papers with nervous hands, the coroner said, "Since this case is obviously connected with that of the young lady whose body was removed from the morgue, Captain Grady, I am going to ask you to tell the jurors the circumstances of her suicide." He turned to the jury. "As you know, gentlemen, another jury, sitting in the case of Miss Ross, has already found that she committed suicide while temporarily insane." He pointed a finger at the empty witness chair. "Tell them in your own words, captain."

Stiffening their backs, the jurors displayed interest. The six looked oddly alike—threadbare clothes, wispy hair, wavery eyes, smudgy skins with the water line just at the Adam's apple. They also shared a common inability to keep awake.

The captain was saying, "The woman's body was discovered by Miss Annie Jackson, the black chambermaid on that floor of the hotel. She was entirely naked (the woman, I mean)—" the captain smiled indulgently while the jurors guffawed "—and she was hanging from a rope thrown over the bathroom door. Under her feet was a bathroom scale which she had obviously used to stand on while she was adjustin' the rope. Before killin' herself she had taken a bath, and you could make out th' places where her wet heels had beat the door."

Hot rays from the sun burned William Crane's back through his shirt. He slid his chair into shadow.

"The body was discovered about one o'clock in the afternoon, and the coroner's physician reported she had been dead approximately twelve hours, so she must have killed herself about midnight." Captain Grady produced a silk handkerchief, rubbed his face, the back of his neck. "We have not been able to find anyone who knew her as yet, but we should have someone soon. It is known she received a visit from a, har-rump, gentleman caller."

There was a whispering, a nodding of heads, among the ladies in the audience. Gentleman caller, indeed!

"We should be tracing him soon, unless, which is likely, he read of her death in the papers and made himself scarce." The captain nodded his head as though that were probably the case. The jurors, hanging upon his words, nodded, too. " 'Tis almost certain the poor lady was worried over financial affairs," Captain Grady went on. "She had only four dollars in her purse."

The coroner bent over his desk. "Captain Grady, have you any opinion as to why her body was taken from the morgue?"

Aluminum-colored eyebrows drawn into a V over his nose, the captain said, "I have a very good idea." He was looking at Crane. "I believe the girl came of a prominent family somewhere and that her people heard she was dead and did not wish her to be identified." He loosened his collar, running his forefinger between it and his neck. "I think the snatchers did not intend to kill poor Augie—Mr. Liebman —but hit him too severely tryin' to knock him out, as Mr. Crane suggested."

Everyone looked at William Crane, while the captain, with the gratified air of a man who has been able to set a motorist on the right road, climbed down from the stand.

The coroner said, "Well, Mr. Crane, you're the last witness."

Deep and fairly comfortable, the witness chair had arms on which to rest his elbows. He gave his name as William Crane, his residence as New York, his occupation as private detective, and then settled back while the coroner rustled his papers, tried to think of his first question.

At last the coroner asked, "You were the last person to see the deceased alive, Mr. Crane?"

"No, sir."

"No, sir?"

"No, sir."

"Well, then, who did see him last?"

Crane's shoulder itched. He scratched it. "The man, or men," he said, "who killed him."

The coroner grunted. Crane said, "I beg your pardon?" The coroner said, "I didn't say anything." Crane said, "Oh."

It was breathlessly hot in the room. Hats, handkerchiefs, handbags were being used as fans by the women in the audience. The air smelled of human perspiration, heavy and salty sour.

In reply to another question, Crane said, "I have no idea who the lady was, other than that she was called Alice Ross by the newspapers." He related how he had received orders to try to determine her identity.

The coroner returned to his probing of the last few minutes of Mr. Liebman. "How long were you down there alone with him?" he asked.

Crane was conscious of Mrs. Liebman's eyes upon him. He said to the coroner, "Not more than two or three minutes." Mrs. Liebman was registering hate.

"You say you had been looking at Miss Ross' body with the two reporters when Mr. Liebman came down?" asked the coroner.

"That's right."

"What did Mr. Liebman do after he told the reporters someone wanted to see them?"

"He looked at Miss Ross' body, too."

One of the cameramen was making a shot of Mrs. Liebman. She was still registering hate. She was registering more than that. She was clenching, unclenching, her hands. She was registering: I would handle that murderer if I were a man instead of a defenseless widow.

"Mr. Liebman looked at Miss Ross' body," the coroner repeated. "Did he say anything?"

"Yes, he did." William Crane paused. He lowered his eyelids, pretended to yawn. "He said: 'I wish I could trade my wife in for a model like that.'" He watched the widow from the corners of his eyes.

Mrs. Liebman took it as well as could be expected. She leaped to her feet, screamed, "Why, the lousy bum!" Nobody could be sure whether she was referring to William Crane or her husband because she immediately fainted at the feet of Captain Grady. She was removed by two female cousins to the ladies' room.

This, the coroner appeared to think, concluded the testimony. He said, "Thank you," to Crane, let the jury through a door at the back of the room. Crane followed the scuffling, perspiring crowd through a corridor into the big waiting room. He had a drink of warm water from the fountain. The clock with the cracked glass read 12:20; the red mercury column in the thermometer on the morgue keeper's desk was a fraction below the line marked 98. His head ached, his eyes smarted, his face was hot; he went into the room marked MEN to wash.

He was pulling a paper towel from a container marked: "Why Use Two When One Will Do Just As Well?" when someone came into the room. He looked in the fly-spotted mirror and saw it was the Italian of the night before. He said, "You've got your nerve, coming here."

The Italian was standing in the center of the floor. He wasn't very tall and he was more than forty, but he was thick and he looked as though he would be durable. He said, "The big shot wants to know something." He didn't seem friendly.

"What does he want to know?"

"He wants t' know what you done with the girl?"

The paper towel broke in Crane's hands. He dropped it in the waste basket, pulled another from the container. "What makes him think I took the girl?" he asked.

"Him and I was at the inquest." The Italian's legs were apart, his

42

body bent forward at the waist. "We heard what they said. We got ears."

"Yeah, you got ears, all right." Crane looked at the Italian's with disfavor. "If you didn't have so much hair on them maybe you could have heard me say I didn't know who took the body."

"We heard what you said." Black hair grew in a reverse widow's peak on the Italian's chest just below his neck. "But you don't need to hand us the old crappo. We wanta know what you did with the girl."

"I didn't take her."

"O.K., smart boy." The Italian moved toward Crane. "The big fellow wants t' see you, then." He took hold of Crane's arm, started to push him toward the door, halted suddenly.

A man dressed in a green ensemble was watching them. His face was swarthy and, except for a jagged scar over the right cheekbone, handsome. He wore an olive-green suit cut square at the shoulders, snug at the waist. He had on a black hat, a dark-green necktie with small red dots in it, a tan shirt, and brown suède shoes.

"Hello, Pete," he said.

The Italian released Crane's arm, stepped backward. "Frankie!" he exclaimed. He held his arms stiffly, away from his body, away from his hips.

Water, freed by the automatic release, gurgled through the urinals.

"You'd better leave—" the man in green was talking to the Italian "—while you can." He smiled with his mouth. "I want to talk to Mr. Crane." His lips were full, cruel.

Sullenly the Italian made a side-stepping progress toward the door, moving in an arc always the same distance from the man in green, as though a pistol was pointed at the pit of his stomach. He went out the door backward.

With his expressionless face inclined toward Crane the man in green had followed the Italian's departure with his eyes until the sockets were filled almost entirely with white. Now the golden irises slid back into position. "I'm Frankie French," he said. He shook hands with Crane, added, "Maybe we can be of assistance to each other in this matter."

Crane was surprised to find he was still holding the paper towel. He dropped it, took another, rubbed his face with it, said, "Why use one when two will do just as well?" He rolled the paper into a ball, flipped it into the basket with his thumb. "What help can I be to you?"

Frankie French talked without moving his lips. "You can give me a little information."

43

"Yeah, I know. I can tell what I did with the girl's body."

"I see we understand each other." The man's carefully plucked eyebrows and the long lashes of his narrowed eyes made exactly parallel lines. "How much will it cost me to find out?"

"It won't do any good for me to say that I haven't the least idea where the lady's body is?"

"No, Mr. Crane, it won't."

Leaning against one of the washbowls, Crane said, "Supposing for a minute that I do know where the girl's body is, how much would it be worth to you to know?"

Frankie French's tapering hands were beautifully manicured. Light reflected from the glossy fingernails. He lifted five thousand-dollar bills from a calfskin wallet, held them out to Crane.

Moving his head negatively, Crane said, "It's too bad I don't know where the body is."

"I'm not going to haggle with you," said Frankie French, still holding out the bills. "My top price is five grand." His voice was low, ominous. "You will be wise to accept it." He spoke precisely, almost the way a foreigner, who had learned English in a good school, would.

Crane shoved himself away from the washbowl, balanced himself on the balls of his feet, repeated: "I don't know where the body is."

There were golden flecks in Frankie French's eyes. He moved back from Crane—lithely, dangerously, like a cobra about to strike. "You goddam cheap dick," he said, almost in a whisper; "I'm giving you five seconds to start talking." The fingers on his right hand fluttered.

Some men came into the washroom. One of them was saying; "—an' on the buck dinner they throw in a glass of red wine." He was a heavy man with a pock-marked face and curly black hair.

Crane went over to him. "Well, for God's sake, what are you doing here?" he asked the man. "How's the wife?" He seized the man's hand, shook it heartily.

For a moment Frankie French hesitated, then said to Crane: "Think it over." His tone was impersonal, courteous. "I'll be seeing you again." He left the washroom.

The man with the pock marks said, "You got the better of me, Mister." His face was puzzled. "I can't recall ever having seen you before."

Crane released his hand. "You never did," he said. "But anyway, thank you very, very much." He left the men staring at him in astonishment, went back into the room where the inquest had been held.

It was only a few minutes before the jury returned. The foreman handed the coroner a sheet of paper before taking his seat with the

44

other five men. The room was filled again and the audience, even the reporters, waited attentively. Crane looked around for both Frankie French and the Italian, but he was unable to find them. His eye caught that of Mrs. Liebman; she scowled, looked away. Between the two homicide men Captain Grady sat unconcernedly, as if he had no interest in the verdict. His eyes, in contrast to his brick-red face, were a startling blue.

The coroner cleared his throat. "The jury finds," he said, "that the deceased, August Liebman, was willfully murdered by person, or persons unknown while trying in the line of duty to prevent the felonious removal of the body of Miss Alice Ross from the Cook County Morgue in the City of Chicago." He cleared his throat again. "The jury further recommends that the police proceed at once in the steps necessary to apprehend the murderer, or murderers."

The coroner stood up, swept the papers off the desk into a black brief case, quickly stepped from the room. The jury followed hurriedly, eager for their free lunch. Crane walked over to Captain Grady and said: "Missed me that time, didn't you?"

Captain Grady snorted, made no reply. The burlier of the two homicide men, however, said, "Listen, smart guy, we're going to keep close to you."

Crane glanced around again for Frankie French, but he couldn't see him. He spoke fervently to the homicide man. "I hope you do."

Chapter Five

WILLIAM CRANE didn't feel sleepy any more, but that was probably because he was scared rather than because of the two-hour nap he had just finished. He didn't feel sleepy, but he didn't feel so good, either. He sat on the edge of his bed and brooded about his connection with the girl who had been stolen from the morgue. He wished he had never become involved in the matter—at least not to such an extent that the police, a gang of gunmen, and the sinister Mr. Frankie French were all convinced he had the girl somewhere. In fact, on second thought, he wished he had never become involved in the affair at all. Not at all.

There was a knock at the door. His startled jump brought him halfway across the room, onto his bare feet. "Who's there?" he asked.

"The waiter. Your drinks, sir."

The waiter was a Greek. He had a tray on which there was a bottle of Dewar's White Label, a bowl of cracked ice, two high glasses and a siphon. He put the tray on a table, deftly caught a quarter, said, "Thank you," and departed.

Crane poured himself a straight one first. Then he filled the glass halfway with the whiskey, dropped in a chunk of ice, squirted seltzer water until the mixture reached the brim. He drank this slowly, sometimes letting the cold liquid stay in his mouth a minute before he swallowed.

Thirty stories above the street, the room was still uncomfortably warm. There was a steady breeze filled with the distant sounds of roaring motor coaches, of streetcar wheels screaming against steel rails on turns, clattering on steel rails at switches; of automobile horns and, faintly, human voices; but it was not a cool breeze. There was not a cloud in the sky.

Well into his third drink, Crane was debating whether or not to take a cold shower when there was another knock at the door. He was surprised to find he was still jumpy. He shouted, "Come in."

A dapper man with a waxed black mustache, button-bright eyes and black hair with a white streak over the left temple stood in the doorway. "Hi," he said. His name was Doc Williams and he worked for the same detective agency as Crane.

"Oh, my God! am I glad to see you?" Crane dragged him into the room, kicked the door shut behind him, shook his hand, pounded his back. "The U. S. Marines to the rescue. Have a drink, marine, have a drink." He poured whiskey in the other glass, ignored Williams' twice repeated "When." He handed him the glass. "My God, I am glad to see you."

"Don't I get any seltzer?" asked Williams.

"Seltzer? Oh my God, yes, seltzer." He squirted seltzer in the glass. "Say, did I tell you I was glad to see you?"

"I think you mentioned it." Williams tasted the liquor tentatively. "What's the matter, pal? Some dame after you?" He took a second, longer drink.

Crane was filling his own glass. "I only wish there was." He didn't add any seltzer, simply filled it to the brim with whiskey. "It's a lot worse than that." He started to tell Williams about the girl in the morgue.

46

"I know about her," said Williams. "She's why me and Tom O'Malley are here. The colonel sent us down to meet the dame's brother."

"The girl's brother!" Holding his glass in mid-air, Crane stared at Williams. "You know who the girl is . . . was?"

"If she's this guy's sister we do. Tom's over gettin' him now. Going to bring him up here. He's a society dude from New York. The family's got a pot of dough." Williams took a long drink. "The name's Courtland, Chauncey Courtland the third."

Crane whistled. "I know that family. His old lady's got something to do with the opera."

"Something to do with the opera?" Williams' voice rose to a higher key. "Say! that old dame *is* the opera. Without her the Metro would be playin' burlesque this very minute."

Crane scowled. "Well, if they got all these rocks, what's the daughter (what's her name, anyway?) doing in a cheap joint like the Princess Hotel?"

"The dame's name is Kathryn, and I don't know nothin' about her." Williams took off his hat, scratched the back of his head, replaced the hat. "We'll ask brother about her when he gets here. All I know is that the brother of old Mrs. Courtland—the girl's uncle, that is—is our client. He's been dealing direct with the colonel." He rubbed the moisture off his glass, let the drops fall from his finger to the green carpet. "And, incidentally, the colonel's plenty sore at you."

"Sore at me? The colonel? The colonel's sore at me? By God! what for?"

"He thinks you were a sucker to let them steal the girl's body from the morgue."

"He does, does he?" Crane got to his feet, steadied himself by holding to the foot of the bed. "Why didn't he tell me he wanted the body watched? Who ever heard of a body being stolen from a morgue, anyway? Hey? If he wanted the body watched all he had to do was to say see, so—I mean so, see? I would have climbed right in with that babe, right in that old steel box."

"That isn't all. He thinks you screwed up the Indianapolis case."

"He thinks that?" Crane's tone was anguished. "Why, I stuck round there at great person'l sacri . . . sacro . . . risk until everybody got killed off except that nasty old lady . . . then had her pinched."

"That's a fine way to look after your clients' interests—let 'em get bumped off."

"Hell," said Crane; "the old lady was my client." He released his hold on the bed.

"Where are you going?"

"I am deeply, deeply wounded. Very deeply, indeed." Crane put his glass on the window sill. "I am going to take a shower."

Under the sobering influence of alternately hot and cold water Crane related the story of the body's removal and the narrow escape he had had in the Princess Hotel.

"Whooee!" exclaimed Doc Williams when Crane came to the account of his flight from the police through the other room. "You climbed right into bed with this floosie?"

"Sure. Why not?" Crane was soaping under his arms. "I'm a desperate man."

"I'd like to have been there." Williams, sitting on the toilet cover, sorrowfully sipped his drink, then brightened. "You'll catch hell, though, when she gives the police your description."

"I'll bet she doesn't say anything about it." The soap slipped from his hand, bounced out of the shower cabinet into the bathroom. Williams tossed it back to him. He caught it, said, "No woman likes to admit a man was in bed with her without making any advances."

"No advances is what you say," Williams said.

"My God!" Crane poked his head out of the cabinet. "You don't think I'd assault a woman bound hand and foot, do you?"

"Certainly," said Williams.

Crane finished with the shower handle turned clear over on COLD. He dried himself with two towels, put on a clean suit of underwear. He told Williams about the inquest and the conversations he had had in the morgue washroom. He pretended to be hurt when Williams thought it was funny everyone believed he had stolen the body.

"Frankie French is a big-time gambler," Williams finally said. "He's supposed to own some joints over on the North Side, around Oak Street."

Crane asked, "But what would he or that other bunch of mobsters want with the body, particularly if she's a New York society gal?"

"Why didn't you ask Frankie when you were having your little chat?"

"He was doing all the asking." Crane shuddered at the memory. "He said he'd be around again, though." He pulled on his right sock. "I'd just as soon meet a rattlesnake."

"We'll handle him all right." Williams twisted his mustache between his thumb and forefinger. "Maybe we can figure some way of partin' him from that five grand he's waving around so careless."

"I'd sooner try to rob the Chase National Bank single-handed." The telephone rang. Crane fastened a button to hold his trousers up and answered it. "Sure, send them up." He hung up the receiver, said, "It's Tom and young Courtland."

48

"We better hide the liquor," said Williams. "Courtland's sort of a client." He carried the loaded tray into the closet, closed the door.

Crane had a clean broadcloth shirt on when they arrived. He shouted, "Come on in." Williams was seated primly on the edge of the bed.

Tom O'Malley came in first. He was a handsome, dissolute Irishman; tall and muscular, with deep-set blue eyes. He said, "Mr. Courtland, this is Mr. Crane." His voice was deep, formal. He weighed 210 pounds, was six feet three inches in height.

William Crane said, "Well, for the love of Jesus!" He circled the room until he was between the door and the second man, added, "How are you, Mister A. N. Brown of San Diego? And how is Cousin Edna?"

They sat around while young Courtland explained. He was a nice-looking man with blue eyes that wrinkled at the corners when he smiled. His features were irregular, but he had nice teeth and a good tan skin. He was saying:

"I grabbed the sleeper plane from New York at midnight last night (had to, because it was the only one I could get after just missing the nine o'clock plane) and landed in Chicago at 3:30. I took a cab right over to the morgue to see if it was sister.

"When I got here I found the place in a devil of an uproar. The body had been taken, but I found that out too late to draw back. I certainly didn't want to drag in the family name, particularly as we weren't at all sure it really was Kit. So I used the name of a passenger on the sleeper plane, Mr. A. N. Brown, and made up the stuff about Cousin Edna. That seemed the only thing I could do."

"That was a good idea," said O'Malley, "but you'll be in a jam yourself if the police catch up with you, Mr. Courtland."

"Hell," said Doc Williams, "if it ain't his sister the police 'll never see him again, and if it is he can explain he didn't want to get mixed up in the thing until he was sure."

Crane asked, "How are you going to find out if it is his sister or not?"

"That's up to you." The lid dropped over one of Williams' bright eyes. "Master Mind!"

Courtland said, "I'm almost sure it isn't Kathryn, after all. You see, I hopped over to the hotel the woman was staying in to look at her clothes. That captain——"

"Grady," said Crane.

"Yes, Grady. He took me over to see if I could identify anything. We had some trouble getting into the room (I think a sneak thief

49

was supposed to have been inside and to have jumped out the window when we tried the lock) and the police had to break down the door, but I examined all the clothes, and I'm pretty sure they weren't the kind Kit would wear. They had Marshall Field's label on them, and she'd been getting things from Best's and Saks ever since I can remember." Courtland thought for a time, then shook his head. "Besides, I'm certain Kit wouldn't have had so few clothes. She wouldn't travel without a trunk."

"Look," said Crane; "we can settle this right away, if you have any pictures of your sister."

Courtland produced an ostrich billfold. "I've got a passport photo taken of her some time ago." He pulled out a small photograph and handed it to Crane. "Always carry it with me. Of course, we have some studio portraits of her at home."

Crane walked to the window with the photograph. It showed the head of a young girl about nineteen—a rather plump young girl with blond hair and an excited, anticipatory expression about her lips and eyes. There was a white background, and that, with the strong light used by the photographer and the fact that the girl's face was turned toward the camera, made it impossible to determine what sort of a nose and chin she had. There was a comb in her unbobbed hair.

Courtland said, "It was taken nearly four years ago, and you know how passport photos are, anyway. . . ."

Crane gave the photograph back to him. "I know," he said. "It doesn't look much like her. Your sister's fatter. . . . I mean fuller in the face, for one thing."

"Kit was fatter, then." Courtland held the photograph, watched Crane's face. "She was fat as a little kid, clear up to the time she was twenty. Then she suddenly lost weight. It showed especially on her face. I used to kid her about dieting secretly. D'you think it might be her, if you made an allowance for the difference in weight?"

"It might be." Crane sat on the bed beside Williams, leaned backward so that his elbows were resting on the green spread. "It might be, but she'd have had to change a lot. A hell of a lot. I don't think that photo is going to do us any good." He looked up at the ceiling. "I bet you could take the photograph of almost any pretty blonde, and she'd look something like the girl in the morgue, especially if you had to allow for a difference in weight and four years in age."

O'Malley had been sitting on the straight-backed chair by the writing desk, his blue eyes attentive. He said, "Maybe you could have one of the portraits sent on to Chicago, Mr. Courtland?" He turned around to Crane. "We'd probably do better, Bill, if we showed it to some of the people in her hotel. They saw her alive."

"Of course." Courtland's face brightened. "I'll wire Mother to send it air mail." He ran his hand backward through his short blond hair, left it tousled. "You know it's damnable to have something like this happen to you. The uncertainty. Most of the time I'm sure it can't be Kit. It isn't like her to kill herself . . . and then there are the clothes and the puzzle of why anybody would steal the body, if it was her." Emotion made his voice husky. "But every now and then I have a terrible conviction she is dead. You know she hadn't lived at home for two years, since she and Mother quarreled, and we didn't know exactly what sort of life she was leading."

Crane sat up on the bed, used Williams' shoulder as an armrest. "She couldn't have been hard up, could she?" he asked. "I mean, your mother didn't cut her off . . . ?"

"Oh Lord, no! Mother couldn't bother her." He laughed, deeply amused. "Mother gets an allowance from the estate, just like the rest of us." He was smiling now. "I'd hate to think what would happen if Mother was in charge of the family purse. Money'd go for a chorus composed of famous tenors or a Theosophist temple the size of the Empire State Building."

Crane asked, "Do you mind saying how much your sister received?"

"Not at all, if it's any help." Courtland was sitting on the edge of his chair, hands thrust in his coat pockets. "She had fifteen hundred a month until she married."

"Then what?"

"She gets one third the estate."

Doc Williams' eyes were black and shiny. "Fifteen hundred should keep her out of the bread line." He wet his lips with his tongue.

Crane asked, "Who has charge of the estate?"

"Father named Uncle Sty in the will as general trustee, but . . ."
Crane interrupted. "Uncle Sty?"

"Yeah," said Doc Williams. "He's our client."

O'Malley said, "Stuyvesant Courtland."

"I'm sorry," said Crane. "Go ahead, Mr. Courtland."

"All I was going to say was that I handle most of the details of the estate."

Crane rubbed his right ear. "Then you know that your sister was receiving her fifteen hundred dollars regularly each month?"

Courtland nodded. "I've been adding it to her account at the Hanover Bank even though she apparently stopped using it six months ago."

"Was that when she quarreled with her mother?" Crane asked.

"Oh no. That was two years ago, as I told you."

"Oh!" Blinking his eyes, as though he were trying to remember,

Crane said, "I think it would be simpler if you told us about your sister chronologically, about the quarrel, I mean, and what she's been doing since then."

Courtland leaned back in his chair, thrust out his legs. He bent his neck so that he was looking over Crane's and Williams' heads. "The trouble with Mother started about the time Kit came back from a year in France—some school down at Tours. Mother hated the crowd Kit took up with, objected to her going down to Greenwich Village all the time with a lot of half-baked artists and writers. She also disapproved of Kit's drinking.

"Finally, one morning, Kit cleared out after Mother had waited up until six o'clock to bawl her out. She packed her clothes, while Mother yelled and raged and raised hell generally. I remember there was some little squirt there—" his voice was faintly amused "—with a beret and a velvet jacket (I thought those things went out with Oscar Wilde) and when Mother screamed something at him he hopped behind Kit and shouted, 'Don't you dare strike me,' and burst into tears. Mother told Kit she needn't bother to come home, that she never wanted to see her again.

"Kit said, 'You never will,' and that was the last time Mother saw her."

There was a momentary pause. The shrill voice of a newsboy floated up from Randolph Street. Wind blowing through windows around the hotel corner sounded as though someone were pulling a heavy rug across a waxed floor. It was still hot.

Courtland continued, "I had sided with Mother in some of the earlier shindigs (I didn't see a damn bit of sense in going around with a lot of unwashed Cubists and Joyceans when Tom Bowers—he's with Dillon, Reed—and half-a-dozen other decent fellows were crazy about her) and Kit told me she didn't want to see me, either. I went around to her place on Fifty-fifth Street seven or eight times, but she was nasty, or maybe I was, so finally I stopped trying to see her.

"I guess the last time I ran into her was at the Cotton Club in Harlem. That was about five months ago. The funny thing was that it was after 4 A.M. and she was at a table all by herself, but she wouldn't join our party. She said she had a date later!"

"The hell!" exclaimed Crane. When Courtland looked at him he grinned, added, "I just thought of something. Please go ahead."

"I got worried about her two months ago and stuck my nose into some of the old haunts in the Village, but they said there that they hadn't seen her for five or six months, either. They said she had just dropped out of sight. Her apartment was closed—she was still paying rent on it, and her things were there—and the janitor said he thought she had gone to Europe. At the Hanover Bank her account showed that she had drawn out six thousand in February and not a cent since then. It did look as though she had gone abroad for a jaunt, until Mother got the letter from her."

"What letter?" asked Crane. "I don't know about any letter."

Courtland gave him a letter he had been carrying in a manila envelope in his inside coat pocket. The letter was postmarked Chicago, Central Station, July 24, 10:15 P.M. It was addressed in blue ink to Mrs. Chauncey Courtland, 835 Park Avenue, New York City. Crane took out the inside sheet. It was undated and it read:

Dear Mother:

I'm afraid I haven't been a very good daughter to you, but I do want to tell you I am genuinely, truly sorry for the trouble and worry I have given you and Chance. We haven't been a very happy family . . . perhaps it has been my fault . . . and I have been a headstrong and foolish girl, certainly.

I am telling you this because I am going into a different, perhaps a better world soon . . . and this may be the last time you will ever hear from me. I am so sorry, mother. . . .

Love,

Kit

Doc Williams was frowning. "Who's Chance?" he demanded.

"That's my nickname," Courtland said.

Crane folded the letter, put it on the bureau. "But you received that more than a week ago," he said. "Why all the delay in looking for her?"

"Mother." Courtland's expression was one of disgust tempered with tolerance. "She didn't show it to Uncle Sty or me until a few days ago. She had been consulting her yogi about it first."

"Her yogi!" exclaimed Williams. "What in hell's a yogi?"

Crane said, "Shut up." He was standing in front of Courtland. "What did you and your uncle do when she finally did show it to you?"

Courtland was smiling at Williams. "We both had the same idea—that it might possibly mean suicide, but more likely not." The crow's feet disappeared from the corners of his eyes. "Kit was always very dramatic. But we were both worried—far more than Mother. She took the letter to mean Kit was entering a nunnery, or a new cult, or something." He offered Crane a cigarette from a leather case, lit one of them himself when Crane refused. "Anyway, we discussed hiring detectives to find Kit. We were actually discussing it yesterday afternoon in Uncle Sty's office when the papers came out with stories of the girl's suicide in Chicago." He drew deeply on the cigarette, exhaled slowly, letting the gray smoke roll from his lips. "Mother discovered it. She came charging into Uncle Sty's office with the News in her hand. 'Kit's dead,' she said, then fell over backward into one of the big leather chairs." He filled his lungs with smoke again, let it come out as he talked. "That was nearly six o'clock in the afternoon. Uncle Sty got hold of your Colonel Black who suggested I come out here and try to identify Kit, and said in the meantime he would put a man to work in Chicago. That's about all, except that I got caught in some traffic jammed up by a fire near the mouth of the Holland Tunnel and missed the nine o'clock plane at the airport."

That was about all. Crane asked a few questions, but developed nothing new. They decided that the best thing was to wait for the studio portrait of Courtland's sister, taken about six months later than the passport photograph, to arrive in the morning, and then take it to the Princess Hotel. Courtland refused Crane's invitation to have dinner with them.

"I have to eat with friends in Winnetka," he explained. "The Paul Bruces. He handles some of the estate's business here. I'll be around the first thing in the morning, though, as soon as I get hold of the picture."

"Fine," said Crane. "I think we'll get somewhere with it." He went to the door with Courtland, shook his hand. "Better get plenty of sleep; may be a tough day ahead."

He closed the door and went back to Williams. O'Malley got up from his chair and stood glowering at them. "Now, you bastards," he said, "where'd you hide the liquor?"

Chapter Six

AFTER THEY finished the two-dollar dinner at the College Inn—actually it came to four dollars each with Martinis and a quart of Niersteiner '29—they moved into a suite of rooms on the twenty-ninth floor and ordered a bottle of Martell's brandy. Doc Williams took off his coat and his shoes and said, "Boy, this is the life." In a way he was responsible for the suite (two Early American bedrooms with twin beds, a very large bathroom and a combination Early American and modern living room) because when O'Malley had suggested such an arrangement he had enthusiastically agreed, pointing out that the price was only five dollars a day more than it would have been if all three of them had taken single rooms; and adding, "—and, anyway, it ain't as if it was just for us. We gotta obligation to old Uncle Stuyvesant. HE wouldn't want HIS detectives to have anything but the best . . . not a man in HIS position."

Crane had been alarmed by this plan at first, but by the time they had finished his bottle of Dewar's he was no longer disturbed. He even thought up an additional reason for taking the suite. It had windows on two sides of the hotel, he explained, and that gave you variety. You could look at the City Hall, or you could look at the Ashland Building. Or, if you wanted to drop bottles, you had a choice. You could drop them on the heads of pedestrians on Randolph Street, or you could drop them on the heads of pedestrians on Clark Street.

When the brandy had arrived, had been poured into slender tumblers with ice in them and slightly diluted with White Rock, they settled back in the soft chairs. That is, O'Malley and Williams settled back. Crane had the davenport and he lay down with a pillow under his neck, his feet slung over the back. He put his glass on his chest.

Williams finally broke the silence. He said, "You know, I think there's something funny about young Courtland's attitude. He don't act like a guy who just had his sister kill herself. He don't seem worried, or broken up . . . or nothin'. . . ."

O'Malley said, "Maybe he didn't like his sister."

The glass felt cool and wet on Crane's chest, right through his shirt. "That may be part of it, but I think he's pretty upset," he said. "Did you notice his hands tremble and the way he was smoking one cigarette after the other? His face and his manner were front—just trying to appear tough, unmoved." He shifted the glass so it would cool another part of his chest. "You can always tell about guys from their hands; they don't think to guard them when they're acting with their faces."

Beads of sweat on the glasses in the indirect light were like drops of quicksilver.

"Maybe he knows the dame's not his sister," suggested O'Malley.

Crane asked, "Why would he and his uncle be keeping us on the job, then?"

"Search me." Williams was putting more brandy in his glass. O'Malley said, "Don't forget me." Williams gave him the bottle, asked, "Could you tell anything from the passport photo, Bill?"

"Not a thing." Crane swung his feet down onto the last cushion on the davenport. "Hell! I probably couldn't have told anything if it had been taken only a few weeks ago. People change when they die. Sometimes relatives who've been seeing them every day can't identify them." He tilted the glass, let some of the cold liquor slide into his mouth. "We'll do better when we get the portrait from Mama."

"Say!" Williams sat erect, spilled some of the drink on his trouser leg. He rubbed the spot with the palm of his hand. "What did that guy mean by his mother's yogi?"

O'Malley snorted. "What! you haven't heard of the song?" he asked; ". . . the song about ol' black yogi?"

Crane thought this was funny. He laughed with O'Malley. They laughed even harder at the indignation in Williams' pink face. They laughed until they were wringing wet, until they noticed three men standing inside the room by the hall door. By the hall door, but inside the room!

The men were all dark and scowling. One of them was the Italian. Another of them, in back, was partly in shadow but yellow light washed the third's face. He was not tall, but he was thick. His chest was the shape and the size of a flour barrel and his neck looked like the base of a fire hydrant. He asked the Italian: "Which one's the punk?" He had bushy eyebrows and coarse black hair, like the hair of a horse's tail, grew from a point on his sloping forehead hardly more than an inch above the brows.

Pointing a thick thumb at Crane, the Italian said, "This 's the guy, Chief."

The thick man shambled over to the davenport and looked down at Crane like a grouchy bear. "Didn't Pete tell ya I wanted t' see ya?" he asked. He slurred his words, as though there was something in his mouth.

Crane didn't want to sit up because he was afraid somebody would misconstrue the motion and shoot him. It was ridiculous, though, having to talk with the man while lying flat on his back. He compromised by shoving his neck against the arm of the davenport, so that his head, at least, was vertical. He replied, "He mentioned it, all right."

The thick man's voice was menacing. "When I wanta see som'-buddy I see 'em." He bent over Crane. "Come on. We go som'where an' have a talk."

"This is a nice place to talk," said Crane.

The thick man, still bending over Crane, said, "I think you come wit' me." When Crane shook his head the man who had been in the shadow walked over to the davenport. He was a young man, and his face was dark and smooth. He was scowling, but the youthful appearance of his face made him seem like a sulky girl. He had an automatic pistol in his left hand. He said:

"Get on your feet, smart guy, or I'll give it to you."

There was no expression in his flat, metallic voice.

Crane struggled to a sitting position. O'Malley was already on his feet. He said, "No! No! Sit there." He walked toward Crane, as if to say something more to him, but when he came abreast of the boy he swung his arm in a quarter circle, stingingly slapped his face. The boy staggered backward, throwing his hands in front of his eyes. O'Malley jerked the pistol away from him, slapped him again across the mouth. "Flash a rod, will you, you punk?" he asked savagely. He wheeled around to face the thick man, who was blinking stupidly at him. "Here," he said, thrusting the pistol in the thick man's hand; "put this where baby can't reach it."

The boy was standing in the middle of the green rug now, with his hands at his sides. His face was blue-white, like watered milk, and from the left corner of his mouth ran a trickle of blood. "I'll fog you for that, you son of a bitch," he said to O'Malley. His brown eyes were hot with hate.

Crane wondered why Pete, the Italian, hadn't taken part in the action. He was standing motionless at the back of the room, an expression of negation on his face, as though he was trying to assure someone that he was in no way responsible for the boy's actions. Simultaneously, Crane saw the reason for this attitude. Doc Williams was holding a Colt .45 in his lap, its mouth pointing at the pit of the Italian's stomach.

O'Malley paid no attention to the boy. He was speaking to the thick man. "If you got some business with Mr. Crane, spill it." His face, his tone, his manner indicated fury repressed with difficulty. "You ought to know better than to come around here with a gunsel like that. Jerking a heater out as though it was some kind of toy. I'll bet you're damn fool enough to let him play with matches."

The boy said, "You son of a bitch."

Gold teeth appeared suddenly in the man's thick mouth. "Jeez!" he exclaimed, "You get mad easy." He started to hand the boy's pistol back to him, then decided against it. "Tony, you and Pete go out in the hall. I come out right away." He put the pistol in his coat pocket. "If ya don' hear from me in ten min'ts call fer th' cops." He was grinning broadly now.

Williams waited until the two had gone out before he put his pistol away. He took a drink of brandy and said, "You came near losin' a couple of your boys just then, Mister Paletta. You really oughta be more careful."

Surprise and pleasure were mirrored in Paletta's heavy face. "You know me, huh?" He was wearing a black suit of tightly woven wool and cotton, and there was a wrinkle around the back of the coat where the collar pushed against his neck.

O'Malley said, "Well, I don't. I don't even like you." His blue eyes were pale. "If you got something to say, say it. If you haven't, get out." He looked slender beside the bulky dark man.

Bushy eyebrows almost concealing his bloodshot pupils, Paletta stared at the Irishman. Then he laughed, appealed to the others, "Goddam, ain't he got the temper?" They looked at him with wooden faces. O'Malley said, "There's the door over that way."

Paletta addressed Crane. He spoke rapidly, more distinctly. "Listen, I'm sorry Tony pulled the cannon, Mister. The bambino's gotta learn some t'ings yet." His gold teeth, each time he opened his mouth, reflected the light in quick flashes, like a radio station sending Morse code. "Me, Mike Paletta, don' hurt nobody unless he has to, see?"

Crane asked, "What do you want?" He made his voice unfriendly.

"It's the dame in th' morgue." The dark face seemed unguarded for an instant. "I wanta find 'er."

"You think I took her?"

Paletta was rubbing his right ear. "Listen, Mister, I ain't sayin' who took her. I jus' wanta find her." The hand was moving over the ear in downward, milking strokes. "Listen. You let me have her, an' I let you fix the price. I don' care about th' dough; I got plenty, see?" He bent down toward Crane, thrust out his lower lip. "What about makin' it ten grand, whadusay?"

Crane didn't say anything for a time. Williams had his lips puckered as though he were whistling, but no sound came out. Lighted windows in the Ashland Building to the east made a geometric design on the side of the structure. Neither cool nor hot now, the breeze had died to a whisper.

Finally Crane asked, "What do you want with this girl's body, anyway?"

"I wanta bury her out at Calvary, out by Evanston."

"Bury her! You want to pay ten thousand dollars to bury that girl?" Crane was really astounded. "Why?"

Paletta thrust out his lower lip, said sadly, "She's ma wife."

Bending double, Crane tried to catch his glass before it struck the carpet. He failed, but the glass didn't break, merely spilled liquid in the shape of a pancake stain on the green surface. He handed the glass to Williams, said, "Fill 'er up, Doc, before I faint." He turned back to Paletta. "How do you know she was your wife?"

The thick man told his story with a curious eagerness. His wife's name was Verona Vincent, and she had been a singer at Colisimo's until he had married her five years ago. That was when she was nineteen. They had lived happily together until a year ago, when his wife had run away with Frankie French, that son of a bitch. He would have had Frankie French knocked off, only he still loved Verona, and if Verona loved Frankie, he wasn't going to spoil her happiness. But then, about five months ago, he learned that Verona had left Frankie, that son of a bitch, and had gone to New York.

He had followed his wife there—found her singing in a Third Avenue "barrel house"—and had given her one last chance to come back to him. Verona had agreed, and he had given her five thousand dollars to buy some new clothes, and then, he asked Crane, "Whad' ya think tha crazy dame done?"

Crane said he didn't have any idea.

"She took it on th' lam . . . wit' all th' dough."

This had made him pretty sore. He didn't get mad easily, see? But this had made him pretty sore. He let word get around that he was planning to bump her off, not really intending to kill her, but just to give her a good scare. It must have scared her, too, because he hadn't been able to find her since that time. Last he had heard she was staying in cheap hotels in Chicago with her money all gone and pretty desperate because both he and Frankie French, that son of a bitch, were looking for her.

Crane asked, "What did Frankie French want with her?"

Paletta wasn't sure, but he heard that after she and Frankie had split up a couple of Frankie's best gambling houses had been raided by the police and that Frankie had blamed her for tipping them off. It seemed that the police had had some inside information, anyway.

Crane asked, "What makes you think the dead woman in the Princess Hotel was your wife?" He added, "Especially when you never saw the body?"

Paletta rubbed his ear. "I ain't sure she is, but you gotta admit it looks a lot like it. In the first place, th' papers say th' dame is a swell-lookin' blonde, an' I ain't blowin' when I tell ya Verona's th' classiest blonde anywhere." He glared at Williams and O'Malley as though one of them had denied this, then continued speaking to Crane. "An' besides, why should anybody snatch any other dame from th' morgue like that?"

Crane asked, "Why would anybody take your wife?"

"There's Frankie French, that son . . ."

59

Crane said, "I know he hasn't got the body."

Paletta stuck his right hand out at Crane, palm downward. "Maybe he ain't got her, but I'm overlookin' nuttin', see? He could be pretendin'." His voice was hoarse. "But there's plenty other guys that'd like to get hold of her, too."

"But why?"

"Listen. I'm business agent of the Amalgamated Truck Drivers and Helpers Union, see? An' there's goin' t' be an election o' officers in a couple months." He had both hands in front of him now, palms upward, like a mammy singer. "What chance 'ud I have if word got around I wasn't big enough man t' bury my own wife?" He added darkly: "Tha's exactly the kind of thing that dirty Monahan would use."

"Is the job of business agent worth so much to you?" Crane asked.

"It's wort' som'pin better than fifty grand a year."

Doc Williams actually whistled this time.

Crane said, "Now look here. You probably won't believe it, but I didn't take the body from the morgue. But there's a chance that I may find it. If I do, and it's your wife, I'll make some sort of a deal with you." He was speaking quickly, earnestly. "I have another client who thinks the girl might have been his sister. If it's her we haven't got any deal at all. But the fact is that I haven't got the body."

Paletta's face turned dark and ugly, his voice rumbled like stones in a barrel. "Listen, buddy, you got the body, or you wouldn't be tryin' t' make a deal." He clenched his right fist. "You either . . ."

Someone knocked on the door. "What the hell!" exclaimed Williams. He walked over to the door and opened it. O'Malley kept his eyes on Paletta. A small, pale, black-haired man with gold-rimmed spectacles entered the room. It was Assistant State's Attorney Samuel Burman. One of the men from the homicide squad was with him. Burman's eyes widened when he noticed Paletta.

"Hello, Mike," he said; "what are you doing here?"

"Hello, Mister Burman." Paletta's face was friendly, respectful. "Jus' havin' a little talk with my ol' fren, Mister Crane." He turned to Crane. "I go now. Tomorrow ma'be we make a deal." He paused at the door. "Good-by, Mister Burman."

When the door closed Burman demanded suspiciously, "What was Mike Paletta doing here?" His eyes were curiously examining Williams and O'Malley. He had on a white double-breasted linen suit.

Crane reached over to the table by the head of the davenport and took up his glass. He drank with evident relish. "Mike and I are planning to enter vaudeville, only we need a stooge," he said finally. "How would you like the job?"

60

"Look here, Crane," said Burman. He put plenty of fury in his voice. "I've stood about enough from you. I could have had you arrested, but I've been leaning over backwards in your case. I've said again and again, give him a chance. But if you keep up this wise-guy stuff I'll have you tossed in the can so quick your head'll swim."

"Sure, you've given me a chance," said Crane. "A chance to hang myself."

The homicide man's black coat and trousers were untidy, wrinkled. He moved forward a step, said, "Just say the word, Mister Burman, and I'll put . . ."

Williams interrupted him. "I'd keep out of this, if I were you, flat-foot," he said. There was something incomparably sinister in the way he was twisting his black mustache.

"Oh, a couple of big city torpedoes," said the homicide man, mockingly. He didn't move forward any further, though.

"Now, what do you want?" Crane asked Burman.

"I want to know why you took that girl's body and what you did with it?"

"I didn't take her body."

"I'm getting tired of hearing you say that."

"I'm getting tired of having to say that."

There was a small diamond ring on the third finger of Burman's left hand. It glinted when he waved his arm. "I told you I was leaning over backwards in your case, Crane. That's why I'm giving you a chance to tell me your story before I get out a warrant."

Crane interrupted a drink, spoke with the glass held to his lips. "Get out a warrant? You haven't any evidence for a warrant."

"Oh, haven't I?" Burman straightened his necktie, brushed imaginary dust from the sleeves of his white linen suit. "Did you know the police found your fingerprints downstairs in the morgue?"

"Why shouldn't they? I told you I was down looking at the girl's body."

"Yeah, but they found these prints on the door leading from the corpse reception room to the driveway—right on the knob of the door."

Through the windows the soft, warm wind made a noise like a sleeping person sighing. Ice, melting in the silver container, slipped down a few inches with a tinkling sound.

Crane said, "Well, if you've got the goods on me, why don't you get out a warrant?"

"I thought maybe you'd like to tell us who hired you." Burman's brown eyes glinted. "We know there's somebody behind you, somebody big."

61

Crane sat up straight on the davenport, his glass resting on his knee. "You mean you want me to turn state's evidence?"

"Now we're beginning to understand each other." Burman was rubbing his hands together in a washing motion. "You see? I've been leaning over backwards in your case, like I told you. I spoke to the state's attorney and he . . ."

"I'm sleepy," Crane broke in, speaking to the others. "I'm sleepy, so I'm going to get rid of this guy." Burman had paused in the middle of his sentence, his mouth an O of surprise. Crane continued, "A police sergeant named O'Connor went around to look at the back of the morgue with me after the body was taken. He and I both handled the door. I'll bet your big friend here knows O'Connor?" The homicide man said in a hostile tone, "Supposin' I do?" Crane said to Burman, "You just trot around and see O'Connor, and that'll clear up all your nasty suspicions."

After a period of silence Burman came to a decision. "All right, Crane," he said. "You don't deserve it, but I'll give you a break. I'll go around and see O'Connor." He opened his double-breasted coat and pulled out a white gold chain with a Phi Beta Kappa key on the end of it. He swung the key in a circle. "Now, in return, don't you think you ought to tell us who the girl was?'

"I don't know who she was."

"But you must have some idea." The key hung straight down on the chain now. "You're representing someone, aren't you? These men are also detectives?"

O'Malley said, "Naw, we ain't dicks. We're members of the Purple mob, outa Detroit." Williams said, "I'm the mascot. I only killed nine guys yet." Crane said, "I told you I wouldn't tell you the name of my firm's client, if I knew."

"All right. All right." The blood drained out of Burman's pointed face, leaving it eggshell yellow. "Remember how smart you sona-bitches were when you're all back of the bars." He put the gold key back in his white vest pocket, buttoned his coat, looked at the homicide man, said, "Come on, let's get out of here."

With undisguised amusement the three watched him follow the homicide man to the door. Williams got up, put his glass on the table and crossed the room so as to be able to close the door in case they didn't. Halfway into the hall Burman paused.

"Listen, Crane, I'll give you one more chance," he said. "I'll give you until tomorrow night to tell me your story." He thrust his pointed face back into the room. "You see? I am leaning over backwards."

Williams said, "Well, be careful somebody don't give you a shove." He closed the door gently in Burman's face.

Chapter Seven

PERSPIRATION, DRIPPING from an arm thrown over his eyes, tickled his neck, finally wakened him. Hot sunlight was beating down on his face, on the uncovered top of his body. He opened his eyes and was slightly alarmed, as he always was when he woke in a room strange to him. It seemed to be a nice room, however, and he admired the racing prints on the walls; bright-colored rectangles of spindle-legged horses carrying jockeys over water jumps and along turquoise patches of sward. He looked at his wrist watch. It was a few minutes of nine o'clock. He remembered he was in the Hotel Sherman, in Chicago and he sat up, knocking one of the pillows on the floor. He had only a slight hangover.

He went into the other bedroom to wake up O'Malley and Williams, but they had already gone. He took a long shower, ending it with the cold fully on, and then he got dressed, putting on an unbleached, natural-tan linen suit. He drank some water, and soon he began to feel quite gay and somewhat hungry. He ordered half a grapefruit, soft-boiled eggs, toast and coffee sent up to the room, and while he was waiting he took out the classified telephone directory and called up the larger photographic studios. At the sixth place he located a picture of Verona Vincent and arranged to have a print sent over to him by Western Union messenger.

Breakfast and Doc Williams and O'Malley all arrived at the same time. Williams and O'Malley appeared unpleasantly cheerful, and Crane regarded them suspiciously.

"You guys haven't been drinking this early in the day?" he wanted to know.

They assured him positively, on their honors, that they had not. Did he think they were the sort of characters who would dream of drinking anything before lunch? Did he think that? They both were deeply hurt.

"All right, you mugs," said Crane disgustedly; "I don't mind your drinking so much as your breaking faith with me." He attacked the grapefruit. "I have been entrusted with the difficult and dangerous (yes, I may fairly say dangerous) task of solving this terrible mystery.

Up with the birds in my devotion to duty, I have already located the portrait of the fair Verona Vincent as the first step in a busy day." He brandished his spoon at them. "And what do I find as I sit down to this frugal repast? What do I find? I find my trusted allies already in the embraces of John Barleycorn." He looked at them cunningly, still pointing the spoon, "I suppose one of you even now has some of this deadly, habit-forming drug concealed about his person."

They looked at him solemnly, protesting their innocence. O'Malley, in all fairness, said, yes, he did think he had a small potion somewhere about him. There was no telling when a man would be overcome with faintness; it was foolish to take a chance. Give him a moment, and he'd try to remember where he carried it. Oh yes, here it was in his hip pocket. He pulled out a half-pint bottle of Seagram's V.O. Rye. You see? He'd hardly remembered he'd had it.

Crane took the bottle from him. "Very interesting," he said. He lifted it to his lips.

After a time O'Malley said, "Hey! you bastard, leave some for me." He rescued the bottle and with the aid of Williams emptied it.

While Crane finished his eggs, which had been boiled too long, and drank his coffee, they discussed the case. Doc Williams observed, "It looks to me as though you better work fast. Either the police or one of Paletta's mob is goin' to catch up with you damn soon."

Crane spread a thin layer of orange marmalade on the last piece of toast. "Listen. Beside Frankie French our friend Paletta is one of the rosy-faced boys." He broke off a piece of the toast. "I feel like screaming for help every time I think of Mister French."

O'Malley asked, "What are you going to do about him?"

Crane shrugged his shoulders. "Wait and see what he does, I guess." He tossed his napkin on the table. "Anyway, I've got something for you and Doc to do while Courtland and I show his sister's and Verona's pictures to the people at the Princess." He grinned at them. "It ought to keep you busy, too. I want you to find me an undertaker."

Williams asked, "Just any undertaker?"

"Well, he may be an undertaker's assistant." Crane went over to a wall mirror and admired his copper-colored Charvet tie. "Anyway, he works in an undertaking establishment. He has red hair, and he's left-handed."

His face suddenly sober, Williams said, "The guy who bumped off the morgue keeper, eh?"

"Not exactly. I think the companion of this fellow did the murder. Our undertaker just held Mr. . . . . what was his name? . . . Augie's wrists while the companion socked him with a pistol."

O'Malley's big tanned face was puzzled. "I see how you figure the guy is red-headed, because Augie had some red hair between his fingers, but how do you get the other stuff?" There was a glint of gray in O'Malley's hair, a trace of white around his temples.

"I'm just using my imagination a little," Crane said, turning away from the mirror. "I'm not even sure I'm right. But this is about all we have to go on. Augie must have been attacked by at least two men—one man couldn't have killed him, removed the girl, put him in the box, and made his escape in such a short time." He sat down on the arm of the bigger of the two overstuffed chairs. "Also, he probably wasn't killed by the man who was holding onto his wrists. This fellow couldn't have held onto Augie's wrists, as shown by the marks, and at the same time held a pistol. Now, we also can be pretty sure Augie struggled with this fellow, got his left hand free and pulled out some of his hair."

Crane paused, his lower lip caught between his teeth, his fingers drumming on the chair.

"The funny thing about this is that Augie should have got his left hand free, because Augie was right-handed. Ordinarily, when a right-handed man grabs your wrists, and you're right-handed, too, it is your right arm that you free. That's because he's holding your right arm, your strongest arm, with his left hand. His strongest hand, conversely, is holding your weakest arm.

"But Augie got his left arm free. That makes it look like the assailant in this case was holding Augie's right arm with his strongest hand, that the assailant was left-handed."

Blond pillars of sunlight on the green carpet, below the two east windows, were becoming squat. No wind stirred the curtains; no cloud rode the sky. It was going to be hot again.

Crane continued: "Now, what sort of a man would you get to help you rob a morgue? You'd get somebody who knew his way around a morgue, wouldn't you? Well, that would be either somebody who worked in the morgue or an undertaker. And it would be too dangerous to try to bribe somebody in the morgue."

Doc Williams objected, "But how do you know the red-headed guy is the undertaker? Why couldn't it have been the man who slugged Augie on the dome?"

"If you grant that an undertaker or his assistant was hired to help take the body," Crane said, "it makes him an unlikely murderer. He was hired to help remove the body, that's all. He wouldn't coldbloodedly kill someone. He wouldn't even have a pistol. He would grab somebody's wrists if they attacked him, but that's as far as he would go." He slid off the chair's arm, sauntered over to one of the east

65

windows. "The violence all belongs to the companion, who was desperate enough in the first place to want to steal the body."

While Crane stared across town at the bulky Palmer House they thought it over. At last Williams said, "I guess the Wonder Boy is right again." He twisted his black pointed mustache, smiled at Crane's back. "When do we start?"

"Now." Crane moved away from the window. "I suggest you try to get hold of a salesman of undertaking supplies or somebody who makes the rounds of all the undertakers. Maybe he'll remember a customer with red hair. I'll wait here for Courtland."

As he went out the door behind O'Malley Doc Williams paused and asked, "Ain't you scared Frankie French'll pay you a call while we're gone?"

Crane said, "I'm going to barricade the door."

He was just finishing a report to Colonel Black when the Western Union boy arrived with Verona Vincent's picture. Crane gave him a dollar. It was a large picture, and he had trouble tearing off the stout brown paper. When he finally got the picture out he whistled, then swore.

The picture was a side view of a woman, and, as far as Crane could see, she had nothing on except a white muff which she was holding in front of her slightly below her hips. She had a very nice figure, tall and slender, with a lovely line from hip to shoulder and small, firm breasts. Her face was toward the camera. She was a blonde, and her features were good. She looked more like the girl in the morgue than did Courtland's sister, but Crane didn't feel at all certain that she was the girl in the morgue. The faces were about the same shape, but this girl was smiling, and there was none of that tragic look about her eyes. Crane looked at her breasts and tried to remember what the breasts of the girl in the morgue had looked like, but he couldn't.

He had the picture down on the floor and was looking at it from above when Courtland arrived, carrying a package under his arm. Crane tossed the picture to Courtland, who stared at it admiringly, then asked, "Who is she?"

"She doesn't look like your sister, does she?" Crane countered.

Courtland shook his head. "Not very much." His face looked tired, and, although small wrinkles around his eyes and mouth made him appear older than he had yesterday, he still was boyish. "She's just about the same build as Kit, but the expression on her face is different. Her eyes, too, aren't as large. She's a honey, though. Who is she?"

Crane told him. He told him about the visit they had had with Mike Paletta and also about his experience with Frankie French in

66

the morgue washroom. He concluded, "It seems they both feel sure the body was that of Verona Vincent and that I got it." He didn't mention the search for the red-haired undertaker, however.

Courtland was impressed. "Gosh!" he exclaimed. "A stolen body, rival claimants, an underworld angle, threats . . . what next?" He handed the package he had been carrying to Crane. It was also wrapped in brown paper, and it had fifty-six cents' worth of stamps on it. "This is Kit's portrait. She's wearing more clothes than the cabaret girl, but maybe you can recognize her." He sat down by the writing desk and picked up the telephone. "Do you mind if I order a drink?"

Crane was trying to untie the string on the package with his teeth. "Not at all," he said. "I might even be induced to have a whiskey and soda myself."

The portrait of Miss Kathryn Courtland was a disappointment, too. She was thinner than she was in the passport photograph, but her cheeks were plumper than those of the girl in the morgue. The portrait was of her head and neck alone, and her face was turned in half profile to the camera. Her forehead, nose, mouth and chin were all good, almost patrician, but they lacked the severity of the really patrician face.

Crane said, "Her eyebrows are heavier than the girl in the morgue."

"Kit started plucking them about a year after that portrait was taken," Courtland said.

Crane took the portrait and that of Verona Vincent over to the south windows of the room and held them to the light. Courtland sat quietly at the writing desk while he looked first at one, then at the other. The two women didn't look anything alike, yet their features were very similar. Those of Verona Vincent were perhaps a shade less marked; her nose was slightly smaller, her chin less determined, her mouth sulkier, but there was little choice between them. The difference lay in the expression. Courtland's sister was serious, thoughtful; there was a feeling of sensitiveness about the face as a whole. The face of Verona Vincent expressed a far more lively temperament; it was naturally gay, but the eyes and the mouth hinted at a furious temper. Her face had a vitality lacked by the other girl. Crane felt that Verona Vincent would be fun to take on a party. He wondered if five years had changed her very much.

He put the pictures down when the liquor arrived. "It's got me," he said, accepting a glass from Courtland. "I'd probably see a resemblance in a picture of Evangeline Booth." He added, "Maybe the gal in the morgue was Evangeline Booth."

Courtland smiled at him, made crow's-feet appear at the corners of his blue eyes. "What's the program?" His jaw was square. He was wearing a white linen suit with a navy shirt and a canary-yellow necktie. He seemed to be enjoying his drink.

"I'll put a last line on this letter to my boss," Crane said, "and then we'll hike over to the Princess Hotel with the two photographs."

In moving from the writing desk Courtland took Crane's glass. He added more whiskey and a puff of soda from the siphon, then did the same with his glass.

Crane looked up from his writing in alarm "Hey! I've already had a drink this morning . . . before you came."

Courtland said, "So've I."

It was 2 P.M. when they finished at the Princess Hotel.

They were both exhausted. It had been hot, unbelievably hot, in the hotel. They had removed their coats and neckties, rolled up their shirt sleeves while they showed the photographs to chambermaids, clerks, bellboys, porters. Outside the sun made the sidewalks griddle hot, set the tar squirming from cracks in the streets. The newspapers carried stories of corn popping in central Illinois fields, of eggs being fried on pavements, of prostrations and deaths. The faces of pedestrians were sullen.

Three of the interviews had been notable enough to make Crane write notes on the back of an envelope. The first had been with his friend Edgar, the bellboy. Crane asked him if he had thought of anything further to describe Miss Ross's visitor.

Edgar admitted he hadn't and added: "There's sure been a lot of hell over your being in the room that night. How'd you get out, anyway, jump?"

"Yeah," Crane lied. "It's a wonder I didn't get my neck broken." He asked Edgar if he had ever cleaned any shoes for Miss Ross.

"You bet. She gave me a quarter."

"Did she have more than one pair?"

"Sure." Edgar was scornful. "She had a bunch of shoes. A couple of pairs of sport shoes, you know, with white on them, and some regular ones." He looked at Crane alertly. "You're not so dumb. The cops are trying to figure out why there wasn't any shoes in the room, too."

The night clerk didn't mind being awakened, especially when Crane handed him a ten-dollar bill. His name was Elmer Glaub and he said, "Next to impossible for a feller t' sleep, anyhow, when it's as hot as this." He was a lean man with an axe-thin face, mottled teeth and a prominent Adam's apple. He had on a soiled violet bathrobe. He didn't recognize Crane.

In response to a question he tried to remember something about Miss Ross's friend. "He was wearing a black hat," he recalled.

"I know that," said Crane, impatiently; "but can't you remember anything else?"

Mr. Glaub remembered the fellow was dark, sort of "slick lookin'," and that he was well dressed. He'd never heard his name, had never seen him except when he passed through the lobby the night before she killed herself. No, sir, he didn't know if he had a scar or not.

Crane asked, "Did he stay all night with Miss Ross?"

The clerk's Adam's apple quivered. He giggled, said, "I don't suppose he sat out in the hall."

Courtland, who had been listening silently, winced.

Crane asked Mr. Glaub, "Did you ever see Frankie French?"

"The gambler?"

"Yeah."

"No. At least, not to my knowledge."

There was a musty odor about the clerk's bedroom. Crane prepared to go, then asked, "Can you remember if you saw Miss Ross' friend on the night she killed herself?"

Mr. Glaub, elbow on knee, chin on palm, thought. Suddenly he jerked erect, exclaimed, "My God!" He leaped off the mussed bed, said excitedly, "You know, I did see that guy come down from her room." His bathrobe came open, exposing thin, hairy legs. "He come in and then come hurrying out again. I remember thinkin' they musta had a quarrel." He stopped in front of Crane. "I don't know how I come to forget that."

"About what time was it you saw him?" Crane demanded.

"About twelve o'clock." Mr. Glaub was positive. "I know, because I just come back from havin' a glass of . . . a cup of tea."

"Did he appear frightened?" Crane asked.

Mr. Glaub couldn't remember. "I just know he was in a hurry—you know, walkin' real fast."

Finally, there was the maid on Miss Ross's floor. Her name was Annie Jackson and her skin was the color of root beer with a dash of cream in it. There were beads of sweat on her fat cheeks.

"You never saw the man who visited Miss Ross?" Crane asked her.

She leaned heavily on the handle of a mechanical carpet sweeper. "No, suh; he come after I gone home."

"Did you talk much with Miss Ross? I mean, enough to find out what sort of a woman she was?"

The mulatto's eyes brightened. "She was awful nice to me, Mister. She gave me a dollar." She added that Miss Ross had been worried about something.

69

"Seemed like she was afraid of someone finding her," she said. "She didn't want strangers to see her. She wouldn't even leave me keep the door to the hall open when I was makin' up her room."

Courtland glanced at Crane, who shrugged his shoulders, and then asked Annie: "Did Miss Ross give you any clothes?"

"No, suh." Annie gazed at her broad bosom with a pleased smile. "I reckon she didn't figure they would fit me."

"Did she have a lot of clothes?"

"I guess so."

"You guess?"

"Well, I never seen them all." She pulled out a man's handkerchief from her bosom and wiped her face. "She done kept her closet locked, an' all I seen was what was out in the room."

Crane tried to think of some more questions. He felt that there should be something more to learn about Miss Ross. He asked, "Did she receive any letters?"

Annie said, "I never seen her git any."

"Did she ever have any visitors? In the daytime?"

"No, suh."

"She didn't have any friends, then? Nobody was interested in her?"

"No, suh." Annie began to move the sweeper back and forth, tentatively. "That is, nobody but that woman."

"That woman?"

"That Miss Udoni." Annie's tone expressed dislike. "I think she was tryin' to spy on Miss Ross. One time I caught her peerin' through the keyhole in the hall." The mulatto snorted. "She pretended she had dropped somethin'."

"The hell!" Crane brightened. "Does this Miss Udoni live in the hotel?"

"She did, but she moved out. The day after they found poor Miss Ross."

"You mean yesterday," said Crane.

"Yes, suh." The mulatto gave the sweeper a jerk. "She didn't remember me, neither."

"Have you any idea where she moved to?"

"No, suh. But I kin tell you where she works."

"Where?"

"At th' Clark-Erie ballroom. She's a hostess there."

"A taxi dancer?"

"I reckon that's what you calls 'em." Annie's face was stern. "Over on the South Side we has a differ'nt name for 'em."

Back in the big parlor of the suite at the Hotel Sherman Crane was both pleased and disappointed. Pleased because of the three interviews and disappointed because there had been no opportunity to compare Kathryn Courtland's handwriting with that of Miss Ross. He had found out that Miss Ross had written nothing, had not even signed her name to the register.

Courtland had sent for ice and was pouring a drink, Scotch and soda, into a glass. He asked, "What is the final tabulation on showing the photographs, Mr. Detective?"

Crane groaned, examined the back of his now completely covered envelope. "Well, here're the final results. Three of the hotel people, including Edgar, the bellboy, identified Miss Ross as your sister. Five thought she must have been Verona Vincent. Four didn't know." He accepted the glass. "We now know positively it either was your sister or it wasn't, or that it was Verona or it wasn't."

Courtland said, "Or that it wasn't either." Crane, as usual, had reached the davenport first, and he stretched out with a groan. Courtland, his drink fixed, sank back in one of the big chairs. The hot wind moved an unruly tuft of blond hair on the rear top of his head. He asked, "What's the program now?"

Crane sighed, said, "I'm going to take a nap."

Chapter Eight

"HI, MURDERER."

William Crane opened his eyes. Soft gray light filled the room, obscured the racing prints on the walls, made the greens and reds of carpet and furniture the tints of a Whistler pastel. He had been asleep six hours, and his legs were cramped from having been bent to fit the davenport. Williams and O'Malley were looking at him. He groaned.

"Ain't you going to eat, murderer?" asked Williams. "It's eight o'clock."

He sat up, rubbing his eyes. "Where do you get that murderer stuff?" he demanded.

Williams gave him a copy of the *Evening American*. He glanced

71

at it, exclaimed, "Well, for God's sake!" On the front page of the second section was a photograph showing Mrs. Gertrude Finnegan Liebman pointing a finger at William Crane. Below, in black type, was: "This Man Killed My Husband!"

Crane said, "Oh, my God!" Then he said, "The old bitch! Now Grady and his crew will have to drag me in, with the papers after me." Alarmed, he stared at Williams. "It's a wonder they aren't here now."

Williams said, "We'll take care of you, pal. We'll see you have plenty of cigarettes while you're in jail."

"Listen," said Crane, earnestly. "I don't want to go to jail. I want to go dancing tonight. I'm jazz cuckoo, see? I gotta go dancin' every Satitdy night, see?" He stood up, pretended to tap dance on the carpet.

O'Malley and Willams exchanged glances. "He's off the trolley again," O'Malley observed.

Crane went into the bathroom and doused his head in cold water. He appeared with a towel in his hands. "Gentlemen," he said, "we have to move fast. The fate of a nation is in our hands." He held out one hand to show them how he was holding the nation's fate. He felt fine after his nap, and he wasn't really scared about the police.

"O'Malley, you call Courtland. Tell him to meet us at Hardings on Clark Street, in the Ship's Cabin on the second floor." He finished drying his face. "He's been resting, too, for the dancing tonight. We're going together."

"Oh, you nasty girls," said O'Malley.

Doc Williams was troubled. "Are you going on another bender like you did in the Westland case?" he wanted to know.

O'Malley said, "You should worry. He broke that damned case, didn't he?"

Crane was cleaning off his tan-and-white sport shoes with the towel. "I solve 'em, drunk or sober," he said. "Gentlemen, I give you William Crane. May he always be sober in foreign affairs, but drunk or sober, I give you William Crane." He flicked the towel at them. "A quotation from Stephen Decatur."

They started dinner with martinis at Hardings.

The room was small and comfortable, and in another booth were some chorus girls from the revue at the Apollo. The room was built to represent the inside of a ship. There were portholes with brass rims, and walls and tables of polished oak, and there were nautical instruments—clocks with mechanical calendars on their faces, huge compasses and a barometer—hung head high. The girls were gay and pretty. A lovely blonde kept glancing at their table. Crane winked at her; she winked at him.

Crane said, "I don't know as I'm going to work tonight, after all."

O'Malley said, "I thought you were going dancing?"

Crane finished his martini. He looked regretfully at the blonde. "That's right. Me and Courtland are going dancing."

Courtland's square face was sober. "I'm afraid I can't. I had a wire from Mother. She and Uncle Sty are coming in on the midnight plane. I'll have to meet them."

"I'm sorry," Crane said. "I'd like to have you along." He beckoned to a waiter, said, "We have come here not to bury Caesar, but to eat him."

The waiter said, "Yes, sir."

"You'll help us Sunday, won't you?" Crane asked Courtland.

Courtland said, "Oh, sure."

They ordered steaks broiled on the charcoal fire downstairs. They also ordered hashed brown potatoes in cream, combination salad, French fried onions, and a bottle of Liebfraumilch. Crane said he thought he'd try some Bass ale.

When the food came O'Malley said, "Don't you want to know what me and Doc did today, Master Mind?"

Doc Williams peered at Crane triumphantly over the bowl of combination salad. "You ain't the only one who gets results," he added. There were crisp slices of green pepper in the salad.

Crane was facing them, sitting beside Courtland in the booth. He pretended to choke on his ale, allowed some to spill on his chin. In wiping his face with his napkin he allowed his forefinger to rest vertically against his lips. He said, "Sure, tell me what you did today. I'm all aquiver." He made horizontal, negative motions with his head, still rubbing his face with the napkin.

O'Malley evinced a sudden coyness. "Maybe we oughtn't to tell him, Doc. He's SO young."

"Aw, come on," said Crane. "Come on. Tell me."

"Okay. He asked for it." Doc Williams cut off a big slice of steak, shoved it in his mouth, spoke between chews. "We shadow the big gangster like you tell us. We stick to him like flypaper. We don't let him out of sight all day. And what d'ya think we find?"

Crane said he couldn't guess.

O'Malley said, "We find it's time for supper."

"Aw, you spoiled the story." Williams pretended to be deeply wounded. "I don't never get a chance to tell things." As a consolation he filled his glass with the pale, green-gold wine.

73

Courtland's blue eyes were incredulous. He stared at first at Williams, then at O'Malley. He started to say something but didn't.

"I know," said Crane. "You're disgusted." He finished his ale. "I don't blame you. I am disgusted, too. A fine pair of detectives. A hell of a fine pair of detectives." He turned to Courtland. "And we're paying them well, too. Twelve dollars a week and carfare."

Courtland decided to be amused. "A fabulous sum," he agreed.

The blonde with the other chorus girls came over to their table. She had a pert nose and her lips were vermilion. Crane thought she was going to speak to him. She spoke to Courtland. "Hello, Chance." She had on a pink silk dress.

Courtland stood up. His voice was cordial. "Why, it's Topsy! My God! I didn't recognize you at all. How are you? What in the world are you doing here? Where is Eva?"

Her laughter was a delighted tinkle. "I'm playing at the Apollo. Eva's in New York with Billy Rose. Why don't you drop over after the show some night and have a visit?" She released her hand. "I have to run. Curtain goes up in fifteen minutes."

Crane watched her retreating back. The silk dress was tight across her small buttocks. Courtland said, "I used to play around with her girl friend in New York. She's an awful nice kid."

Williams' black eyes glistened as he enthusiastically agreed. "Yes, sir, she does look like a nice kid. Yes, sir, an awful nice kid." He would have said more, but O'Malley said, "Shut up."

Crane ordered a round of whiskey and soda from the waiter.

Courtland looked at one of the clocks on the wall. It read 8:27. He asked, "How long does it take to reach the airport?"

"About three quarters of an hour," Crane replied.

"Then I have until around eleven. Isn't there something we could do in the meantime?"

Crane said, "We could go to a movie."

"No. I meant some work."

"Oh!" Crane regarded him blankly. "Work? Oh yes, to be sure. Work." He pondered for a second. "No. I prefer a movie."

Williams looked at him with disapproval. "Listen. You better get busy. If the colonel hears . . ."

O'Malley interrupted. "We're going to work, anyway. I think we can get cleaned up on this—" he caught Crane's warning glance "—on this gangster tonight. I mean, we can shadow him some more," he finished lamely.

"Yeah," Williams confided. "We have to run up some carfare. That's how we make our dough. The streetcar company gives us a commission."

74

The waiter came with the drinks. Crane helped him distribute them, then said, "One of you two mugs is coming with me to the taxi-dance joint. I think I'm going to need an assistant."

He explained how he and Courtland learned of Miss Udoni from the colored chambermaid at the hotel.

O'Malley shook his big head. "You don't want anybody to go with you. That'd be foolish. Two persons would make them suspicious. They'd think it was the cops, and everybody'd close up like clams."

"No, I thought about that." Crane took a long, reflective drink of whiskey. "They won't think we're cops if we get drunk enough, not if we get blind drunk." He waved an arm at Courtland. "That just goes to show you nothing is wasted, not if you're wise. You and I have been drinking all day. If we were to go to bed it'd all be wasted. Yes, sir, every drop. Every sweet little drop." He sampled his own drink to show what he meant by a sweet little drop and continued, "But I'm wise. You think I drink just for amusement? Or because I'm scared of Frankie French, that son of a bitch? No. A thousand times no. I have a purpose. I waste nothing. I build up a foundation so I can get drunk and go to the Clark-Erie dancin' establishment without having people suspect I, he, I am a cop." He blinked at them. "The fact is, I am not a cop."

Doc Williams said, "Boy! you really got a foundation."

"Well, gentlemen," Crane demanded; "which one of you are willin' to sacrifice your integrity and get drunk so's you can come with me?"

It turned out they were both willing to make the sacrifice. So willing, indeed, that they had to flip a coin to determine which would be the victim. O'Malley won. He brushed aside Williams' condolences, ignored his offers to take his place. He said, "Let's have another round of sacrifices."

Crane asked, "Shall it be a Scotch sacrifice, or a rye sacrifice, or just a good old plain gin sacrifice?"

They decided on Scotch sacrifices.

Later they said good-by to Courtland and Williams. Courtland wanted to go to his hotel before meeting his mother and uncle, and Williams was determined to finish the work he and O'Malley had been doing. Crane and O'Malley hailed a Yellow cab. "Chicago Theater," O'Malley directed the driver.

"Now, you bum," said Crane when they had started. "What'd you and Doc find out?"

The cab went south on Clark Street and made a left turn at Washington Boulevard in violation of a traffic ordinance. O'Malley said, "I think we got your undertaker for you. At least we found a red-headed guy who's an assistant in a joint on the South Side."

Crane caught sight of the lights of the Chicago Theater to the left, to the north, as they crossed State Street. They were going at right angles to the theater. "What are you trying to do," he asked the driver, "creep up on the place?"

"With these new traffic regulations," said the driver, "to cross the loop you gotta go by way of Gary, Indiana."

Crane asked O'Malley: "What's Doc going to do?"

"He's going to find out if the guy's left-handed."

"Good," Crane said magnanimously. "Couldn't have thought of a better idea myself."

O'Malley was looking out of the back window of the cab. "Jesus!" he exclaimed. "I think somebody is following us!"

They swung up in front of the theater, and a tall doorman opened the cab door. Crane paid the driver, said to O'Malley, "I hope it's that cute little blonde."

Chapter Nine

WHEN THEY came out onto the street again, a few minutes before midnight, air as hot and stale as the wind from an electric hair drier in a beauty parlor met their faces. They elbowed their way through the crowd under brilliantly illuminated theater signs on Randolph Street, pushed into Henrici's where they each had two glasses of Planter's punch. Then they took a cab.

"Excuse me," said the driver when Crane gave him the address, "but that's a dive. You gentlemen would do better somewhere else."

"Listen," said O'Malley, "if we'd wanted a guide we would of hired a rubberneck wagon."

"O.K., boss," said the driver.

As they pulled away from the curb Crane leaned back in the seat, closed his eyes and sang softly:

"Don't bring me posies when It's shoesies that I need."

"What the hell made you think of that?" demanded O'Malley. "I ain't heard that song for ten years, I guess."

76

"That Miss Ross. I keep thinking about her. What's a dame like that doin' without shoes?"

O'Malley said, "Maybe she was Japanese."

They crossed the Clark Street Bridge and went at a good clip past the rundown section nearest the river. Later the street grew brighter, and there were cabarets, restaurants, and dollar-a-night hotels. As the cab slowed in front of Ireland's, its windows filled with huge lobsters, sea turtles and solemn salt-water fish, O'Malley said:

"I think we lost them guys."

Crane asked, "What guys?"

O'Malley said, "Oh my God!"

The twinkling sign above their heads was green and red and white, and it read:

CLARK-ERIE—50 BEAUTIFUL HOSTESSES

Paint long ago had been worn from the surface of the stairs, and each step was splintered and cracked. The steps creaked under their feet. As they neared the top they could hear the noise of a jazz band playing with plenty of volume and using a great deal of brass. At the rear of the second floor landing was a booth, with a counter along two thirds of its front and a steel cashier's cage with a fat black-haired woman in it. There was a sign in red paint over the cage reading:

COSTUME BALL TO-NIGHT! ! !

Two Filipinos wearing light-gray Hart, Schaffner and Marx suits were leaning against the counter drinking orange crush from bottles and talking to an unshaven man with a bandage over one ear. The woman had yellow tickets on a roll. She asked, "How many?" Her voice had no inflection at all, no rise in tone to mark an interrogation.

Crane leaned against the steel bars. "How many what?" he inquired.

Small eyes gelid, the woman examined him.

Crane turned to O'Malley. "She wants to know how many," he said. "What do you think of that?"

O'Malley reached over Crane's head and seized one of the bars, and pulled himself to the counter with a tremendous effort, as though he were breasting a gale. "Tell her there's two in our party," he said. "Ask her if she'd like to join us."

The woman's face was watchfully sullen.

"I'd rather she didn't join us," Crane said. "I don't like her looks." He cocked his head, examined her. "Too fat."

Leaving the two Filipinos, the man with the bandaged ear came over to them. His face was furious. "You bastards can get out of here," he said. "We don't want your business."

O'Malley, with an air of pleased surprise, said: "Well, well, look who's here!"

Crane pulled ten dollars out of his pocketbook, shoved it under the curved opening of the cage. "Madam, I am sorry," he said. "Give us that many tickets."

"Better not, Mame," the man with the bandaged ear warned her. "These guys are crocked to the gills."

With no change in her plump, impervious face, the woman handed Crane a long block of tickets. The man watched them, frowning. Crane gave half the tickets to O'Malley, started for the burgundy-colored velvet curtain hanging across the hall at the end opposite the stairs. O'Malley said to the man, "It's been a great pleasure," and shoved himself from the cage and followed Crane.

Taking hold of the curtain just below the sign NO CHEWING GUM OR LIQUOR ALLOWED, Crane swung it open, stepped inside, tried to peer through the strange, red-glowing semi-darkness of the ballroom. Trumpet notes from the orchestra, going hot and heavy and raucously on "I'm a Ding-dong Daddy from Duma," beat against his eardrums, almost obscured the sush-sush of leather on the waxed floor. There was in the torrid, heavy, humid air a sickening odor; a combination of human sweat, penny-a-squirt perfume, gin breath. Red and green and orange crepe paper, cut in strips, hung from the ceiling everywhere, like Spanish moss.

"My God!" whispered O'Malley in Crane's ear. "What kind of a joint is this?" His hand hurt Crane's shoulder. "What've them dames got on?" He pushed up beside Crane. "For God's sake, look!"

Crane was looking. He shook his head, looked again. He said, "Either we got X-ray eyes, or those babies are dancing in their underwear."

They finally decided the girls were dancing in their underwear. Each one had on a brassière, silk panties, silk stockings and high-heeled slippers. There was a line of flesh on each girl from breast to hip and from one third the way down their thighs to their knees. The men were mostly Filipinos, and they were all completely clad.

Crane felt sobered and a little disgusted. He noticed, however, that some of the girls were quite pretty. O'Malley didn't say how he felt. He signaled a tall blonde who was dancing with a red-haired girl, boldly put his arm about her bare waist and plunged out into the crowd on the floor. Crane noticed the blonde had pimples on her face, on her back. She had a good figure, though.

The red-haired girl came up to him, asked, "How about it, honey?" She was a trifle plump and her face was heavily powdered and rouged. She had on green silk panties.

Crane said, "Sure." His right hand rested on a bulge of warm flesh just above her hip; his left hand, holding her right, instantly became damp. He said, "It's hot, isn't it?" They moved out onto the floor and presently he asked "You don't have to dance like that, do you?"

She said, "What's the matter? Don't you like me?"

"I'm crazy about you," he said. "I just don't like to dance that way."

Under their heavy coating of blue-black mascara her eyes were surprised and angry. "Okay," she said. "It's your dime."

She turned out to be a good dancer and they moved easily about the floor, swishing past other couples and whirling on the turns. When the piece ended and she started to leave him he held her hand.

"That wasn't so bad," he said. He gave her five of the yellow tickets. "How about another?"

She stared at him coldly, but she left her hand in his.

The orchestra began to play "My Disposition Depends on You" from *Hit the Deck*, and he put his arm around her waist again. He always danced well when he was drunk, and the music seemed excellent, too. He wondered if he would have thought so, sober. The trumpet player had long black hair, and it fell over his eyes when he bent down over his instrument and then fell back of his ears when he raised it to the dark ceiling. He swung off on several wild, inspired riffs, and when the orchestra came to the part of the song which goes:

> "Sometimes I'm happy,
> Sometimes I'm blue,
> My disposition
> Depends on you . . ."

he barrel-housed the "you-ooo" with wailing blue notes that sent shivers up and down William Crane's back.

Entranced, he slowed the pace of their dancing, watched the man. "He *can* play!" he said.

"He plays a gang-o-horn," the red-haired girl agreed, "but you oughta hear the boy on the sax swing it when he's feeling right." Her voice was friendlier.

As they continued to dance Crane examined the other couples. They moved their feet very little, shuffling about on one spot, sometimes with their hands out to the side in the conventional ballroom manner but more often with the woman's arms about the man's neck and his around her bare waist, Apache style. The women stared over their partners' shoulders, their expressions rapt, contemplative, oblivious, while the men, mostly, stared down at the women's faces. There was practically no conversation except among the extra girls, who danced together, taking short, jerky steps.

79

After several dances, Crane said, "I've got a friend who comes up here a lot. He asked me to give a message to one of the girls."

The red-haired girl glanced up at him suspiciously. "What's her name?"

"That's the trouble," he said. "I've forgotten."

"Well, what does she look like?"

He thought for a while. "I think he said she was dark."

"That's a big help." They paused for one of the thirty-second intermissions, and she accepted five more tickets. "There are only about forty dames up here with dark complexions."

"Wait a minute. I think I remember her last name." He pulled at his lower lip with his teeth. "I think it's something like Alone, or Adone, or something."

"You don't mean Angela Udoni?"

"Sounds something like it, all right."

She pulled him a half turn to the left. "That's her, over there with the grease ball in the purple suit. The black-haired girl."

Miss Udoni was dancing with a Filipino in a suit which certainly looked purple. She was slender, and she had on yellow silk panties and a yellow brassière. He couldn't make out her face in the dim light. Back of her, all at once, he caught sight of the man with the bandaged ear and another man, slender and dark. They were staring at him. He looked around for O'Malley, found him just as he and the tall blonde with pimples came to a sudden stop on the floor. The blonde pulled herself out of O'Malley's arms, slapped his face sharply, walked away from him.

"For God's sake!" exclaimed Crane.

He stopped dancing. "You'll have to excuse me. I think my friend is in trouble over there."

He went over to O'Malley, asked: "What happened?"

Other couples were looking curiously at O'Malley, who was rubbing his face and grinning. "I insulted her."

"Christ!" said Crane. "How could you?"

O'Malley said, "We were talkin' about theme songs, and I said the chorus of hers ought to begin: 'You're the acne of perfection.'" There was an angry red mark on his cheek. "So she slugged me."

"Listen," Crane said. "We've got to get to work. I've located the gal, but the management doesn't seem to like our looks." He pointed to where the man with the bandage and the slender man were standing. "Keep your eyes open, and I'll see what I can find out from Miss Udoni."

He located her by her yellow brassière and tapped her partner on the shoulder. "There's a guy out in the hall wants to see you, buddy,"

80

he said, making his voice gruff. "I think it may be a copper." He put his arm around Miss Udoni, shook his head at the Filipino's puzzled face. "Better be careful."

The skin over Miss Udoni's hip was smooth and firm, and her muscles were supple. Her shoulders were rounded, but he couldn't see her face very well. She danced beautifully.

"How come you don't dance like the others?" he asked.

She said, "I do if they ask me to." Her voice was fresh, her enunciation cultured. "Do you want me to?"

"God, no!" They were passing the orchestra, and he was surprised to notice the trumpet player watching him. "I'm no wrestler." He sniffed appreciatively. "Nice perfume, that Shalimar. Expensive, too."

"How did you know?" She raised her head until her eyes met his. He saw they were gray-green.

"I know everything. I know your name is Miss Udoni. Angela Udoni. That's pretty."

He felt her back muscles stiffen under his hand. "How did you know my name?" Her voice was suspicious but not unfriendly. "Did you just make up that story about the man wanting to see Pedro?"

"Pedro?"

"The boy who was dancing with me."

"Yes. I made it up." He danced evenly, smoothly. "I noticed you on the floor—I like yellow, you know—and I asked the girl I was dancing with who you were. Then I came over. You look very nice in yellow."

She blushed, pressed closer to him so he was unable to see her brassière. "You needn't make fun of me. I'm just earning a living."

"I'm sorry. But I think you do look nice."

She didn't reply, and they danced silently for a while. Suddenly he saw coming toward him from the curtained entrance, the slender man. With him was Tony, the boy who had pulled the gun on him in his room at the hotel. They were coming toward him, not hurrying, but moving rapidly. In a line that would intersect their course before they reached him, and moving still faster, paced O'Malley. The orchestra was playing "Lullaby of Broadway," and outside an automobile horn was honking.

Crane swung Miss Udoni around and danced towards the end of the floor opposite the entrance, away from the two gunmen. In the center of the floor, in the midst of swaying couples, O'Malley encountered the pair. He planted himself in front of them, spoke to the slender man. They halted, answered him furiously, motioned for him to get out of their way. From the entrance fifty feet away, almost running, came Pedro the Filipino, and the man with the bandaged ear. Pedro looked as though he were going to cry.

81

Outside the horn had stopped honking.

The slender man attempted to push O'Malley out of his way. O'Malley struck him lightly on the chest with his left hand, then let him have a stiff right to the chin. Whirling in a half turn to the left, the slender man lost his balance, sprawled upon the floor. The boy had the automatic pistol in his hand. He crouched, sidled around his companion's form, spoke as though he was spitting. Crane could hear him say:

"Nobody's going to stop me this time, you son of a bitch."

The man with the bandaged ear and the Filipino were running now, right behind the boy. Their feet pounded the floor. O'Malley's face was joyful. He shouted, "Good work, boys; you've got him now."

The boy swung around like a coral snake to face the running feet.

O'Malley leaped, threw his arms around the boy, reached for the pistol. There was a hollow report and the Filipino, still running, his angry, almost weeping eyes fixed on Crane and Miss Udoni, plunged headlong onto the floor, slid twenty feet across its polished surface on his face, bowled over two couples like a well-trained blocking half-back, and came to a stop almost at Crane's feet. He was either dead or unconscious.

Someone by the curtained entrance screamed:

"The police!"

More than a dozen men, some of them in uniform, ran into the room. O'Malley had the boy's pistol, was beating him across the face with it. The slender man was trying to rise from the floor, comically, because his feet couldn't get traction on the wax.

Crane seized Miss Udoni's hand. "A raid!" he said. "How can we get out of here?"

She said, "Through the girls' dressing room. There's a fire escape."

They ran toward the dressing room, but the attendant with the bandaged ear got in front of them, said, "No, you don't."

Crane hit him on the bandage with a tremendous roundhouse swing, and he faded away.

Gas burning under a red globe set red shadows flickering in the dressing room. Back of a large, half-opened window Crane could see the fire escape. He said, "Come on." His hand hurt.

She halted. "I can't go out on the street like this. I'll have to find my dress."

"My God!" He spied a pile of dresses on a table. "Here!" He scooped up an armful. "One of these will fit you." He pulled her out the window, down the steel steps into a pitch-black alley. They ran along it until faint light from the street reached them, then halted while she put on one of the dresses, a black one with an imitation gardenia pinned over the left hip.

"This is much too big," she said.

"It'll have to do until we get to some place where you can change. We've got to get away from here before that bandaged gent tips off the police." He led her out into the street, still carrying the other dresses. "We'd better get a cab."

Inside the cab, he said, "Whew! that was a close one."

She said, "Do you know, you look familiar to me."

"That's funny. I was just thinking the same thing." He tried to see her face, but in the darkness of the cab he couldn't make it out. "My name's Crane, Bill Crane. Does that mean anything to you?"

It didn't.

When they reached her hotel—the Alexander, on Wilson Avenue— she tried to say good-by. "My gosh," he objected, "after all we've been through, don't you think we ought to have a bite to eat?"

"All right, but I'll have to put on one of my own dresses."

Crane paid the driver, came into the hotel lobby with her. It was dark, and there was only a light over the automatic elevator. "What'll I do?" he asked. "Sit down here?"

"Oh, you might as well come up. I have a dressing room."

She got her key, and he followed her into the elevator, and they went up to the seventh floor. It was dim in the elevator, and in the corridor. She unlocked the door, switched on a brilliant indirect light and motioned for him to enter. She closed the door and they turned toward each other, curiously. Swiftly the half smile on her lips was erased; her eyes, green-gray, became as large as poker chips. She crossed her arms over her breasts and screamed.

Chapter Ten

"LISTEN," said William Crane earnestly, "I'm sorry to always have to be tying you up this way, but you *do* seem to like to scream." He was sitting in a moderne white-leather chair, his legs thrust out in front of him. He had found some whiskey and was drinking it mixed with cold water. "I think we might have a very beautiful friendship, if you just wouldn't scream. Why don't you try not screaming for a while—just as an experiment?"

She shook her head. Her strange, greenish eyes, over the towel around her mouth, were angry. She was lying on a scarlet-cushioned chaise longue, and her hands and feet were bound with tan silk stockings.

"I am really sorry about the other night," Crane continued, "but that was the only way I had of dodging the police, short of leaping to my probable death on a roof below Miss Ross' window. You wouldn't have wanted me to do that, would you?"

She nodded, yes.

He grinned. "Listen, I didn't hurt you when I got in bed with you. I didn't even hurt your boy friend. I put him back right where I found him. You can't say I'm not considerate . . . or neat." He took a long drink. "You still want to scream?"

She nodded, yes.

He stood up, stretched his arms over his head, yawned. "Pardon me." He examined the room with interest. "Not a bad place for a taxi dancer."

Miss Udoni's apartment consisted of a large room, the walls of which were two shades of white, a dressing room and a bathroom. Scarlet curtains hung at the windows of the large room; one chair was covered with white leather, another with red leather, and the combination couch-bed was the color of cherries. A tall silver-and-black lamp on a pencil-thin metal stand threw light up at the white ceiling, so that the reflected rays lit the room indirectly.

There was a checkbook lying on a small table with chromium legs and a black composition top, and William Crane picked it up. It was for the First National Bank of Chicago, and the last stub (number 7) showed a balance of $3,251.68. He whistled.

She watched him move about the room. Her eyes, now darker, more green-blue than gray, were apprehensive. The too-large black dress had slipped down over one rounded shoulder, exposing white skin and a triangle of yellow silk.

In the closet off the dressing room were dresses and coats. He looked at the label in a light-green evening wrap with a summer ermine collar. It was Saks, Fifth Avenue. A black silk dress also had a Saks' label. On a dressing table, among combs and manicure instruments, was a bottle of Guerlain's Shalimar perfume. He stuck his head into the bathroom. A red-rubber shower cap hung from a hook over the tub; back of the door were pink mules, a pink robe-de-nuit.

On a stool beside the tub was a large round bottle half filled with black liquid. A white label read: "Armaud's theatrical Hair Tint—Black." The medicine cabinet was filled with cosmetics, gargles, two toothbrushes, a blue metal container of Dr. Lyon's tooth powder.

Crane went back into the large room and said: "Three grand in the bank isn't bad for a girl who's just trying to earn a living." He bent over Miss Udoni, said, "Listen, if I was going to rob, rape or murder you I would have done it long ago. My intentions are very honorable, indeed. I simply want to talk with you. Won't you talk to me?"

She nodded her head, yes.

"You won't scream?"

She shook her head, no.

He took off the towel gingerly, ready to shove it back in her mouth. Her face was composed, however, and he stepped back, smiled, said, "There, that really improves your appearance."

Unsmiling she said: "Aren't you going to untie my hands and feet?"

He took out the clipping from the *Evening American* showing Mrs. Liebman pointing at him and saying: "That Man Killed My Husband."

"You see, I'm a desperate guy. A hell of a desperate guy. I don't want any funny business." He felt her tremble as he undid the stockings around her feet, her hands. He looked up at her face. She was laughing.

He sat down on the chaise longue in the love seat made by her bent knees. "Want a drink?" She said, "No. What do you want with me?" He said, "I've got some questions I want to ask you." She said, "Well . . . ?"

"First, I want to know why you were so interested in Miss Ross at the Princess Hotel?" He arched his back, added, "Say, if you jump like that again you'll have me on the floor."

The blood had drained from her face, leaving only a raspberry smear on her lips. "You sit in that curved white chair," she said. "You make me nervous here." Her eyes were a cloudy aquamarine. "I promise not to scream."

He found his drink, sank back in the chair. "Well, how about Miss Ross?"

She bit at the narrow, highly polished, flesh-tinted nail on her forefinger. "I was curious to see . . ." she began. White light reflected from the ceiling came down across her face, made shadowed pools of her eyes, hollowed her cheeks. Suddenly she looked directly at him. "You knew my husband had eloped with her?"

Crane said, "Well, I guessed it. When did this happen?"

"About five months ago . . . in New York."

"Your husband was a musician, wasn't he?"

"Yes. He played with Vallee."

He drained the glass. "Why didn't he stick with Rudy?"

"He wanted to form a band of his own—that is, one in which he would have a part interest. That's why we quarreled in the first place. He gave up two hundred a week with Vallee for nothing a week with his new band."

"That *is* quite a cut." He filled his glass a third the way up with whiskey. "Won't you have some?"

She said, "I might as well, since I paid for it." She found another glass, let Crane pour her an equal amount of whiskey. She took both glasses. "I'll get some water in the bathroom."

He was uneasy while she was gone, but she came back almost at once. She saw his troubled face and her lips were faintly contemptuous. "I told you I wouldn't scream."

He accepted the glass. "Thanks." The liquor was cool and tasted faintly smoky. "That certainly hits the spot." He put the glass on the black composition table. "Now, where did your husband meet Miss Ross?"

"Somewhere in New York. While he was playing at the Savoy-Plaza, I think. She got him to leave his job with Vallee."

"Why did she do that?"

"She told him he could make a name for himself with a hot band instead of spending all his life with the long-underwear boys." She drank the whiskey as though she didn't like it. She drank it in gulps. "Of course, her real reason was to get him for herself."

Crane was frowning. "The long-underwear boys?"

"The big commercial sweet bands."

"I guess I get the idea. Anyway, how'd they ever get to Chicago?"

"The new band had a contract in the Kat Klub on Walton Place. They played there for a couple of months, and then the place went broke." She had nearly finished her drink. "I didn't know they had come to Chicago until I got a letter from him asking me for a divorce so he could marry her. Of course, I couldn't do that."

Crane said, "Of course not."

Faint color seeped into her cheeks. "So I came here myself. I got a room next to hers at the Princess Hotel, so I could watch her."

"Why did you want to watch her?"

"I knew sooner or later she'd double-cross him, and I wanted to be able to tell him about it. I didn't want him to get hurt."

"You still love him, then?"

She shrugged her shoulders, "Something like that." Her voice was defiant. "Some women are fools." She held out the glass. "Another."

As he filled her glass he asked, "If you'll pardon my getting personal, I'd like to know who that gentleman was I had to remove from your bed that night." He stopped pouring, held the whiskey bottle over the glass. "Your brother?"

She sat up angrily. "No!" For an instant Crane thought she was going to throw the whiskey at him, prepared to duck. "That was Sam."

"Oh! Just old Sam, eh? Good old Sam."

"My husband." She leaned back in the chaise longue again. "He was drunk . . . he got drunk after he found that woman's body, and I had to do something with him."

"So you took him to bed with you."

"I couldn't get him to go to his room . . . he was afraid."

"Of whom?"

"The police."

"Why the police?"

"I don't know." She drank, but her cloudy eyes never left his face. "He didn't tell me."

"Maybe he didn't want to get mixed up in the suicide because the publicity would hurt him professionally?"

"Maybe."

With his glass to his mouth, the edge touching his lower teeth, he pondered. "What did he do the night Miss Ross died?" he asked finally.

"I don't know."

"Well, how did you happen to find him the night I so rudely burst upon you?"

"Oh, I've been keeping my eye on him."

"Where can I find him?"

She took a long drink of the amber liquid before she answered. Then she spoke in such a soft voice that he was barely able to hear her. "I don't know."

"You mean you won't tell me?"

"Yes."

Her eyes, her mouth, her chin were resolute. Crane stared at her admiringly, said, "I sort of go for you." He leaned over so that his elbows were on his knees. "Look. I just want to find out one thing. Then I'll leave you and your husband alone."

Her face guarded, she watched him.

He said, "I want to know who Miss Ross really was."

She shook her head. "I'd like to know myself."

87

"Do you think she was a society gal?"

"I don't know." She handed him her empty glass. "I never had an opportunity to talk with her." Her voice was grudging. "She was beautiful, though."

Crane drained his glass, put whiskey in both the glasses and went into the bathroom for water. As he let the cold run into the wash basin he noticed the bottle of hair restorer had been taken from the stool. He opened the medicine cabinet and saw that the bottle had been placed on the top shelf. He brought the filled glasses out to her.

"Do you think your husband would know who she was?" he asked as he gave her the glass.

"I don't think he had any idea she was anybody but Miss Ross." She peered up at him. "What makes you think she was somebody else?"

"Well, in the first place it's funny nobody claimed her. And, in the second, it's funny somebody would think it worth while to rob the morgue to get her body."

She drank, agreed. "It is funny."

"You don't know of any friends she had, or any family?"

"No."

"Do you think your husband would?"

"I don't know."

"Do you know why he didn't live with Miss Ross instead of just visiting her?"

"I don't think she would let him live with her."

He tapped his fingers against his glass. "We don't seem to be covering much ground." He frowned at her. "How do you happen to be working in that taxi-dance place when you've got three thousand in the bank?"

"Oh, I can't touch that."

"Why not?"

"Sam gave it to me when he left me." Her eyebrows curved like the arches in a Romanesque cathedral. "I won't touch a cent of it until he comes back."

Crane looked at her with admiration. "You've got looks and character, baby." He lifted his glass in a toast to her. "If he doesn't come back you can send for me."

"He'll come back, all right."

"Well, listen, baby. I'm sort of a detective. All I want to do is find out who Miss Ross was. I don't want to hurt your Sam, but I'd like to talk to him. Maybe he can help me." He glanced at her composed face. "Won't you tell me where I can find him?"

She shook her head.

"Well, tell him this. If he feels like helping me out and at the same time avoiding trouble tell him to get in touch with me at the Sherman Hotel." He finished his drink, stood up. He found he was quite a little drunk. "The name's William Crane to him but Bill to you, baby."

Her murky eyes were questioning. "Avoid what trouble?"

"The inquest is still open on Miss Ross' death, and the police would be glad to have him for a witness if I tipped them off." He swayed slightly.

She didn't seem especially frightened. "If I see him I'll tell him that." She followed him to the door, stood there beside him. Her hair was fragrant. She said, "Thanks for escorting me home."

"That's quite all right." He wondered if he dared kiss her. He decided she'd probably kick him. "You're not afraid to be alone, are you? I mean, if you'd like me to stay I'd . . ."

"I'm not afraid."

He nodded sadly. "I didn't think you would be."

She said, "Well, good-by."

"Good-by."

He said, "There's no harm in asking, is there?"

"No. Good-by."

He reached over and lightly pinched her cheek between thumb and forefinger. "I like you, baby." He started down the hall, using his left hand as an additional means of locomotion by shoving himself from the wall every time he veered into it. At the end of the corridor he turned to wave to her.

She had already closed her door.

Chapter Eleven

AFTER HE had paid the cab driver at the Randolph Street entrance of the Hotel Sherman Crane paused to appreciate the sunrise. He felt that he was becoming a connoisseur of sunrises, and as one authority to another he spoke to the milkman.

"Pretty nice," he said.

The milkman was loading cases of empty bottles on his white truck. He held one of the cases for an instant, looked east on Randolph Street. "Yeah," he agreed, "it's good and red. Only I wish it'd rise in the west once in awhile, just for variety."

Crane said, "I'll do what I can for you," and entered the hotel.

In two of the tapestry-backed chairs, asleep, were Williams and O'Malley. Williams had his legs thrust out so that his heels alone touched the floor; his head was thrown back and his mustache quivered a little each time he snored. He awoke with a start when Crane touched his shoulder.

Crane asked, "What's the matter with your bed upstairs?"

"Nothing, except there's a couple of guys in it."

"Cops?"

O'Malley was awake now. "A flock of 'em, all lookin' for you. They got a warrant."

"The hell!" Crane's face expressed extreme distaste. "I need some sleep, too." He thrust his hands in his trouser pockets, glanced at Doc Williams. "What'll I do?"

Williams was unsympathetic. "If you can just keep that nasty old sandman away for a couple of hours we could go out and see the left-handed, red-haired, undertaking gentleman."

Crane simulated overwhelming vitality. "All right. We'll go. Right now." He assumed a military posture. "The Queen expects every man to do his part." He walked over to O'Malley, who had stood up, and embraced him, pretended to kiss his cheeks. "Sir, I wish to thank you for saving my life."

O'Malley shoved him away, said, "Nuts."

Williams eyed Crane with disgust. "You can stay drunk the longest . . ."

"You didn't have to sit up all night with a swell babe, did you?" Crane demanded. "You didn't have her ply you with drinks until your head whirled, did you? You bet you didn't."

"All right. All right."

Crane shook his head sadly. "The things a man has to do in the line of duty." He led the way to the door. "It's ruining my character."

O'Malley said, "I'll sit up with that Udoni babe any time."

Once the cab had reached the outer drive and was heading south at forty miles an hour Crane asked:

"Where does this undertaker hang out, Doc?"

"Right by the Hyde Park police station, at 5217 Lake Street. It's called the Star Mortuary. The guy's name is Theodore Connell, and he works the night shift from mid-night until eight o'clock."

Crane looked at his wrist watch. It was 6:11. He said, "We'll catch him easily." He spoke to O'Malley. "How'd you ever get out of the jam in that dance hall?"

Suspended over the lake like an Orange Pekoe tea ball on a string, the sun was already uncomfortably warm.

O'Malley replied, "I'm a hero. It seems the dicks wanted that gunsel, Tony, on a murder rap, and they were glad to take what was left after I finished cuffin' him around." He smiled reminiscently. "My story was that I bumped into them two accidentally on the floor and naturally got sore when they started to swear at me. When Tony pulled a gun I tried to take it away from him, and it went off and shot the Filipino."

"Kill him?" asked Crane hopefully.

"Naw. You can't kill them Hershey bars. Anyway, some of the dancers backed up my story, and the cops thanked me very politely, and took Tony to the hospital, and tossed the other torpedo in the can."

Crane nodded. "Naturally, Tony and his pal couldn't tell the police they were sent up there by Mike Paletta to get me."

"I don't think they wanted to put you on the spot; just pull you in so's Mike could talk to you." O'Malley grinned again. "You're a popular guy."

"How'd the police get there so quick?"

"That guy with the bandaged ear—the one you slugged—called them when Paletta's boys got there. He recognized Tony and knew he was going to make trouble."

"I suppose Tony was the one who shadowed us."

"Somebody from Paletta's gang."

With the whish of a sudden exhalation a compact seventy-mile-an-hour electric train on the Illinois Central tracks passed them. The broad drive was dotted with automobiles now, carrying people to seven o'clock jobs. The lake was so calm it looked frozen.

O'Malley was chuckling again.

"You seem to have gotten a lot of fun out of that dance hall," Crane said.

"I was just thinking about those floosies working there. Boy, were they mad! Somebody stole the dresses of about twenty of them, and they had to go home in their B.V.D.'s."

Crane said, "I stole 'em." He told them how he and Miss Udoni had escaped down the fire escape and related his conversation with her. They were both amazed when he told them she was the woman he had been in bed with at the Princess Hotel. He concluded: "She's a nice dame. I may have to go back and see her again."

"I'll go with you," O'Malley said.

"No, you won't."

Doc Williams asked, "How are you going to locate her husband? All you know is that his name is Sam and that he plays in a band."

"I'm thinking about that." Crane scratched the back of his neck. His hand still hurt, and he examined his knuckles to see if he had broken them in hitting the man with the bandaged ear. "I got an idea the guy's a swing artist."

O'Malley said, "I thought you said he was a musician?"

The knuckles seemed sound. Crane turned his hand with a flourish. "You fellows don't know how us musical artists talk. A swing artist is a hot musician."

After another mile along the lake they turned right on Fifty-third Street, went under the Illinois Central tracks and turned left on Lake Street. It was just 6:30. They came to a stop in front of a two-story, gray-stone building with a smudgy display window, the upper portion of which was decorated with gold lettering, reading STAR MO TUARY. The first R in mortuary was missing.

Groaning, the glass-paned front door opened under Williams' hand. The air in the green-carpeted reception room was musty. There was an odor of floor polish and embalming fluid, aromatic, sweet and sickening. Williams said, "Mr. Connell." Three-quarter-drawn blinds made the light gloomy.

Williams spoke louder. "Mr. Connell!"

"Maybe he's in the back," suggested O'Malley.

Under their feet the uneven floor creaked, trembled. At the end of a corridor was a large room with bare walls. A shaft of molasses-colored sunlight angled from an east window, disclosed coffins on the uncarpeted floor. Beside an imitation ebony coffin with ornate silver handles was half sitting, half lying, a man, his head bent so that his chin rested on his chest. Blood from a wound on his neck had pooled on the floor, marooned the seat of his white Palm Beach trousers.

Williams bent over, touched the back of the man's neck, drew his hand away quickly. "Somebody beat us to him."

"It's the red-haired guy!" O'Malley exclaimed.

Crane said, "Sure it is. How long has he been dead, Doc?"

On hands and knees Williams was examining the floor. "Quite a while. He's cold." He rolled the body away from the ebony-finished coffin. "I wonder what they cut him with?"

"Looks like a slash from a good-sized knife," O'Malley observed, examining the red-haired man's throat. "Damn near took his head off."

There were freckles on the red-haired man's face; his eyebrows were

92

the color of straw after it has been on a stable floor for a time; his ears were large and they stuck out from the sides of his head. He was about thirty years old.

Crane examined his wrist watch again. It was 6:47. He said, "We've got time to take a look around. Doc, you go through the guy's pockets. O'Malley and I'll case the joint."

They searched through drawers, desk pigeonholes, cabinets, even two cutaways hanging in a closet, but all they found was that a nice funeral with two cars for mourners could be secured from the Star Mortuary for as little as ninety-seven dollars and fifty cents. Crane discovered an imperial quart of Dewar's White Label (his favorite whiskey) standing in the bottom drawer of a maple filing cabinet, and, judging that it was kept there for the use of too affected relatives, he pulled out the loosened cork and took a long drink.

He dropped the bottle, closed his eyes, clutched at his throat and tried to yell, but he couldn't. His vocal muscles were constricted. He could feel the inside wall of his stomach being burned away. He tottered blindly about the room.

O'Malley's eyes goggled in amazed alarm.

Crane staggered to the water cooler, poured glass after glass of tepid water down his throat, spilled some of the liquid on his coat. His breath came in gasps.

"For God's sake!" exclaimed O'Malley. "What's the matter?"

Crane dramatically pointed his free hand at the Dewar's bottle, said between gulps: "Embalming fluid."

O'Malley's deep laughter, rumbling like a cannon fire, brought Williams on a dead run from the back of the building. His face was indignant. "For the love of Mike, cut it out. You'll wake somebody up."

Between convulsions O'Malley described Crane's pleased expression at the discovery of the whiskey; the shocked surprise, the pain after the long drink; the blind search for water; but Williams didn't think the incident funny at all.

"There's a murdered guy lying back there," he said, "and you horse around like a couple of comics in a burlesque show. Besides, we're supposed to be working."

Crane had a partially filled glass of water in his hand. "I'm dying," he said. "Do you call that horsing around?"

Williams snorted and disappeared down the corridor.

Crane finished the water. He felt better. He looked at the Dewar's bottle. "What in hell do you suppose they do, embalm the relatives, too?" he wanted to know.

O'Malley thought maybe it was a sample. He thought maybe they had different flavors in embalming fluid. Like raspberry. Or chocolate.

Crane said, "This must have been lye." He filled his water glass.

O'Malley had a heavy paper account book on one of the desks; he was thumbing through its pages. "Here's where they list all the burials," he said.

Crane said, "Yeah?" Then he said, "Oh! Say, that *is* an idea."

He went over and helped O'Malley find the page for Friday, August 5. There were only two entries.

Patrick Morgan, 59, 6123 Woodlawn Avenue.

St. Ann's. $237

Agnes Castle, 25, 5454 Cornell Avenue.

Edgemoor. $150.

Crane turned over the page to see the entries for Saturday, but there weren't any. He excitedly copied the Agnes Castle entry. "Unless I'm wrong as hell," he said, "that's our girl."

"How are you going to find out?" O'Malley asked.

"I don't know, but I'll figure out something." Crane filled another glass at the water cooler. "There's nothing like a little embalming fluid to make the brain function."

They went back into the large room. Williams was still grubbing around among the empty coffins. "I can't find that knife," he said in an aggrieved tone.

"Never mind," said Crane. "You just putter around. We'll do the real work."

He had a piece of paper torn from the burial ledger in his hand, and, placing it on a coffin, he began to write with a pencil stub.

O'Malley asked, "What are you doing?"

Crane showed him the paper. It read:

TO THE POLICE—

YOU WILL FIND IT INTERESTING TO COMPARE THE HAIR OF THE LATE MISTER CONNELL WITH THAT CLUTCHED IN HAND OF THE LATE MISTER AUGUST LIEBMAN, MORGUE KEEPER, AND NOW IN POSSESSION OF THE ESTEEMED CAPTAIN GRADY.

MERRY XMAS!

SHIRLEY TEMPLE

Williams, reading over O'Malley's shoulder, said, "What the hell?"

Crane accepted the paper from O'Malley, bent over the corpse and tucked the note in the left hand, saying: "I figure this is the easiest way to find out if the hair really does match."

O'Malley said, "Let's scram out of here. I'm getting the jumps."

On their way to the street Crane halted in the office. O'Malley asked, "Going to have another nice sip of that Dewar's?" Crane ignored him, lifted the French telephone, called Andover 1234, asked for the city editor. The operator put the city room on the phone, and he told the copy boy who answered that he wanted to speak to the man in the slot. When he got him he said:

"You'll find a man murdered in the Star Mortuary at 5217 Lake Street. I'm tipping you off before the police, because I want the facts to get in the newspapers."

The slot man kept asking, "Who is this calling? Who is this calling?" but Crane hung up. He said to the others, "We better beat it."

In the street saffron sunlight hurt their eyes.

Chapter Twelve

EXACTLY AT noon Crane and O'Malley and Williams left the Turkish bath run by Olaf Jensen on West Madison Street to meet the Courtland family at the Blackstone Hotel. On their way they stopped at the Crystal Bar and ordered a quart of Cook's Imperial Champagne and three bottles of stout. Mixed, this made a drink called Black Velvet, which they drank with considerable gusto, for, as O'Malley said:

"Uncle Sty wouldn't want his boys to come up smellin' of something common like gin, for instance."

There was just enough for two glasses apiece, and when they came out onto the street again they all felt fine, especially Crane, who reflected that in the matter of sleep he was acting like a really first-class detective.

"Do you guys know," he said, "that I haven't been to bed for twenty-eight hours? How's that for devotion to my profession?"

Williams asked, "You're just overlookin' that nap yesterday afternoon?"

"Oh, you can hardly count that." Crane waved a hand, airily dismissed the nap. "Why, it was just a short wink, not more than four or five hours."

In front of the La Salle Hotel they hailed a Checker cab, started for the Blackstone along nearly deserted streets. It was hot again, and the liquor made them perspire. Their faces were still flushed from the heat of the Turkish bath, the skin fresh and pink; their eyes were dark and sunken, the whites bloodshot; their linen suits had been pressed by the bath attendant. Crane was thinking they must look like a particularly sinister trio of adventurers out of the tropics, when there was a loud report behind them. He threw himself at the cab floor just ahead of O'Malley. Williams was already there, fumbling for his pistol.

The noise was not repeated, and O'Malley cautiously peered out the back window. "Hell!" he said. "Another cab backfiring."

Crane put his hand over his heart. "Whew! I thought it was my old pal, Frankie French."

Williams was putting the pistol back in the under-arm holster. "If they do shoot you, Bill, we'll have to kill a lot of people to avenge you," he observed. "It might be French; it might be Paletta; it might be the guy who murdered the undertaker; it might even be the coppers."

Crane was interested. "What makes you think French or Paletta didn't kill the undertaker?"

"I never heard of a gangster killin' anybody that way." Williams buttoned his coat, settled back in the cab. "They either squirt some lead at 'em or take 'em for a ride. Even the wop mobsters don't fool around with knives no more."

O'Malley said, "I think he's right, for once."

Crane thought about this until they reached the Blackstone. The Courtlands' suite was on the eleventh floor, and they went up without telephoning. Young Courtland let them in. He seemed surprised to see them. "I've been trying to reach you all morning," he said. He had on another gabardine suit, sky-blue in color, and a pair of black-and-white sport shoes.

Crane explained that they hadn't gone to their room because of the police.

A blue-gray Chinese rug hid the sitting-room floor. There was a real fireplace with dragon-headed bronze andirons. They sat down gingerly on the fragile Chinese-Chippendale chairs, eyed the soft tints of the Parisian water colors on the walls.

"I'll call Mother," Courtland said, going out one of two doors at the back of the room.

Williams examined the furniture, shook his head, said, "Hell, our joint's got this beat a mile."

Crane agreed. "It wouldn't take much of a brawl to break that stuff up into firewood. This may be artistic, but ours is durable."

O'Malley said, "This ain't got any cops in it, though."

Through a door other than the one Courtland had used, walked a woman and a man. She had steel-gray hair, diamond rings, a violet dress about the color of a three-cent stamp, a double string of beautifully matched pearls. She stared at them through a lorgnette, said:

"Why! what odd-looking men!"

The man with her was about the same age, past sixty. He was half a head shorter than the woman; he wore pince-nez glasses with a black ribbon, a cutaway coat and striped trousers, an Ascot tie, and a white carnation boutonnière. His face was round and the skin hung in folds around his mouth, over his jawbone, as on the face of an English bloodhound.

William Crane stood up. "Mrs. Courtland?"

The woman studied him through the lorgnette. "I presume so," she said.

Young Courtland came into the room. "Oh, there you are. Mother, these are the detectives Uncle Sty hired." He introduced them to Mrs. Courtland and Uncle Stuyvesant.

"Oh, detectives!" Mrs. Courtland raised her lorgnette again. "Dear me! What an unpleasant occupation!"

There was a harassed expression in Uncle Stuyvesant's pale-blue eyes. His tone disowned any responsibility for the detectives. He said, "It takes all sorts of people to make up a world, Evalyn."

"Oh yes!" Mrs. Courtland's voice was loud, deep, assured. "But does one have to receive them?" As she said the word "them" she tossed her head, held it at such an angle that to see the detectives she had to look down her nose.

What the hell! Crane thought. What the hell!

Young Courtland said, "Now, Mother. These men are trying to help us find Kathryn."

"Oh yes! My poor daughter!" She leaned forward, peered at Doc Williams. "Have you found her?" She enunciated each word so vigorously that she quivered. "Have you at last . . . found her?"

Williams gulped, said, "No, ma'm." He kept turning his Panama in his hands.

"Really!" She spoke from the chest, like one of the Barrymores. "Isn't it about time?"

Williams said, "Yes, ma'm." He looked appealingly at Crane.

97

Young Courtland said, "But, Mother, they've only been working three days."

"I don't propose to argue." She glided majestically to one of the doors, paused for a last look through the lorgnette, said, "Have the room properly aired when you complete your business, Chauncey."

Williams sank into one of the chairs, mopped his forehead with a wrinkled handkerchief.

Young Courtland said, "Mother's upset by the trip and the heat. She doesn't like hotels, either. You mustn't mind her."

Crane spoke to Uncle Stuyvesant. "I haven't much to report, sir." He summarized what he had learned from Miss Udoni. "If I can locate her husband," he concluded, "I believe we may learn something from him."

Young Courtland agreed. "He certainly should know who Miss Ross really was."

Uncle Stuyvesant sat primly in his chair, his hands folded in his lap. "Time alone will tell," he said.

"There's one thing I would like to know," Crane said. "What was the color of Miss Courtland's eyes?"

"Blue," said young Courtland.

"No, I mean exactly. What sort of blue?"

Hand over mouth, Courtland pondered.

"Were they a greenish blue?" asked Crane. "Or a deep blue, like the gulf stream? Or gray-blue?"

Uncle Stuyvesant said, "Gray-blue."

Young Courtland shook his head. "It's hard to tell. They were sort of greenish some of the time, and gray-blue, too. They changed."

"That's right." Uncle Stuyvesant beamed. "They changed."

"Okay." Crane rose from his chair. "The next thing on the program is to locate Sam, the trumpet player. I've got a hunch we can find him this evening."

Williams had been huddled in his chair, staring apprehensively at the door through which Mrs. Courtland had disappeared. "Where?" he asked, not taking his eyes from the door.

"At the taxi-dance place. One of the players looked sort of familiar to me."

"Oh, ho!" exclaimed O'Malley. "That long-haired guy." His eyes were bright with interest. "I noticed him. He can play, what I mean."

Crane said, "Us artists say, he can swing it."

"I'd like to go with you," said Courtland. "May I?"

"Sure." Crane moved toward the door. "I wish you had been along last night, although O'Malley came in mighty handy."

Eyes rounded behind the pince-nez glasses, Uncle Stuyvesant had been watching Crane. He asked, "Have you been able to find the red-haired undertaker yet?"

Crane said, "What?" He frowned, looked at Uncle Stuyvesant's round, innocent face with narrowed eyes. Then he looked away, pretended to brush some lint from his trousers. "Oh, that fellow." He rubbed the palm of his hand on his right trouser leg. "We haven't done anything about him yet."

Young Courtland glanced at Crane curiously. "You didn't tell me anything about a red-haired undertaker."

"It was such a silly process of reasoning," Crane grinned derisively, as though he was ashamed to speak of it, and told them how he had deduced the occupation and left-handedness of August Liebman's assailant. "The chances are that I'm all cockeyed," he added.

Uncle Stuyvesant said, "Nothing ventured, nothing gained."

Courtland asked, "What are you going to do this afternoon?"

Crane hid a yawn under his hand. "I'd like to get some sleep, but I suppose I'd better do some work."

"Sure, let's do some work." Courtland's square, boyish face was eager. "I'd like to go along. You can sleep tonight." He squeezed out his cigarette on a brass ash tray. "You go downstairs, and I'll meet you as soon as I fix things with Mother . . . that is, if you're ready to start now?"

"I'm ready," said Crane, opening the hall door.

Uncle Stuyvesant beamed at him. "That's right, young man. No time like the present."

Crane held the door for O'Malley and Williams, said, "Not unless it's daylight-saving time," and closed the door.

When they reached the lobby Williams said, "Phooey! What a dame!" He sank in one of the divans to the left of the reception desk.

"That's the high society crap," said O'Malley.

Crane agreed. "She was handing us a touch of the old hauteur." He sat down beside Williams. "Doc, this business has taken a turn for the worse."

"You mean about Old Uncle Sty knowing we were lookin' for the undertaker?"

"Yeah. How in hell could he have known about him?"

"Well, he don't know the guy's dead, anyway."

"Maybe. . . ."

"Maybe! You mean . . . ?"

"There's nothing to prevent him from hopping off that midnight plane and going out and killing Mr. Connell, is there?"

It was cool in the lobby and quiet, and they sat in silence for a while, their eyes half closed. Through a shaded window they could see the sun-bathed pavement of Seventh Street, passing pedestrians in shirt sleeves, summer dresses. Traffic on Michigan Avenue made a fitful rumbling.

Finally O'Malley asked, "But that means he must have bumped off the morgue keeper, doesn't it?"

Crane opened his eyes. "I don't know. We'd better check and see if he could have been in Chicago then." He sat up on the divan. "In fact, I think we better have a check made on the old lady, and on young Courtland, too. It won't do any harm to find out about all of them." He turned to Williams. "You and O'Malley better wire the colonel an account of all we've done so far, including my tête-à-tête with Miss Udoni, and ask him to make the check on the Courtland family. Ask him to check on the Courtland trust fund, too, and find out if young Courtland, Uncle Sty or Mrs. Courtland stand to benefit from Kathryn's death."

Williams nodded.

"Also, and this is important," Crane continued, "ask him if he told Uncle Sty about the undertaker." His eyes followed a slender, dark-haired girl from the reception desk to the elevators. "Then, after you write the wire, I want you two to go out to the Edgemoor Cemetery and see if you can find exactly where Miss Agnes Castle is buried. You can pretend you're relatives and want to put flowers on the grave."

"What are you going to do?" asked Williams.

"Courtland and I will see if we can find where Sam, the plumber, hangs his derby."

"You better keep your eyes open," O'Malley said. "I'll bet them thugs of Paletta's are still looking for you."

"How can they when they're in jail?"

"Hell, I bet he's got more guys workin' for him than Harry Hopkins," said Williams scornfully. "He's a big shot."

"How do you spell shot?" asked Crane. He watched a small, compact girl in a tight-fitting custard-colored linen suit descend the Michigan Avenue stairs. She was in a hurry and her buttocks moved in petulant jerks. He sighed, said, "Seems like I have to work all the time."

Williams and O'Malley stared at the girl until her head disappeared. Williams said, "You couldn't get to first base with a dame like that. She's got class."

"I got class myself," said Crane. "You should have seen those babies in the taxi-dance hall fight to get a chance to step around with me."

O'Malley said, "It was either you or a Filipino."

Crane's indignant reply was halted by the sight of Courtland coming from one of the elevators. "What do we do first?" he wanted to know.

"Eat," said Crane.

<h1 style="text-align:center">Chapter Thirteen</h1>

O'MALLEY AND Williams decided to go about their business, so Crane and Courtland ate lunch alone at Henrici's. Crane had a double martini, very dry, and then astonished the management by consuming seven Vienna rolls with an order of combination salad. He also drank three fifty-cent bottles of imported Pilsener beer.

"I can hardly remember back to the last meal I ate," he sighed, buttering the final piece of the seventh roll. "And then this weather gives you an appetite."

Courtland peered out at the sweltering street and grinned. "Nothing like a crisp spell to tone a fellow up," he agreed. His eyes crinkled at the corners. He was having a club sandwich and three bottles of beer.

The restaurant was air-cooled and dark, and Crane wished he could slide under the table and take a nap. He resisted the impulse, however, paid the bill and said gloomily, "I suppose we better be going."

Courtland appeared to have plenty of energy. He stood up and said, "Sure. As Uncle Sty would say, don't put off till tomorrow what you can do today."

Crane looked up at him sourly. "Yes, but does Uncle Sty know this one?" he demanded. "A rolling stone gathers no Ross?"

Courtland's face was appropriately pained, and Crane followed him out the door. They took a cab to the Clark-Erie Dance Hall.

"You better go up and inquire about Sam," Crane said. "I don't think they like me so well."

Courtland was gone only two minutes. "Nobody around at all," he said. "The place is locked up."

"The hell!" said Crane. "I wonder if the management was pinched last night."

He took Courtland around to show him the fire escape he and Miss Udoni had descended. They were both staring at it when three men came down the alley behind them. One of the men walked up beside Crane and stuck a pistol into the small of his back. "We want to talk to you, buddy," he said. His voice rumbled like a truck crossing a wooden bridge.

Crane straightened his back, said, "O.K. What do you want?"

"Just button your gabber," said the man, "an' come along."

Another of the three men had a high, metallic voice. "What'll we do with this other mug?" he asked. "Conk him one?"

"Naw, we better bring him along," said the man with the rumbling voice. "Frankie might want to talk to him." He shoved the gun into Crane's back. "Come on."

"Don't do that," said Crane. "I'm ticklish."

They prodded him and Courtland into the back seat of a Lincoln sedan parked across the mouth of the alley. A fourth man, squat and with a bulge of flesh over his collar, was in the driver's seat. One of the men got in front with him, and the other two got in back. The man with the rumbling voice had his pistol in his coat pocket. He sat in one of the folding seats and kept the pistol pointed at Crane. His nose had been broken and badly set, his face was pockmarked, his teeth were stained with tobacco juice.

Crane asked, "Where are we going?"

The man's voice sounded as though he were talking around a hot boiled potato. "The duke wants t' know where we're goin', Charley," he said.

"The duke wants t' know where we're goin', does he?" said Charley. He was sitting between Crane and Courtland, and his voice sounded as though he had a tin larynx.

"Yeah, the duke wants t' know where we're going," said the man with the rumbling voice.

That seemed to end the matter. There was silence until the car drove up in front of a two-story stucco building with a green-and-white canvas canopy over the entrance. A sign on the building read: LIBERTY CLUB. In a small window by the entrance were photographs of young ladies with shawls draped in different places over their bodies. Printed on a card below the photographs was: "Eight Gorgeous Beauties."

"Come on, duke," said the man with the rumbling voice to Crane. He climbed out of the car and waited on the sidewalk, holding his pocket in such a way that the pistol's outline was visible. Crane and Courtland followed him into the bulding, up a narrow flight of steps, and into a large room with a square dance floor and an orchestra platform. Close on their heels came the other three men.

Around the dance floor were bare tables and chairs; around the room were vivid green and red and blue and orange murals of naked South Sea islanders bathing, dancing and carrying baskets of fruit. Eight girls, in various types of shorts, stood on the dance floor in two lines of four. A frowsy man with a cigarette dangling from his lips sat at the grand piano on the orchestra platform; another man wearing patent-leather shoes, violet trousers pulled up almost under his armpits, and a baby-blue polo shirt stood in front of the girls, his hands, knuckles inward, pressed against his sides just above his hips. All of these people stared wonderingly at the six men.

"Where's Frankie?" the man with the rumbling voice asked.

"He'th back in hith offith," said the man with the violet trousers. As he spoke he shook his body from side to side like a woman.

They went through a door beside the orchestra stand into a room with a large roulette table. There were no windows and there was a gray carpet on the floor. Next they went into a smaller room equipped with one window and a set of moderne office furniture made of steel tubes. Frankie French was seated at a red-surfaced desk, his darkly handsome face turned toward them impassively. Light from a chromium desk lamp slid from his sleek hair.

"Who is the other gentleman?" he asked.

The man with the rumbling voice said, "He was with the duke here, so we brung him, too."

"Very unfortunate," said French. "It means we will have to dispose of two of them."

"Listen," said Crane. "This man is Chauncey Courtland of New York. He's a client of our firm. We're looking for a relative of his. He hasn't anything to do with Miss Ross."

Frankie French gazed at Crane with his golden eyes. "Search them, please," he said. His lips were full, cruel, contemptuous.

Roughly, two of the men went through Crane's pockets, two through Courtland's. They piled the wallets, keys and change they found on the red table. French went through the wallets, handed Courtland's back to him, said:

"I'm sorry, but I shall have to detain you. If Mr. Crane will answer my questions I shall let you both depart. If he doesn't I shall be forced to . . ."

Frankie French shrugged his shoulders.

Courtland's face was angry. He stepped toward French, said, "Crane's a friend of mine. If anything happens to him I'll see that you . . ."

"Can that stuff," said one of the men. He seized Courtland's arm, shook him.

Frankie French said, "Take him outside and tie him up. I may want him later." His golden eyes regarded Crane speculatively. "Charley, you stay here and help me talk to Mr. Crane."

Courtland left, escorted by the other three men. Charley closed the door in back of them, his thin face expressing anticipation. French adjusted the desk light so that the rays fell on one of the chairs.

"Sit down," he said. His voice was polite, frigid.

Crane said, "I don't want to sit down."

"Sit down!"

"No," said Crane.

Charley hit him on the head with a pistol butt. Blue-white light blinded his eyes; his ears rang; he sank to the floor. He lay there for a time, the two men silently watching him. He wasn't knocked out, but he was badly dazed. From the floor he could see the men's faces. Charley's eyes glistened, his tongue kept wetting his lips. A vein vibrated just behind the jagged scar on Frankie French's jawbone, but his expression was coldly composed.

Finally Frankie French said, "Now sit in that chair."

Crane got onto his hands and knees, then onto his feet. He sat in the chair. The light dazzled his eyes, sent stabs of pain through his head, made him dizzy.

Frankie French asked, "What did you do with Miss Ross' body?" His hands, palms down on the table, were in a patch of light. They were slender and nervous, like a violinist's, and the nails were glossy.

"I didn't take her body," Crane said. He put his hands on the arms of his chair to keep from toppling over. "I've been trying to find out who did."

Frankie French repeated his question. "What did you do with her body?"

"I didn't take it."

The slender fingers drummed on the table. "Mr. Crane, I think you will do better to tell me." French's voice was lazy, faintly amused. "You will spare yourself needless pain."

"But I really don't know where the body is."

Charley opened a drawer in the red-topped desk, drew out a pair of black pliers. "Which nail will I start on, Mr. French?" he asked.

French's thin eyebrows, his lips, made parallel lines. "I believe the loss of a thumbnail is quite painful," he said.

Charley had some rope. He advanced on Crane.

"Wait a minute," said Crane. "Wait a minute." He leaned forward in his chair, toward French. "I've told you I don't know where Miss

104

Ross' body is, but there's nothing to prevent my lying to you to get myself set free. Why don't you take my word for it that I don't know who took the body?"

"It will do you no good to lie, Mr. Crane. I intend to hold you here while my men check on whatever story you tell. I imagine there is little need to remind you that some very unpleasant things will happen if the story proves to be false."

"All right," said Crane. "I do know where the body is." He half closed his eyes, let his chin rest on his chest. "But I'm damned if I'll tell you."

Golden flecks swam in French's eyes. "Go ahead, Charley," he whispered, barely moving his lips.

Crane pushed himself from the chair, drove his right hand into Charley's face, sent the man spinning against the wall. Frankie French pushed a finger on an ivory button set in a black-lacquered wooden block on his desk. Crane hurled his chair at him, but French ducked and the chair crashed against the wall. Crane seized the block from the desk, tore it loose from a wire, threw it in French's face as he came up from behind the table, turned just in time to avoid a kick aimed at his groin by Charley. He caught Charley's foot with both hands, twisted it until something cracked with the hollow report of a popgun.

Charley lay face upward on the rug, screaming horribly.

Hands fluttering, shoulders hunched, French came around his desk, grappled with Crane. As they fell to the floor Crane swung his body on top, broke French's hold, punched him twice on his neck, on his Adam's apple. Turning on his right side, French caught hold of Crane's left arm and bit the wrist to the bone. Crane pulled his arm away, heard someone behind him, turned his head . . .

A man was kicking him in the ribs, not violently, but hard enough to make them thump. The man kept saying: "Get up, you son of a bitch; get up."

Crane opened his eyes, struggled to a sitting position on the floor. The man kicked his hip, said, "Ah-ha! The duke's on tap again."

Frankie French was seated beside his desk, daubing at his lips with a red-stained handkerchief. "Tie him in a chair," he ordered the man. His face was grim, his voice no longer amused.

Two men jerked him into a chair, tied his hands and feet. One of them was the driver; the other was the man with the rumbling voice. Charley had disappeared. The rope tore the flesh on Crane's wrist where French had bitten him, sent warm blood trickling between his fingers. Blinding flashes of pain, like sheet lightning, crossed his head irregularly; his ribs hurt with every breath; his face was numb on the right side.

"Where are the pliers?" demanded French.

The driver located them on the carpet.

"Pull out one of his thumbnails," ordered French.

The man approached Crane, the pliers held tightly in his right hand. His breath was strong with garlic. Crane closed his eyes.

"Wait a minute," said a voice from the doorway. "All of you put up your hands."

It was young Courtland. He had an automatic pistol, was pointing it at the pit of Frankie French's stomach. The three men raised their hands above their heads.

"Now go over and face that wall," said Courtland. "And keep those hands in the air." As they obeyed he slid behind Crane's chair, unfastened his hands. "You better undo your feet," he said.

Crane fumbled with the knots at his ankles, finally loosened the rope so that he could pull out first one foot, then the other. He went over and searched the men. The man with the rumbling voice had a pistol under his arm; the driver had a police-model revolver in his underarm holster, an automatic on his hip, and French had a palm-sized .25 Colt automatic in his coat pocket.

"Pretty good haul," said Courtland. "Now let's lock them in here."

"In just a second." Crane picked up the wallet, keys and change from French's desk. He jerked the cradle-type telephone from its wire, tossed it on the floor. He looked out the window, saw that it was a long drop to a cement driveway. "I guess they won't get out right away."

Palms touching the wall, the three men stood in silence.

"I'll lock the door," Crane said. "You clear the way ahead."

Crane unfastened the snap lock on the door, pulled the knob until he heard it click. Courtland was waiting for him.

"All we have to do is walk out," he said. He examined Crane. "They certainly beat you up, didn't they?" His tone was anxious. "Do you think you can make it to a doctor?"

Crane said, "Boy! I never was so glad in my life to see anyone as I was to see you." The pistols in his coat pockets clinked as he walked past the roulette wheel into the dining room with the murals. "Where is everybody?" He looked wonderingly at Courtland. "And by the way, how in hell did you get free?"

"The girls and those two fellows have gone home, and one of the mobsters took Charley to a doctor. I think you bunged up Charley's leg a bit, from the manner in which he was moaning."

Crane led the way down the narrow stairs. He said, "I hope they have to amputate it." He wrapped a handkerchief around his bleeding wrist, pulled a knot tight with his right hand and his teeth. He was considerably relieved to find that his teeth were intact. "But how did you get free? I thought they tied you up."

Courtland said, "They did." He followed Crane into the street. "I'll tell you as soon as we get away from this place."

Crane halted and stared at the stucco front of the club. "I'd like to burn the goddam joint up," he said, "but I don't suppose it would be such a smart thing to do."

Courtland had secured a taxi. He helped Crane into it, instructed the driver: "Drive around until you find a good doctor."

"All right, Mister Houdini," said Crane, as the cab started. "How did you do it?"

"Well," said Courtland, "in that chorus was a girl I used to know, and . . ."

"You seem to know 'em all," said Crane.

"When I was younger I used to get around a bit." Courtland gave Crane a Camel, took one himself, lit both cigarettes with a silver lighter. "Anyway, the men tied me in the roulette room, as French ordered them to, and then they went down to the bar with the girls and the two musical fellows who had finished their rehearsal." Courtland blew a puff of smoke at the ceiling of the cab. "This girl (her name's Sue) stayed behind, and slipped into the roulette room and asked me what it was all about.

"I told her that French thought you had taken the body of his girl from the morgue and was trying to make you tell him what you'd done with it. She said, 'My God! doesn't he know Verona's still alive?'"

Crane straightened up so quickly it hurt his head. "She said that?"

"Yes. And I said, 'Presumably not.'"

"Presumably not," echoed Crane. "Say, there was no 'presumably' about it."

"Well, that's what I said. Then she loosened my ropes so I could free myself in case I saw a chance to escape, and told me there was a gun in a drawer below the cash register. Then she became frightened. . . ."

"I should think she would," said Crane.

"And went downstairs to join the others. In a short while I heard the girls leave, and then, a few minutes later, I heard sounds of a struggle going on in French's office."

"Sounds of a terrific struggle," corrected Crane.

"The three men supposed to be watching me dashed through the roulette room and into French's office, hardly glancing at me as they went by. In a moment one of them came out with Charley. I heard him mention a doctor. The office door was closed, so I slipped off the rope, got the pistol out of the drawer below the cash register, and you know the rest."

"I'll never forget it," said Crane warmly.

Courtland was embarrassed. "Anybody would have done what I did." He blew smoke through his nose. "What happened before I got into the office?"

Crane related as much of what had taken place as he could remember. When he recounted how he had told Frankie French that he did know where the body was hidden Courtland asked:

"Do you, really?"

The taxi driver slowed the cab, said, "Here's a high-class medico, gents." They were on the corner of Huron Street and Michigan Boulevard. There were doctors' offices on the third floor of a white-stone building.

"I think I do," said Crane.

"You were in a nasty position, then," said Courtland. "Knowing, yet naturally not wanting to tell so as to protect your client's interests."

"Naturally." Crane got out of the cab, gave the driver a fifty-cent piece. "Keep the change." He tried to smile at Courtland, but it hurt his lips. "Maybe French was bluffing about that torture."

"But what if they actually started to pull off one of your finger-nails?" Courtland persisted.

"Hell!" said Crane. "I would have told 'em!"

Chapter Fourteen

DOC WILLIAMS and O'Malley gaped at Crane's face, circled him wonderingly. They were in the incense-scented lobby of the Congress Hotel, in a corner by the marble stairs leading to the second-floor convention rooms. A bellboy with a blue-and-white uniform was watching them curiously.

"Just some concussions and lacerations," said Crane, "as well as a bruise or two. The chances are I will live, though."

Williams' face became serious. "They really cuffed you around. Who did it?"

"Some people who objected to my collecting a few rare old weapons." Crane turned to O'Malley. "Perhaps you were not aware, Mr. O'Malley, of my interest in the panoply of war?"

O'Malley asked, "What are you talkin' about?"

Williams said, "Quit foolin' around. Who did it?"

"Frankie French." Crane put his hand in a coat pocket. "But I secured a few trophies."

Williams said, "Yeah, I can see 'em all over your face."

"No, I mean some rare old weapons." Crane produced five weapons: the three pistols and the revolver he had taken from French and his men, and the pistol Courtland had found in the cash-register drawer. "Not bad, eh?"

"Jay-zus!" exclaimed O'Malley. "You musta stuck up the Capone gang."

Crane told them how he had acquired the armory and the wounds, and how Courtland had saved him.

"It was a good thing for you he knew that doll," stated O'Malley. "And a good thing he had plenty of guts. He's quite a guy. What'd you do with him?"

"He went back to have dinner with his family. We're going to pick him up about midnight."

Williams was thinking about Frankie French. "I'll fix that guy," he asserted. "He can't pull that kind of stuff on us."

"He can't, but he did," said Crane.

"Why didn't you slug him after you and Courtland had him covered?" Williams demanded. "You could've busted his nose, or knocked out a few teeth or something to pay him back."

"I thought of that," Crane admitted, "but I decided to let him alone. He'll figure nobody would take a beating like mine without planning some sort of revenge, and he'll spend most of his time figuring out how he can dodge me. In other words, he'll decide the grievance is all mine and not his, as it would be if I'd done something to him. So he'll sit tight for awhile."

"I guess that's smart," agreed Williams, "but I'll put a tack in that sonabitch as soon as we clean up this case."

"That reminds me," said Crane. "Did you find Miss Agnes Castle's grave?"

"Sure," said O'Malley. "We put lilies all over it."

"Forty bucks worth," supplemented Williams, disapprovingly.

"Holy mackerel!" Crane stuck out his lower lip, looked down his nose at O'Malley. "You must have been knee deep in them."

"Well, Uncle Sty . . ." O'Malley began.

"Yeah, I know," said Crane. "Uncle Sty wouldn't want HIS detectives stinting on flowers for the girl who might be his niece. Not *Uncle Sty*." He gave the police revolver and one of the pistols to Doc Williams, the two other large pistols to O'Malley, and kept the .25 Colt automatic. It had "F.F." set in silver letters on the handle. He dropped it in his pocket. "Let's see if the colonel has answered any of our questions."

At the Hotel Sherman, in the name of O'Malley, was a telegram from Colonel Black. Williams learned from his friend Dwyer, one of the house detectives, that the police were still watching their rooms, so they didn't go upstairs. Instead, they went across the street to the Bismarck Hotel's German grill and ordered potato salad and assorted cold cuts, rye bread and beer. Crane opened the telegram and read it aloud:

ESSENTIALS COURTLAND TRUST: MRS. COURTLAND LIFE INCOME OF FORTY THOUSAND A YEAR. KATHRYN FIFTEEN HUNDRED A MONTH. UPON MARRIAGE KATHRYN RECEIVES ONE THIRD TRUST AND AT THIRTY COURTLAND RECEIVES ANOTHER THIRD. AT DEATH OF MRS. COURTLAND BEFORE 1950 HER FORTY THOUSAND A YEAR REVERTS TO TRUST. SHOULD COURTLAND DIE WITHOUT CHILDREN ONE THIRD OF THE ESTATE GOES TO PRINCETON UNIVERSITY FOR BOOKS AND LIBRARY IMPROVEMENTS. SHOULD KATHRYN DIE WITHOUT CHILDREN ONE THIRD GOES TO SMITH COLLEGE FOR SIMILAR PURPOSE. SHOULD KATHRYN AND COURTLAND DIE UNCLE STUYVESANT GETS REMAINING THIRD FOR PHILANTHROPIC PURPOSES AS HE SEES FIT LESS ONE MILLION FOR MRS. COURTLAND. IN 1950 THE TRUST IS DISSOLVED. MRS. COURTLAND, IF ALIVE, IS TO RECEIVE ONE MILLION AND COURTLAND AND KATHRYN, WITH OR WITHOUT CHILDREN, TO SPLIT REMAINDER. COURTLAND HANDLES AFFAIRS OF ESTATE WHICH AT TIME OF PROBATE WAS ESTIMATED AT THIRTEEN MILLION.

Crane stopped reading long enough to eat a piece of tongue liberally coated with mustard and finish his stein of cold beer.

O'Malley, holding a piece of chicken breast on a fork, said, "If I had thirteen million I'd throw one away just to make sure I didn't have no bad luck."

"Yeah," said Williams scornfully. "You'd throw it, and the other twelve, too, away on some babe." He delicately wiped beer foam from his mustache.

"You mean, on some babes," corrected O'Malley.

Crane signaled the waiter, ordered more beer, tried a piece of boiled ham and said, "I'll finish the telegram." He read:

YOUNG COURTLAND LEFT NEW YORK THURSDAY EVENING AFTER A CONFERENCE WITH MOTHER, UNCLE AND ME WHICH LASTED UNTIL 7:05. HIS NAME ON PASSENGER LIST OF MIDNIGHT SLEEPER PLANE AS IS THAT OF A. N. BROWN OF SAN DIEGO. WOULD HAVE ARRIVED IN CHICAGO ABOUT 4 A.M.

UNCLE STUYVESANT PRESUMABLY SPENT NIGHT AT HIS APARTMENT, WHERE HE LIVES ALONE. MANSERVANT, WHO CAME IN FOR BREAKFAST AT 10 A.M. SAYS HE AWAKENED UNCLE FRIDAY MORNING AS USUAL.

MRS. COURTLAND PLAYED BRIDGE WITH FRIENDS UNTIL MIDNIGHT, AROSE SATURDAY AT 11 A.M. SHE AND UNCLE STUYVESANT LEFT NEW YORK FOR CHICAGO AT 9 P.M. SATURDAY.

YES, I DID TELL UNCLE STUYVESANT ABOUT UNDERTAKER. FELT WE OUGHT TO BE ABLE TO SHOW HIM WE ARE MAKING SOME PROGRESS, EVEN IF WE ARE NOT.

BLACK.

"I wish he was around to absorb a beating or two," said Crane bitterly. "Maybe he wouldn't holler so much about progress then."

"Look," said Williams. "Let's see if we can figure out who'd gain by having Kathryn out of the way."

Crane's eyes were alert. "Why do you want to do that?"

"It don't seem reasonable Uncle Sty would hire an undertaker to hide the girl's body and then kill the guy later just to protect the family honor."

"No, it doesn't." Crane reluctantly put down a piece of bread, examined the telegram. "Should Kathryn and Courtland die," he read, "Uncle Stuyvesant gets remaining third for philanthropic purposes as he sees fit, less one million for Mrs. Courtland."

"Jeeze!" exclaimed O'Malley. "All the old guy has to do now that Kathryn's croaked herself is to knock off Chauncey, and he has about three million bucks for himself."

"Sure." Crane cut into a piece of very rare roast beef. "But why would Uncle Sty go to all the trouble to hide the girl's body?"

"He don't want to frighten Courtland, see?" O'Malley waved a piece of chicken in the air. "He'll let the body be found after Courtland's dead."

"And he could've easy killed that undertaker after he and Mrs. Courtland got here on that plane." Williams tapped the table with a butter knife for emphasis. "He could've slipped away from the hotel."

Crane said, "That reminds me." He summoned the waiter, asked him to get the evening newspapers. Then he asked, "But who helped the undertaker remove the body from the morgue? There must have been two persons."

"It could've been anybody," Williams assured him. "Some pal of the undertaker's, or a guy sent by Uncle Sty from New York."

"O.K." Crane nodded his head. "That gives us suspect Number One." He drank half his stein of beer in one breath.

Williams said, "I guess that's about all, too."

"Yeah," said O'Malley, examining the telegram. "It doesn't look as though young Courtland would have anything to gain by his sister's death. Her third goes to Smith College."

Crane said, "Maybe it's a plot on the part of the board of trustees at Smith." He finished the stein of beer. "Maybe the college needs a new book."

"Aw," said Williams, "a collidge wouldn't do that . . . ?"

A waiter picked up Crane's stein, looked at him inquiringly. Crane nodded, then faced O'Malley. "Look," he said, taking the telegram. "I think I see how young Courtland can be suspect Number Two."

"How?"

"Well, here's the way the will goes: if Kathryn marries she's to have one third of the estate. If she dies, Smith College is to get the third." Crane accepted the new stein from the waiter. "In the event of either death or marriage the estate has to be broken up to make that one-third payment.

"Now, let's suppose Courtland has been embezzling a lot of money from the estate. Maybe he's been playing the market, or the races. . . ."

"Or women," said Williams. "My guess is chorus girls."

"Anyway, if this is so," Crane continued, "Courtland can't afford to have his sister marry anybody. The marriage would end the trust and disclose his peculations. Neither could he have her dead, for the same reason."

"Then, what the hell?" asked O'Malley. "What does this prove?"

"Well, suppose he learns his sister is dead, that her body's in the morgue in Chicago? What does he do?"

Williams said, "He hides the body."

"You see," said Crane. "It fits. By taking his sister's body before anybody identifies her she becomes a missing person. It would be a year or more before she would be officially declared dead, and in that time Courtland could make good his embezzlements or leave the country."

O'Malley nodded. "It sounds good—provided the dame in the deadhouse proves to be Kathryn."

Williams said, "I guess we'll have to get an order from the coroner to exhume the body tomorrow."

"No, we won't," Crane said. "We're going to get the body tonight."

"What!" Williams was genuinely startled. "Rob a grave?"

"Certainly." Crane saw the waiter coming with the papers, flipped him a quarter. "Do you mean to say you've never cracked a sepulcher?"

Williams said indignantly, no, he hadn't.

The newspapers gave a very satisfactory play to the new development in the Morgue Mystery. The *American* took a proprietary interest in the affair; it was almost as if a member of the staff had murdered the undertaker. It announced with pride that the red hair on Mr. Connell's head matched that found in the morgue by Captain Grady, told in detail of the strange telephone call which enabled its reporters to be first on the scene, irritably denied the assertion of the rival *Daily News* that the signature "Shirley Temple" on the note proved the crime was the work of a deranged mind. The signature was evidence of a macabre sense of humor on the part of the author, the *American* asserted, and added, as a final bit of triumphant proof, that "the voice on the telephone was that of a cultured man."

"For God's sake!" exclaimed Williams, when Crane read that part. "How did you manage that?"

"Oh, I've picked up a little culture listenin' to youse guys," said Crane.

Further reading added little to the story. Mr. Connell had been dead about seven hours before the police found him, or, as Crane mentally calculated, about six hours before 6:30 A.M. Mr. Connell was twenty-nine years old, unmarried, and he had been employed by the Star Mortuary for thirteen months. Before that he had worked as a bouncer in the Venice Club in New York, had got into trouble by beating up a disorderly but influential customer, and had been forced to leave the city. The *Daily Times*, the tabloid newspaper, played this bit of history as a "gangster angle," suggested that the theft of Miss Ross's body, the murder of August Liebman and the death of Mr. Connell could be laid to a "half-world feud" between the leaders of two Chicago gangs. The story sounded as though the reporter had heard a rumor of the quarrel between Frankie French and Mike Paletta.

Crane crumpled the papers, tossed them under the table. He yawned, closing his eyes and holding the palm of his hand over his mouth. "Do you know it's thirty-five hours since we've been to bed?"

113

he demanded. "Thirty-five hours!" The beer tasted fresh and dry-sweet in his mouth. It left his mouth clean and cool, as though he had taken a breath of Montana air. "And I'm still going."

"Where?" asked O'Malley.

"To bed," said Williams.

"Don't be cynical." Palms against the white tablecloth, Crane slid back his chair. "I'm going to send a couple of telegrams."

They paid the bill, gave the waiter a dollar over Williams' violent objections and went to the Western Union booth in the lobby. There Crane wrote two telegrams.

One read:

A. N. BROWN, MISSION HILLS, SAN DIEGO, CALIF.
DID YOU RIDE SLEEPER PLANE NEW YORK CHICAGO THURSDAY? PLEASE ANSWER COLLECT.

THOMAS O'MALLEY, HOTEL SHERMAN.

The other read:

COLONEL BLACK, CHRYSLER BUILDING, NEW YORK CITY
PLEASE WIRE O'MALLEY ACTIONS UNCLE STUYVESANT, COURTLAND AND MAMA WEDNESDAY NIGHT, THURSDAY MORNING. HAS COURTLAND BEEN LOSING MONEY WOMEN, HORSES, MARKET? MY PROGRESS FINE. DOCTORS SAY WILL LIVE. LOVE.

CRANE.

From the Bismarck Hotel they took a taxi to the Clark-Erie. The building was dark and Williams was unable to locate anyone connected with the dance hall. Crane got out of the cab to help him make inquiries and finally, in the basement, they encountered the janitor of the building. He answered their questions around a chew of tobacco the size of a walnut.

No, he didn't think the musicians would be around this evening. He didn't think they'd be around any evening, in fact. The reason he thought so, he averred, squirting cinnamon-colored juice into an ash can, was that the joint had been closed by the cops. And about time, too.

Yes, he knew Sam, the trumpet player, but he didn't know where he lived. He didn't know where any of them musician fellers lived. They hung out a lot at a saloon called the Cavern, though, over in the two hundred block on Grand Avenue. He thought it wouldn't hurt to try there.

Before going to the Cavern, Crane told the driver to stop at the Liberty Club. The place wasn't open, but there was a lemon-yellow bulb burning in the window with the photographs of the chorus girls.

Crane pressed his nose against the window and examined the eight photographs.

"I'll take that blonde in the left-hand corner," said O'Malley, who was standing right behind Crane. "I like a big diz."

"You're old-fashioned," said Williams, jostling Crane to get a better look. "A big diz has gone out of style."

"Style or no style——" O'Malley began.

Crane interrupted: "There's our baby—down at the bottom." He indicated a photograph of a small blonde holding a shawl in such a way that it exposed exactly half her body. She was a trifle plump, but her leg was muscularly slender. Under the photograph was written "Sue Leonard." "Now we have to find her," he added.

O'Malley bent over, holding Crane's arm for support. "Not a bad little twitchet."

Williams was looking at a small sign above the girls. "It says the show don't open for a week."

"We'll find her, anyway," Crane assured him.

O'Malley demanded, "What are you going to do? Walk in and ask your old pal, Frankie French?"

"God forbid," said Crane.

"I got an idea." Williams faced them. "Mike Fritzel, over at the Chez Paree, keeps a list of girls wanting work in his chorus. I'll give him a jingle an' see if he's got her down."

They drove to a drugstore and presently Williams came out, beaming. "She lives at 201 East Delaware," he announced.

Leaving O'Malley in the cab, Crane and Williams took an elevator to Miss Leonard's apartment on the third floor. An elderly woman with carmine lips, bright rouge on her cheeks and white hair answered their knock. She had on a red kimono.

"Miss Leonard's not at home. Is there any message?" she asked, adding, "I'm her mother." Under Williams' frank stare she altered this, saying, "—or rather . . . her aunt." She smirked at them.

Crane said, "She did a great service for a friend of mine today, and I wanted to thank her." He let his voice emphasize the word "thank." "I'd like to find her, if I could."

"Dearie, if it's money, you can leave it here *just* as safe. . . ." She simpered at Crane. "I'm like a *mother* to her."

"No. My friend wanted me to deliver our thanks in person." Crane liked gin, but not second hand. He moved back, out of range of the lady's breath. "When will she be home?"

She broke into a trill of laughter. "Not until late, I'm afraid." Her smirk suggested that girls will be girls. "She's going to a party at a gentleman's penthouse at eleven."

"But where is she having dinner?"

"I *really* don't know, dearie. She went out with two gentlemen and Miss Thompson, another sweet girl who lives here with me."

"Miss Sadie Thompson?" asked Crane.

"Oh, now you're joking me," exclaimed the woman. "This girl is *Anabel* Thompson. She worked with Sue in New York, at the Venice Club."

Williams looked grimly at the lady. "You're not letting the girls go to a party at that gambling penthouse on Surf Street, are you?" His tone was accusatory.

"Oh! Dear me, no!" She shook her head, her whole body. "She's going to Mr. Lawrence's penthouse, on the Orlando Hotel. I'm sure he's a perfect gentleman." In a dramatic gesture she held out both arms, then, giggling, clutched at her kimono. She smiled at them coyly. "I'm afraid I'm not properly dressed to receive gentlemen callers." The skin on her shoulders, her breast, was heavily powdered, like a chicken which has been dusted with flour preparatory to frying.

"That's quite all right," Crane assured her.

"Sure," supplemented Williams. "We're no gentlemen."

This set the lady into a paroxysm of laughter which threatened to let the kimono slip open again. Between gasps she asserted they were the funniest men! They were, they agreed, hastily departing.

O'Malley was asleep in the back seat of the cab. Awakened with difficulty, he rubbed his face, inquired: "Did you find her?"

"No." Crane climbed in beside him, held the door for Williams with his foot. "But we've been invited to a swell penthouse party."

"Hot damn!" exulted O'Malley. "Ain't we the society pooks?"

Chapter Fifteen

THEIR FEET scraped on the cement stairs, halted while the basement door swung open, then shuffled along a dim corridor. Another door let them into a brick-walled room with a wooden floor, two brown-stained tables with chairs and a bar with a mirror behind it. A

116

man was feeding a white English bulldog beer on one end of the bar, holding a glass to the animal's mouth. The bar was made of Cuban mahogany, and in front of it was a brass footrail and three heavy stools.

The bartender was polishing a glass. "What'll it be, gentlemen?" he asked. He breathed on the glass, held it to the light, then rubbed off the fog with his cloth.

They ordered three double shots of Bushmills' Irish whiskey.

The bulldog had stopped drinking, was looking at them. The man was saying, "Come on, Champion; finish it up." He tried to pour the beer into the bulldog's mouth, but the dog snorted, wouldn't drink.

Williams, who was nearest the dog, shuddered. "I hope he ain't as fierce as he looks." He moved his stool nearer Crane's.

The bartender's jaw champed as he talked, as though he were chewing grass. "That dog won't hurt nobody. He's gentle as a kitten." He added with three movements of his jaw, "—unless he's drunk."

"Jesus!" said Williams. "How is he now?"

Cloth in one hand, glass in the other, the bartender gazed reflectively at the bulldog. "He's just a little beered up. That don't mean nothin'. Takes hard liquor to make him ugly."

The dog swaggered along the bar toward Williams. He had the rolling gait, the bowed legs of a cowpuncher. Peering at Williams through topaz eyes, he sat three feet away, barked once, explosively.

"That means he wants a drink," the bartender explained.

"My God! Give him one." Williams' shoulder pressed against Crane's arm. "Give him some beer."

"No," said the bartender. "He wants whiskey."

"But you said hard liquor makes him ugly."

"It makes him worse to be refused."

Williams slid his glass of Irish whiskey toward the dog, but before the animal could get to it his master had the glass. He drank three quarters of the liquor, gave the rest to the dog. "We thank you," he said, pulling the dog back to the end of the bar.

"Quick, pour me another shot," ordered Williams. "A double one."

He took the glass from the bartender, drained it without pause for breath. "Wa-ah!" He wiped his mouth with the back of his hand.

The bartender grinned at him. "Don't worry. That purp ain't really ugly, drunk or sober. It's just a racket. That's the way the guy that owns him cadges drinks—through the dog." He picked up the glass and towel. "I always let him get away with one drink. That don't hurt nobody, and the dog's got some good tricks to amuse the customers. I figure it helps trade."

Crane asked, "What does he do?"

117

"You know. The usual stuff, like playing dead, and barking, and turnin' some'saults." The bartender again held the glass to the light. It sparkled like polished crystal. With a sigh he placed it on the shelf in front of the mirror. "He knows one good one, though. You give him a glove or a hanky belonging to somebody, and he'll pick that person out for you right off. From the smell, I guess." He reached under the bar for another glass. "It don't matter whether the person is in the back room or under the bar; Champion'll find him."

Williams was impressed. "Like a bloodhound," he said.

From somewhere in the back of the building came a few bars of "The Wabash Blues" played on a saxophone. Loud for a few beats, the music quickly died away.

"What was that?" asked Crane.

"One of those musicians," the bartender said. "A bunch of them hang out here."

Crane nibbled on a potato chip. "That reminds me." He stared at O'Malley. "Wasn't the Cavern the place they said Sam went to?"

"You mean that trumpet player?" asked O'Malley.

"Sam Udoni," said the bartender. "He used to be with Vallee. He's back there with the boys now."

Crane said, "I'd like to see old Sam." He finished his drink, slipped from the stool.

"You can see him, all right," said the bartender; "but I don't know as you'll be able to talk with him."

"Why not?"

"Gin and marijuana. They don't mix so well."

"Hell!" Crane shook his head sadly. "I didn't know old Sam hit that stuff."

The bartender accepted a ten-dollar bill, pondered over the cash register, finally, tentatively, pushed three keys. Black numbers leaped into the glass-windowed top of the register, read: 4.20. Fumbling with silver, he said over his shoulder: "I guess all them musicians hit the smoke." He gave Crane a five-dollar bill, three quarters and a nickel.

"Maybe we could go in the back room and see how Sam is getting along before we try to speak to him." Two of the quarters fell from Crane's hand to the mahogany counter. "Is there an extra table in the back room?"

Deftly the bartender scooped up the coins. "Thanks." They jingled against other silver in his apron pocket. "Sure. There's plenty of tables."

Crane started to leave, halted, said, "Maybe you better bring in a pint of that Irish and some fizzy water." His reflection in the mirror, although dim, showed a discolored left eye, a cut on the left temple, and another scratch below his left ear, half on the jawbone, half on the neck.

"Make it a quart," said O'Malley. "We gotta get ready for that penthouse party."

"Okay." The bartender put both hands on the counter, shouted, "Hey! Ty!"

Ty came out of the back room just as they started to enter it. He shied at them like a locoed horse, rolled his eyes until the pupils disappeared, staggered around them. He was the waiter and his white coat had rust-colored stains on the front. They ignored him, went on through the door.

Smoke as thick as fine gray silk sheeted the back room from ceiling to floor, eddied around a peach-colored overhead electric bulb, made indistinct the silent figures of men grouped about a central table. Crane led the way to another table near the door, felt for a chair and sat down. The other two, walking carefully, blindly, joined him. Their eyes were slow in becoming accustomed to the haze. "Whew!" Williams whispered. "Like a fog off the East River."

Against their skin, on their lips, the smoke actually had texture, body. It was warm and moist, like human breath. It was sweet and thick, like chloroform; only it was not medicinal.

At last they managed to see the entire room. Its walls were of cerise brick, darkened in patches by sweat; its ceiling was of rough plaster. There were no windows, but air came in through a chess-board ventilator. Six men were seated around the central table, their heads bowed before a seventh who perched, cross-legged, on top of the table. His head was bald; his face was fat and round and yellow; his arms were folded over his chest. His expression was tranquil. He had no cigarette, but the other six were smoking.

"What the hell?" whispered O'Malley.

Crane shook his head, kept his eyes on the men, who smoked in silence, apparently unaware that anyone had entered the room. The round-faced man on the table had his eyes open, but he didn't seem to be seeing anything through them. The pupils didn't move when the waiter, Ty, came with their bottle of whiskey, glasses, seltzer water and ice, made a clatter setting them on the table.

Crane put a finger to his lips. "Sush."

"Don't worry 'bout them guys," said the waiter, loudly. "Don't even worry a little bit. They ain't on the same plane with us." He filled each of the three glasses nearly half full of whiskey. "They're bein' absorbed."

Crane's eyes widened in wonder. "Absorbed?"

Ty pressed the lever on the siphon bottle, sent liquid over the table top. " 'Scuse me." He wiped the table dry with a napkin. "Yeah, absorbed. See that guy on the table? Well, he's Bray-mer. He's doin' the absorbing."

"For Christ's sake!" said Crane. He really was astonished. "For Christ's sake!"

The waiter aimed the seltzer carefully this time, filled all three glasses. "Those other guys," he stated, "they're undergods. But they ain't on the same plane with Bray-mer yet. They gotta keep smokin' to make it."

Accepting his glass, Crane asked, "How do you know so much about them?"

"Hell! ain't I been watchin' 'em for the last month?" He leaned over the table, spoke confidentially, "They're goin' to make me a god next week."

"Gosh, that's fine." Crane's eyes were wide over the upper rim of his glass. "That's just fine." In contrast with the sweet smoke in the room the whiskey was cleanly bitter. He let it roll around in his mouth, then asked, "Which one of those fellows is Sam Udoni?"

The waiter examined the men. "That's Sam. The dark guy, right across the table from you. He's Nar-sin."

"Nar-sin?"

"The lion-god."

"Oh!" Crane nodded his head as though everything were clear. "The lion-god."

The waiter gave them change for another ten-dollar bill, accepted a dollar and turned to leave. Crane said: "Wait a second." The waiter swung around. Crane asked: "How long do they keep this up?"

"They're just gettin' under way." The waiter frowned thoughtfully. "They ain't even reached the fifth plane yet."

"How many do they have to go?"

"They gotta hit the seventh plane before they can even talk with Bray-mer." The waiter frowned again. "That'll take three more rounds of gin, an' three more cigarettes, not counting the rest periods."

"God!" said O'Malley. His voice was awed. "You *really* gotta get steamed up to talk with Bray-mer."

"Look." Crane showed the waiter a five-dollar bill. "We want to talk with Sam Udoni. Is there any way we can get him out of here?"

"I dunno." The waiter's face was dubious, but he kept looking at the bill. "I *might* be able to get him for you."

Suddenly the round-faced man on the table spoke. His voice was in the lower human register. He said, "Matsya, extinguish the sacred incense."

One of the six men bowed twice, then chanted in a shrill voice: "Lord Brahma orders the sacred incense extinguished."

The men stood up, bowed twice in unison, mashed their cigarettes on the table, sat down again.

O'Malley and Williams watched them with eyes like fried eggs. Crane slipped a ten-dollar bill from his wallet, held it in place of the five. The waiter's eyes glistened. "You go in the little room back of that door," he said. "I'll bring him in to you." Delicately, he took the bill between thumb and forefinger.

They carried the bottle of whiskey, the charged water and the glasses into the little room. There was a window in the room, looking out into a moon-lit back yard with a wooden fence, and the air was fresh. They felt dizzy for a second, then their heads cleared.

O'Malley said, "It wouldn't take much of that stuff to conk you."

Williams was pouring himself approximately eight fingers of whiskey. "I don't like the looks of those guys." He gulped the liquor. "When I was workin' with Narcotics in Frisco we knocked over an opium joint, and about six of them Chinamen came after us with knives as big as . . ."

Crane said, "These fellows haven't got any knives."

Williams was holding his glass as though somebody were trying to pull it out of his hand. He eyed Crane, asked, "How do you know?"

O'Malley stuck his head out the window. "If they come at us we can scram out this way," he said. "I see a gate in the fence."

Williams said, "That's good. We'll let Buffalo Bill Crane, here, cover the rear with his trusty Remington—" he twirled his pointed mustache with a flourish "—while we ride for help."

The waiter appeared at the door. "These are the gentlemen, Mister Udoni," he said, and shoving a man into the room he backed out, closing the door behind him.

Udoni was somberly handsome. His skin was cream-colored; his hair was black and long, slicked back over a narrow head; his mouth was generous and sensitive. He had on a pale linen suit, a blue shirt and yellow necktie. His eyes, the size of half dollars, were blank.

Crane held a chair for him. "Sit down, Mr. Udoni."

There was a flicker of light in the distended pupils. Udoni sat down, moved his head to look at each of them, like a feebleminded child. "They say Narsinh know you." He blurred his words. "Narsinh does not know you." He started to rise from the chair.

"Wait a second." Crane leaned toward him. "We want to ask you about Miss Ross."

For a fractured second Udoni's face twitched, the blankness left his eyes. Then he said, "Narsinh go."

"No." Crane put his hand on Udoni's arm. "Why didn't Miss Ross have any shoes?"

Udoni stood up, his sleepwalker's face composed. "Brahma calls."

O'Malley said, "The hell he does!" He seized the seltzer bottle, sent a stream of ice-cold water into Udoni's mouth, nose, eyes. Udoni took three gasping breaths, tossed hands in the air and crumpled on the wooden floor.

"That'll bring him down to our plane," said O'Malley.

For five minutes they watched the man on the floor, listened to his heavy breathing. "That's the guy who was in bed with Miss, I mean Mrs. Udoni, all right," said Crane; "but he looks better with his clothes on."

Finally Udoni opened his eyes and sat up. "I think I'm going to be sick," he said.

Williams helped him to the window. He vomited into the back yard. "That closes our last avenue of retreat," said Crane.

"Not for me," said O'Malley.

When Williams brought him back to the table Udoni's eyes were normal. "Could I have some water?" he asked. They emptied one of the glasses, filled it with ice and seltzer water. He drank it gratefully.

"Feel better?" asked Crane.

"Yes." Udoni looked about him. "Where am I?"

"In the back room of the Cavern." Crane studied his face. "We were trying to ask you some questions."

"Questions? About what?"

Crane opened his billfold, showed Udoni his card. "We're private detectives. We want to ask you some questions about Miss Ross, if you don't mind."

"Miss Ross!" There was terror in the man's eyes. "I don't know any Miss Ross."

"Listen. We're not working for the police. We don't want to get you into any trouble, unless we have to." Crane paused to sip whiskey. "But if you won't answer our questions we'll take you down to the detective bureau."

Udoni asked, "But what could they arrest me for?" His eyes moved from one of them to another, furtively.

"Well, for one thing," said Crane, "you found her body and didn't report it to the police."

"Yes, I did." Udoni shrugged his shoulders. "But I was afraid to tell anyone. I'll go to the police, if you like."

"No. You don't have to go to the police at all, if you'll just answer our questions."

Udoni's face was puzzled. "Certainly, I'll answer them. I have nothing to conceal."

"Then why didn't you notify the police when you found Miss Ross' body?"

"I was frightened. I was afraid . . ." he stared for a full thirty seconds at Crane, continued: ". . . that the publicity would ruin my chances of obtaining a job in Chicago for myself and my band."

Crane watched him curiously. "You're sure that was the reason?"

Udoni nodded firmly, but his throat trembled.

"What about her shoes?" Crane made his voice harsh. "Why didn't she have any shoes?"

"I didn't know she didn't have any." Udoni's face was bloodless, his lips quivered. "Better have a drink," Crane urged, but Udoni said, "No, thanks." He added, "She always had shoes while I knew her."

"And you left everything in her room just as you found it? You didn't remove any of her clothes, or anything?"

"Why, no. I was only there a minute or two. I saw her hanging from the door, and . . ."

"Her body was naked?"

"Yes. And so . . ."

"That's all right." Crane wrinkled his forehead. "Now, Mr. Udoni, of course you knew who Miss Ross really was?"

"Really was?" Udoni's expression was startled. "I didn't know she was anybody but Alice Ross. She never told me. Who was she?"

Crane shook his head. "That's what we're trying to find out. We're sure of one thing, though."

Udoni's tone was apprehensive. "What's that?"

"That she wasn't Miss Ross. Somebody would have been asking about the body if that was her real name." Crane put his arms on the table. "You better tell us the history of your affair with Miss Ross. There may be something . . ."

There was anguish in Udoni's voice. "It wasn't an affair." His face worked, as though he were about to cry. "I loved her."

"And you were going to marry her?" Crane asked, surprised.

"Of course, only my wife wouldn't set me free."

"Then why did Miss Ross commit suicide?"

Udoni was actually crying. "She was so temperamental. Gay one minute, sad the next. Everything with her was all white or all black." He shook his head. "She felt my wife would never give me up." Tears rolled past his thin nose, over his lips. "Several times she threatened to kill herself if we do not get married."

"And you think she just got one of her despondent spells and killed herself?"

"Yes." Udoni dragged a handkerchief from his trouser pocket, wiped his face, blew his nose. "I'm sorry, gentlemen."

"That's all right," said Doc Williams. His eyes were bright. He blew his nose, too.

Crane added a little whiskey to the mixture in his glass. "Let's start at the beginning."

Udoni practically repeated his wife's story. He had met Miss Ross at the Savoy-Plaza. She was beautiful, intelligent, educated and musical, and he had fallen in love with her.

Crane asked, "But what was the matter with Miss—uh—Mrs. Udoni?"

"We had been married five years. In five years . . ." Udoni lifted his shoulders ". . . well, I had become bored with Angela."

Crane looked at him dubiously. "It hardly seems possible," he said reminiscently. "But go on."

"Miss Ross felt there was no future in strictly union work . . ."

Crane whispered to Williams, "Commercial jobs with the big bands."

". . . and thought I ought to form a band of my own with some ride-men," Udoni continued, "and pick up some of the dough going to the jungle boys from Harlem."

Williams' eyes were questioning, but Crane shook his head.

Udoni went on: "I had been thinking that myself, so I got hold of Frankie Thomas for the sax and Clem Packard for the clarinet, and Fats Wolman to handle the drums, and some other boys and we grooved a couple of tunes in New York and caught a wire at a nitery here in Chicago."

"Wait a minute! Wait a minute!" Crane held both hands in the air. "You're getting too deep for me. What's grooving a tune?"

"Making a record."

"What in hell's catching a wire at a nitery?"

"A contract to broadcast from a night club."

Crane waved a hand. "Proceed."

"Well, Miss Ross loaned me some money to make the trip to Chicago."

"How much?"

"Five thousand dollars."

Crane turned to O'Malley. "How much was it Kathryn drew out before she disappeared?"

"Six grand," said O'Malley.

Crane swung around on Udoni. "But why did you have to borrow from Miss Ross? You had some money of your own, some savings, didn't you?"

"No. I had saved nothing."

Crane nibbled at his right forefinger, thought for nearly a minute before he said, "Well, go on."

Miss Ross had come to Chicago with him, Udoni related, and tried several hotels before she went to the Princess Hotel. She wouldn't let him live with her, although he was able to visit her at any time. When the Kat Club closed he had been forced to take his band to the Clark-Erie while looking for another opening. That was about two weeks before Miss Ross had killed herself. Now he had lost the taxi-dance job.

"Now about Miss Ross' friends. Didn't she have any in New York, when she first met you?"

"I didn't meet any. She said she had heard me play when she was at a party at the Savoy (once in a while Rudy would let me take a lick), but when I first noticed her she was alone. She always came to meet me alone."

Crane's teeth clicked on the glass. "Did you know anything about a letter Miss Ross wrote to her family saying they would never see her again?"

"No." Udoni shook his head vigorously. "I didn't think she had a family. She told me her parents had died when she was young and that she had no near relatives." His eyes were wet again. Suddenly he pounded the table, words jerked from his mouth. "It was my wife who killed her. She killed her."

"The hell!" Crane's hands tightened on the table edge until his nails were white, "How?"

"By spying on her—following her."

Crane's breath moved through his mouth, whooo. "You mean, that drove Miss Ross to commit suicide?"

"Yes. Every time Alice saw Angela it made her despondent, ashamed of herself." Udoni twisted the handkerchief in his hands. "She moved from the Wacker Hotel to the Princess to escape her, but my wife followed her there, and when she learned that Angela was working in the taxi-dance hall where I was playing it made her ill." His lips trembled. "I believe that's why Alice . . ." His voice died, then came strong again ". . . because she felt so sorry for Angela."

"Didn't you worry about Angela working in the dance hall?"

"Angela can take care of herself."

Crane agreed. "Yes, I guess she can." He turned his glass so that the ice clinked against the side. "What color is your wife's hair?"

Udoni's eyes opened wide. "Why, black. It used to be blonde, but it's black now."

"Did your wife know you wanted to marry Alice?"

"Yes. I wrote her, asking for a divorce, and that's how she found out where Alice was living in Chicago."

"And she came here and watched Miss Ross; first at the Wacker Hotel and then at the Princess?"

"Yes."

Crane took a drink, rubbed melted ice from the tip of his nose. "You loved Miss Ross, yet you would have let them bury her in potter's field?"

"No! No!" Udoni moved his hands up and down. "I was waiting to see if anyone claimed her. I would have buried her, had a friend claim her if nobody took her." He turned to Crane. "I am not altogether a scoundrel."

Crane asked a great many more questions, but he learned little. Udoni reiterated his belief that Miss Ross had no relatives, repeated that she had more than once threatened suicide, expressed surprise that only a few dollars had been found in her room. He said, "She never told me she needed money." He said he wanted to help them in any way he could to find out who she really was, if not Miss Ross.

He asked about the theft of the body from the morgue, wanted to know if Crane had any idea who had taken it. Crane said he hadn't the faintest idea, asked, "Just as a matter of record, Mr. Udoni, where were you on the morning the body was stolen?"

Udoni said he had played with his orchestra at the Clark-Erie until 4 A.M. that morning.

"If that's true," said Crane, "you certainly couldn't have snatched the body."

"But why would I steal the body?"

"I give up." Crane smiled at the others, took Udoni's address—the Mozart. "You'll stick around?" he asked.

Udoni promised he would.

As he rose to leave Crane asked Udoni how he happened to be mixed up with the cult in the next room.

"Those are my boys," said Udoni. "Many musicians have cults, as you call them. It makes the dreams beautiful, instead of sordid, as they ordinarily are from marijuana. I myself rarely smoke, but now it helps me . . . forget."

"You mean you get so you really believe in Brahma?" Crane demanded.

Udoni said, "After the second cigarette one believes anything."

Chapter Sixteen

THE LOBBY of the Hotel Sherman looked like the waiting room of a small-town railway station. Men in shirt sleeves, with loosened ties, sat in the big leather chairs fanning themselves, between puffs of cigar smoke, with magazines, newspapers. A few talked, but most of them simply sat, concentrating on breathing the warm, moist air. It was eighty-three degrees above zero in the lobby, ninety-one in the street. There were circular sweat marks under the men's arms.

O'Malley crossed the lobby to the Western Union counter, collected two telegrams. Williams went to look up his friend Dwyer, the house detective. Crane sank limply in one of the leather chairs. It was exactly 11:41.

Crane had his little finger in a corner of one of the telegrams, was about to slit it when Williams returned. "Dwyer says the cops have beat it," he announced. "He says we can use our rooms if we want, and he'll tip us off if they come back."

Crane put the telegrams in his pocket, found a wilted handkerchief and rubbed his forehead. "That's swell. I could use a shower."

"Yeah," said O'Malley; "and we can get dolled up for that penthouse party." He looked critically at Crane. "You could use a shave."

Crane ran his palm over his cheek. It came away wet. "What do you care?" he asked. "I'm not planning on kissing you."

Williams snorted, allowed them to enter the elevator ahead of him. "I wish I was in Greenland," he said.

"Okay," said Crane. "You take Greenland. I'll take Siberia. But what'll be left for O'Malley?"

"I'll take Miss Udoni," said O'Malley.

When they entered their suite of rooms they saw it had been gloriously ransacked by the police. The rug had been moved and not replaced, pictures were askew, and the Early American furniture had been bunched in a corner by the east windows. In the bedrooms their luggage had been opened and clothes were strewn on beds and floor. Broken glass and a brown stain on the bathroom floor marked the place where one of the policemen had fumbled a bottle of iodine.

Williams whistled in amazement. "What in hell were they looking for?"

"They probably thought we had Miss Ross' body concealed up here," said Crane.

O'Malley was examining the living room. "Yeah," he said disgustedly, "that's why they moved all the pictures. You always hide bodies behind pictures."

Crane pulled the davenport around in place, sat down and read the first telegram:

O'MALLEY . . . HOTEL SHERMAN . . . CHICAGO.
     YOU DIDN'T THINK I SWAM, DID YOU?
          A. N. BROWN . . . SAN DIEGO . . . CALIF.

Crane grinned, said, "I guess that puts him on the plane, all right."

The other telegram was from Colonel Black and read:

COURTLAND PLAYED BRIDGE AT HARVARD CLUB WEDNESDAY EVENING UNTIL AFTER MIDNIGHT. ALIBI ABSOLUTELY AIRTIGHT. THURSDAY LEFT CONFERENCE WITH ME AT SEVEN P.M. TO PACK FOR CHICAGO. CAUGHT MIDNIGHT PLANE.

UNCLE STY LEFT OFFICE 5:30 WEDNESDAY P.M. NO CHECK UNTIL HE WAS AWAKENED AT 10 A.M. THURSDAY BY VALET. SPENT EVENING WITH MRS. COURTLAND AFTER CONFERENCE WITH ME.

MRS. COURTLAND PLAYED BRIDGE HOME ALL WEDNESDAY EVENING. WITH UNCLE STY THURSDAY EVENING. EXCELLENT GUESS ABOUT COURTLAND IN MARKET, BUT HE SEEMS TO BE MAKING MONEY HAND OVER FIST INSTEAD OF LOSING. NO HORSES, NO WOMEN.

                     BLACK.

They flipped a coin to see who would take the first shower, and Williams won. While he was undressing Crane telephoned American Airways, asked the clerk if Chauncey Courtland had been listed as a passenger on the sleeper plane which left New York at midnight Thursday.

After a pause the clerk said yes, he was.

"And the ticket was collected?"

"Yes. It was collected."

Crane thanked him and hung up.

"What's the idea?" asked O'Malley.

"Just checking," said Crane, removing his shirt.

"I can see why you want to know where he was when the body was lifted from the deadhouse," said O'Malley, "but I'm damned if I see what difference it makes where he was Wednesday night when the dame was knocking herself off."

"I'm not sure myself." Crane rubbed his chin. "But whatever I was thinking of seems to be out. Courtland was in New York playing bridge at the time Miss Ross was kicking her heels against that bathroom door, and he was riding in an airplane when somebody was raiding the morgue."

O'Malley shuddered. "Hangin' gives me the creeps."

"Yeah," said Crane; "'to dance to flutes, to dance to lutes, is delicate and rare; but it is not sweet with nimble feet to dance upon the air.'" He pulled his underwear top over his head.

From the shower Williams shouted, "I wonder if the coppers are digging up that graveyard for Miss Ross?"

"They're too dumb to look in the burial book," Crane yelled back. In a lower tone, to O'Malley he said, "And even if they did, they'd have to go to court to get an order to exhume the body, and that would mean they'd have to wait until tomorrow."

O'Malley was removing his shoes and socks. He held up a sock. "Look, it's wringin' wet. I bet I've lost ten pounds in the last couple of days." He put the sock in one of the shoes, added, "I don't like that Udoni."

"Why?"

"There's something phony about him . . . the way he acts . . . like his nerves was all shot . . . as though he was scared to death."

A towel wrapped around his middle, Williams padded into the room. His face was damp and contented. "Wouldn't your nerves be shot," he asked, "if your best gal knocked herself off?" His feet left wet prints on the rug.

"Sure, but I wouldn't be scared," O'Malley said.

Crane agreed. "He did act as though he was frightened."

"I bet I know why," announced Williams after a moment's thought.

They stared at him questioningly.

"That money." Williams held the towel with one hand, gestured with the other. "I bet he took that dough from Miss Ross and gave it to his wife. You remember she told you he had given her the three grand in her bank account?" Crane nodded and he continued. "Well, he's afraid somebody'll either make him pay it back or toss him in jail for taking it from Miss Ross."

Crane's teeth chewed on his lower lip. "You may have it, Doc."

"May have?" Williams made a flat, horizontal gesture with his free hand. "Hell! I *have* it."

O'Malley started for the shower, paused in the doorway, "Why did you ask Udoni about his wife's hair?"

Crane said, "I saw a bottle of black hair dye in her bathroom. She tried to hide it, and I wondered why." He glared at O'Malley. "For Christ's sake, take your shower. I'm going to melt in a minute."

129

O'Malley said, "O.K., Bray-mer."

Williams put on a clean set of underwear, began slapping Ed Pinaud's lilac water on his face. "Do you think Miss Ross is really Kathryn Courtland?"

"It looks like it." Crane was fingering a newly discovered bruise on his back, just below the shoulder blade. "It certainly looks like it. There's the similarity in money (where're you going to find another blonde with five grand to toss around?) and then there's that stuff about Harlem."

"What about Harlem?"

Crane decided that the sore place on his back was the result of a kick. "Don't you remember Courtland told us he saw his sister sitting all alone one night at some club in Harlem? Well, she was probably waiting until Udoni finished playing with the band."

"But—" Williams' voice was outraged "—those guys are all niggers."

"Sure, but a lot of the good white musicians go down to Harlem after they finish playing and practice with the black bands. They get a chance to make up their own variations in Harlem, while they have to stick to the straight music with the commercial bands."

Williams thought for a moment, then said proudly, "You mean Udoni went down to Harlem to blow a lick or two on the horn."

"That's it," said Crane. He heard the shower stop and stood up. "He wanted to swing it with the jungle boys."

Williams said indignantly, "Well, why didn't you say so in the first place? What's the matter, can't you speak English?"

"The trouble is," said O'Malley, appearing in a pair of shorts, "that you two guys ain't on the same plane."

"Oh my God!" Crane started for the shower. "I don't know how I put up with you two."

"Wait a minute." Williams handed the bottle of lilac to O'Malley, who said, "For the love of Mike! Why don't you buy some of this stinkwater if you like it so well?" Williams continued, "Then you aren't going to look for the gangster's gal any more, now you think it is Miss Courtland?"

"What? No penthouse party?" demanded O'Malley.

"Hell, yes." Crane walked into the shower. "I want to find that babe." The wet tile felt nice on his feet. "I'm getting tired of having those two mugs, French and Paletta, slap me around." The water, cool and refreshing as a Tom Collins, sang around his ears.

It was nearly one o'clock when they reached the Blackstone. They were dressed in fresh linen suits, pressed by the night valet at the Sherman, and each had a red carnation in his buttonhole. They felt fine, even Crane, who had just computed that he had been without sleep for forty hours. The clerk who phoned the Courtland suite told them: "Please go up."

Mrs. Courtland had on a black satin evening gown trimmed with lace and festooned with diamonds. She said, "Well! It's *about* time." She had on a diamond choker, was regarding them coldly through a gold lorgnette.

Courtland moved toward them. "We've been trying to find you." He was wearing a white mess jacket, black trousers, patent-leather shoes and a midnight blue cummerbund. "Here's something for you to look at." He handed Crane a letter.

Mrs. Courtland pursed her lips, looked at Crane through the lorgnette. "Now we shall be able to stop this *foolish* waste of money."

The letter had been addressed on a typewriter and was postmarked Pennsylvania Station, N.Y., 9:40 A.M., August 5. It was addressed to Mrs. Evalyn Courtland, 835 Park Avenue, New York City. He took out a folded sheet from the envelope. It read:

Dearest Mother.

Today I suddenly realized that my last letter must have sounded dreadfully like suicide to you and the family. Nothing is further from my real intention. . . .

The new and perhaps better world I spoke of is merely the world shared by the majority of people . . . a world where people are united by the necessity of finding food, of making homes, of earning comforts and necessities. I have learned that money, unless it has been earned, is a burden, and I know, really, that my only chance for happiness lies in working for myself and for another.

I have found that "another," and that is why I must cut myself off from my selfish past, so as not to be tempted to give up if the going is rough.

Believe me, Mother, I do not blame you for my old unhappinesses, but money, and if things go well, perhaps . . . perhaps . . . perhaps . . .

All my love,
Kathryn.

Crane fumbled around in his coat pocket, found the first letter from Kathryn. As far as he could tell the writing was the same. So was the cream-colored writing paper. He gave the two letters to Doc Williams, turned to face the family.

Uncle Stuyvesant, in white flannels and a dark coat, took a deep breath. "Ha, ha, ha," he said; "it looks as though we were barking up the wrong tree, ha, ha, ha." His eyes weren't amused.

"I don't understand it at all," Crane said. "Are you positive this came from Kathryn?"

"Oh yes," said Mrs. Courtland. "It means your job is over, young man."

Crane glanced at Uncle Stuyvesant, who said:

"I'm sorry, but I don't see how any further expense is justified."

Bewildered, Crane blinked at them. Finally, he said, "Would you mind if I sent the letters to a handwriting expert in the city? There's just a chance . . ."

"I consider the matter closed," said Mrs. Courtland, tossing her head.

"Now, Mother," said Courtland. "It can't do any harm." He turned to Crane. "Will it be expensive?"

"It won't cost you anything." Crane took the letters from Williams. "I simply want to satisfy myself."

"Oh, very well," said Mrs. Courtland. "But I hope you won't be forcing yourself——"

"Now, Mother," said Courtland.

"Good evening," said Mrs. Courtland, fixing her lorgnette in order upon O'Malley, Williams, and Crane. "GOOD EVENING!"

Courtland followed Williams and O'Malley out into the corridor. Crane started after them, then turned back, said, "Mrs. Courtland, this is a very serious business. There have been at least two murders in connection with the search for the girl in the morgue."

"Well?"

"As a private detective I am also an officer of the law." Crane made his eyebrows frown, his mouth grim. "And as an officer of the law I want to ask you two questions."

Mrs. Courtland turned indignantly to Uncle Stuyvesant. "Such impertinence!"

"I think you had better answer him, dear."

Crane said, "The night you arrived here, Mrs. Courtland, an undertaker whom we believe was connected with the case was murdered. He was murdered between midnight and two o'clock." He took a quick breath, demanded, "Where was your son at that time?" He braced himself for an outburst.

Surprisingly, she was perfectly calm. "My son met me at the airport and came back to the hotel with me. We talked until after two o'clock." She still held the lorgnette to her eyes.

"Is this true, Mr. Courtland?" Crane asked.

"I suppose so."

Mrs. Courtland said, "Stuyvesant doesn't know. He wasn't with us."

"He wasn't! Where was he?"

"Suppose you ask him."

"All right. Mr. Courtland, where were you?"

Uncle Stuyvesant was making a washing motion with his hands. "Why . . . why, I went out to see a friend from the airport." His eyes moved from Crane to Mrs. Courtland, back to Crane.

"Did you see him?" asked Crane.

"Why, no. No. He wasn't there."

"What time did you get back to the hotel?"

"A few minutes after two."

"Nearer three," said Mrs. Courtland.

"And who was this friend?" asked Crane.

"Yes, who was this friend?" echoed Mrs. Courtland.

Crane stared at her in surprise. She stared at Uncle Stuyvesant in something like triumph. Uncle Stuyvesant stared at the floor.

After a time Uncle Stuyvesant said, "His name is Peter Hamilton and he lives at 3800 Sheridan Road."

"Yes?" said Mrs. Courtland. Her voice was smooth. "Well, good evening, Mr. Crane."

Crane blinked at her, wandered out into the hall. "I'll be God-damned," he repeated under his breath. "I'll be God-damned."

Courtland was standing with the others. "You don't know how glad I am that sister's alive," he said. "I may not have shown it, but I was really worried." His eyes crinkled at them.

"You showed it all right," said Williams.

Courtland asked Crane, "What are you going to do now?"

"I guess we're pretty well washed up." Crane shrugged his shoulders. "However, I think we'll go to a certain penthouse party tonight, anyway."

"Hot damn!" said O'Malley.

"How come a party?" asked Courtland.

Crane told him how they had traced Sue Leonard. "If she knows Verona Vincent is alive," he went on, "she should know where she is. And if I can find where she is I can turn her over to either French or Paletta and stop them shooting at me. I can't have them gunning for me the rest of my life." He suddenly grinned at Courtland. "It's positively embarrassing."

Courtland said, "Yes, I should think it would be." His teeth were strong and white. "Say! Could I come along? Sue might talk to me as an old friend."

"Swell." Crane adjusted his carnation, stared admiringly at Courtland's mess jacket. "You'll give us just the class we need to crash the party."

133

Courtland started for the door to the suite. "I'll tell Mother," he called over his shoulder.

Crane said, "We'll wait for you in the lobby."

As they came out of the elevator Crane said to O'Malley, "We better order a cab."

"Now that Uncle Sty ain't payin' the bills," Williams objected, "we better walk."

"God will provide," said Crane. "You order the cab and talk to Courtland while I make a phone call."

He bought five dollars' worth of quarters from the night clerk, and went into one of the telephone booths and closed the door. He got the long-distance operator and asked for Butterfield 8-4040. Fugi, Colonel Black's Japanese man, answered the phone, said: "Very nice to hear voice again, Mister Bill Crane." Crane said, "Yeah, Fugi; nice, but expensive. Will you put the colonel on the extension?"

In a moment the colonel's voice, lazy and good-natured, came through the receiver. "Hello, Bill."

"Hello, Colonel. I thought I better tell you we just got fired."

"So I understand. Uncle Stuyvesant wired me to call you off."

"It was on account of a letter. . . ."

"Yes, from Kathryn."

"Well, I'm not so sure about that letter. I thought I'd give it to Carlson, the handwriting man. It might be a forgery."

"I wouldn't bother. It's Kathryn's handwriting, all right."

"For the love of Mike!" Crane let the receiver slip from his hand, had to bend his knees to recover it. "How do you know that?"

"We opened the letter when it arrived Saturday and examined the handwriting before we forwarded it to Chicago."

"Then you think the letter's legitimate?"

"I know she wrote it. But you might give some thought to why a typewriter was used to address the envelope."

"But how about the case? Do you want us to drop it?"

"What do you think?"

"I think there's one really good reason why we should go on."

The colonel's voice was soft. "You mean, because Miss Ross was murdered?"

The receiver fell to the end of the cord, banged against the wooden wall of the booth. Crane retrieved the receiver, spoke passionately into the mouthpiece. "Good God! Isn't there anything you don't know?"

Colonel Black chuckled. "Many things, including the identity of Miss Ross. But tell me, what made you conclude she was murdered?"

"A lot of things—the bathtub full of water, the missing shoes . . ."

"Yes, but wasn't there one thing in particular?"

Crane's voice was exasperated. "The bathroom scales."

"Exactly."

Perspiration ran down Crane's face, tickled his neck. He was very angry. "What the hell good am I?" he demanded. "What do you need anybody in Chicago for, when you know everything already?"

"I can hear you quite well," Colonel Black said. "You needn't shout." His voice was good-humored, drawling, "I am very glad you are in Chicago, particularly as it centers the unwelcome attentions of the rival gangsters on you. I like to feel that if anyone is killed in this business it will be you, not me."

Crane clung weakly to the coin box.

"I think it would be advisable to go ahead for a time," the colonel continued. "We can afford it, fortunately, as I received a five-thousand-dollar retainer from Stuyvesant Courtland. You will find Miss Ross' body sometime tonight?"

"Yes," said Crane, hoarsely. He no longer felt surprise.

"Fine. I believe that's about all. . . . Oh, yes! The police."

"Yes. They're after me."

"No. No longer. I had a conversation with the state's attorney which cleared up several misapprehensions. However, he would still like to have a chat with you. I wish you would try to see him sometime tomorrow."

"All right."

"And Bill. About Shirley Temple. Do you think it gentlemanly to involve a young lady with a stainless reputation in a dubious case of this sort?"

"I don't know. . . ."

"If you wish to cast glamour and mystery over the case I suggest you use some name such as . . ." the colonel's voice grew faint . . . "Gertrude Stein." There was a click at his end of the connection.

Muttering to himself, Crane allowed the operator to persuade him to drop three additional quarters into the coin box. "That son of a bitch," he kept saying. "That son of a bitch." He staggered into the lobby, fanning his face with his Panama hat. His skin looked like faded red-flannel underwear. He was still mumbling when he joined Courtland, O'Malley and Williams in a corner of the lobby.

"Who's got nothing to do but sit around all day and think?" asked Williams, catching some of Crane's words.

"Huh?" Crane was startled. "Oh! That handwriting expert," he lied, and asked, "Do you know what I'm going to do?" They shook their heads. He said, "I'm going to get so drunk you'll be able to bottle me."

135

Chapter Seventeen

EVEN BEFORE their elevator halted at the twenty-seventh floor they could hear laughter. It sounded as though the party were already nicely organized. The elevator man said, "You'll have to walk up one floor to the penthouse, gentlemen." He pointed to carpet-covered stairs.

The door to the penthouse was ajar, so they walked right into the hall and tossed their hats on top of other hats on a table. There were screams and laughter, and men's and women's voices coming from a room at the other end of the hall. They were moving in that direction when another door swung open, disclosing a red tile floor and an electric stove, and a man and a woman nearly collided with them. The woman was slender and dark, and she had on a crimson dress cut very low in the back. She jerked her hand free from the man's, widened her eyes at them, said:

"Oo-oo! Lookut big handsome mens!"

She seized Crane's and O'Malley's arms, linked her own under them, inquired, "Does handsome mens like Vangie?" Her companion was an elderly man and he stared at them as though he, at least, didn't like them. He walked down the hall toward the room from which the noise was coming.

They assured Vangie they liked her. Yes, indeed. They were very fond of her, and later they would duel to see who would win her. But, in the meantime, did she know where they could find a drink?

Vangie giggled and led them into the penthouse living room. It was a large room with a high white ceiling and walls painted a vivid blue-green. Soft gray carpet covered the floor; ash-blond light filtered from parchment-shaded lamps; the big chairs, the two davenports facing each other in front of the fireplace, were slip-covered in solid colors, reds and greens and blues, but faded, as though they had been left for a long time in the sun. Someone cried, "Look at Vangie with four men!" and a redhead with dimples and a green dress detached herself from a group of men and women and ran toward them. Across from the fireplace French windows opened on to the terrace. A radio was playing a Wayne King waltz and moonlight, like spilled talcum powder, dusted the shoulders of dancers. . . .

"This one's mine," said the redhead, taking Doc Williams' arm.

He smiled at her, gave his mustache a twirl. "You've got the grand prize, lady," he said.

"That's Dolly," said Vangie.

Crane said, "Dolly, meet Doc."

"Oo-oo! I just adore doctors," cried Dolly, squeezing Williams' arm with both hands. "You're so *safe* with them."

"You better be careful with him," said Crane. "He's an obstreperous one."

Dolly's eyes rounded. She exclaimed, "Oh! A *baby* doctor?"

"Well, for Christ's sake!" said Crane.

They moved across the living room, past women drinking cocktails, men drinking highballs, toward a closet which had been converted into a silver-and-black bar. The air was heavy with cigarette smoke, with the mingled odors of tobacco, champagne, lemon, perfume, hair slick, real-flower corsages, whiskey, shaving lotion and gin. Crane noticed that the men were all elderly—fifty or over. The bartender wanted to know what they would have.

The ladies said they'd have champagne cocktails. Courtland, O'Malley and Williams ordered Scotch and soda; Crane ordered a champagne cocktail. The bartender used Haig and Haig from a pinch-bottle for the Scotch and soda, and Crane knew at once that the party was going to be a good one. The champagne was Mumm's Cordon Rouge, and the bartender poured it into crystal glasses on top of a piece of lemon peel and a lump of sugar partially soaked in bitters.

Like the noise a manicurist makes with a chamois nail buffer, the shuffle of dancing feet on the terrace floated in to them. Wayne King was playing a tango, using wood-winds and stringed instruments, and the music was subdued, sweet.

Vangie took hold of Crane's hand. "Come on, baby, let's dance." She shook her shoulders. "I just love to tango."

Crane put the empty champagne glass on the bar. "I need one more to give me rhythm." He accepted another from the bartender, drained it in a breath. "O.K. Let's go."

In the sky hung a waning moon, lemon yellow and shaped like a portion of honeydew melon. The orchestra was playing a fox trot, and the dancers were moving faster. The air was soft and moist and fragrant.

Crane danced with Vangie for three numbers, learned that she was from the Vanities. She said most of the girls at the party were from the show or from Frankie French's new night club revue. She didn't know Sue Leonard.

O'Malley, leaning against the three-foot stone wall along the edge of the roof, signaled them. "When do I get to dance with this gal?" he demanded. He was carrying two champagne cocktails; gave one to Vangie, the other to Crane.

Vangie tasted her drink, then set it on the wall. "I'll be seeing you," she said to Crane. She danced away with O'Malley.

Crane drank his drink. He watched until Vangie wasn't looking and drank hers. He started out to look for Courtland and almost bumped into a woman. "Sorry," he said, bowing from the waist with continental elegance. "May I offer you a drink, madam?"

There was a noise of ice tinkling against glass in the living room.

The woman was smoking a cigarette in a red holder. Diamonds on a bracelet sparkled as she took the holder from her mouth. Her voice was low and harsh. "Why not?" she asked. Her voice sounded as though she didn't give a damn either way. She walked with him into the living room.

She didn't walk, either. She slouched. She was a blonde and her face was coldly beautiful. Her hair was held back from a low forehead by a lacquered gold fish net; there were blue hollows under her high cheekbones; her lips were full and disdainful. She had on a lace gown which clung blackly to high breasts, thin waist, suave hips, and then, gorgeously, turned to Chinese red in a stiffened flounce exactly midway between her head and her painted toenails.

Crane saw that the diamonds on the bracelet were real. He said, "What'll you have to drink?"

"Gin."

The bartender said, "Yes, Miss Renshaw." He filled a water tumbler half full of Gilbey's gin, handed it to her.

Crane gaped at the glass. "Don't you mix it with anything?"

Her lips smiled scornfully.

Crane said, "Give me the same."

There were sounds of cheering from the terrace. An overhead light had been turned on and in its bright circle Williams and the red-headed girl were doing a Cuban rumba. The girl had a bath towel, was rubbing it around her hind-quarters as she would a shawl, and Williams had another, wound sash-fashion around his waist. His teeth were white under his mustache.

Crane and Miss Renshaw walked to the corner of the terrace over-looking Lake Michigan. A yacht was passing the end of Belmont Harbor and its lights made lemon stains on the still water. Behind them a small fountain gurgled. He tried the gin. It didn't taste so bad, but it was a little difficult to speak for a second or two after a sip. He finally managed to say:

"Silver spray falling on a velvet blotter."

Miss Renshaw's voice was harsh. "What?"

"Moonlight on the lake."

"The moon's all right, if you like it," admitted Miss Renshaw. Her voice was incredible. It was like a waitress' voice in a Greek restaurant. "It don't make me romantic, though."

"No," Crane said. "It wouldn't." He eyed the diamonds.

Miss Renshaw faced him. "Just whatd'ya mean by that crack?" she demanded.

"Nothing," said Crane. "Nothing at all." He drank some more gin. "I was thinking that a full moon is much nicer than one like this. It's so much bigger, for one thing."

Louis Armstrong replaced Wayne King on the radio. It was like jumping from Vienna to Africa. Crane said, "Would you care to dance?"

"Not now," said Miss Renshaw negligently.

"Well, how about a swim?"

"In the fountain here?"

"No. In the lake."

Miss Renshaw looked at him with interest for the first time. "You got a yacht?"

"Well, no. Not exactly," Crane admitted. "But I could probably get one."

"I got one," said Miss Renshaw.

The music was throbbing, moaning, torrid. Saxophones, an inspired trumpet, the piano made wild improvised flights from the written melody. Louis Armstrong was swinging it.

"It's dangerous to swim under a waning moon," said Crane. "Maybe we better postpone that ride on your yacht."

"Who invited you?" asked Miss Renshaw.

"I need a drink," said Crane weakly. He was surprised to find his glass had somehow been emptied. "How about you?" He knew when he was licked.

Miss Renshaw's glass was empty. Crane suddenly realized what her voice made him think of. She said, "My tonsils is dry, too." It made him think of the raucous voices invariably possessed by the female stooges of second-flight vaudeville wisecrackers.

They went back to the bar, secured two more glasses of gin and came out on the porch again. Williams had thrown away the towel and, apparently, his coat, and was dancing Bowery style with Dolly, whose red hair had fallen over her shoulders. There was a circle of people around O'Malley, amazedly watching him produce lighted cigarettes from his pockets, ears, mouth; from other persons' pockets, ears, mouths. Courtland was standing in the doorway of the living room, talking to a pretty blonde in a gown of floating gray marquisette with a garland of yellow daisies over her breast. He seemed fairly sober.

There were seductive hollows just above the V formed by Miss Renshaw's breastbone. They shifted when she moved her neck, sometimes almost disappearing, leaving only smooth flesh, pale in the moonlight. There was an exotic odor of jasmine about her.

Crane thought he could almost forgive her voice. "Getting any warmth out of that gin?" he asked.

She looked into his eyes. "You think I'm cold?"

"Perhaps a trifle reserved . . ."

She stared at him reflectively, then took a long drink of the gin. He said, "I think I've seen you somewhere before."

"Have you?" She looked at him again, then drank the remainder of her gin. "No, I don't think so. People don't forget me."

"I can forget anybody," Crane said. "Anybody."

"You won't forget me again."

"Oh yes, I will," said Crane obstinately.

She put her glass on the wall and took Crane's face between her two palms and kissed him. Her lips were hot. She released him roughly, asked, "You still think you will?" and walked into the living room.

Crane said, "What the hell?" He stared at her back until she disappeared. "Why, my God!" He gulped the rest of his gin.

A man came up behind him and tapped his shoulder. "I'd be careful with that lady, young man," he said. He was about fifty. "She's the host's personal guest."

"Next time she comes around," Crane promised, "I'll scream for the police."

People were watching Williams' girl, Dolly, doing some sort of a buck and wing to the music. She had her skirts pulled above her knees, was moving her feet with unbelievable rapidity. She had on black garters. Crane pushed past the circle, ran into Williams as he stepped into the living room. He asked Williams a question.

"I'm looking for it, too," said Williams.

They wandered down a hall and encountered a woman coming out of one of the bedrooms. She was wearing a dress of pink chiffon. It looked like a nightgown, but you couldn't see through it, so it wasn't a nightgown.

Crane bowed and said, "Pardon, madam."

Williams said, "Hi, tutz."

She said, "Go right through that bedroom across the hall." She smiled at them.

Coming out of the bathroom, Crane and Williams admired the double bed in the bedroom. It had a pale-blue spread and the sheets were silk. Williams fingered them and said, "My God! Look!"

The sheets weren't plain white like most sheets but were sprinkled with royal blue flowers. Crane bent close to them, but Williams said, "No, you don't."

"I just want to try the springs," said Crane.

"No, you don't." Williams tugged at his coat. "We still have work to do. You can sleep tomorrow."

Crane allowed himself to be pushed into the hall. Williams asked, "What did the colonel have to say?"

"What makes you think I talked to him?"

"You don't buy five dollars' worth of quarters to call a handwriting expert in Chicago. Come on, what did he say?"

"He said, keep on working, the son of a bitch."

"Did he have any ideas?"

"He always has ideas," said Crane, bitterly.

"Well, don't let it worry you," Williams moved on ahead into the living room.

"Don't let what worry me?"

"That the colonel's smarter than you."

This put Crane in such a fury that Williams was forced to bring him a quart bottle of champagne to calm him. They each drank from the bottle and watched the progress of the party.

Somebody had turned up the radio until the music sounded as though it were being played by the United States Marine Band. A girl was dancing on the terrace in an orange-colored chemise. Somebody was smashing crockery in the kitchen. Two men were being dissuaded with difficulty from fighting. A baby-faced blonde borrowed a dollar from Crane for cab fare home. A couple were necking on one of the davenports. Three men were bitterly arguing politics on the other. A man in shirt sleeves asked O'Malley if he was having a good time. O'Malley asked him what the hell business it was of his. The man said he was sorry. He said he wouldn't have asked except that he was giving the party and wanted everybody to have a good time. O'Malley accepted his apology. A baby-faced blonde borrowed a dollar for cab fare home from Williams. Somebody fell over a chair on the terrace. Two girls were wading in the fountain. A gold watch flipped from the pocket of a man trying to Charleston on the terrace, shattered itself on the polished tile. Williams asked the girl in the nightgown which wasn't a nightgown for her telephone number and she tossed him a handkerchief, and what do you think? The number, Superior 7500, was printed in green thread on one corner, so all you had to do was to keep the handkerchief. A baby-faced blonde borrowed a dollar for cab fare home from O'Malley. The redhead, Dolly, passed out and had to be put to bed.

Courtland came over just as Crane was finishing the bottle of champagne. His face was excited. "I've been talking to Sue," he began.

"A nice little tambo, too," Williams said.

"You will please be silent," Crane carefully placed the empty bottle on the gray rug. "My friend, my pal, my old pal Mister Courtland, has a message."

"Well, Sue says that Verona Paletta is alive." Courtland grinned at Crane. "She is positive about it."

"That's a strong statement—a very strong statement," Crane wheeled around on Williams. "Isn't that a strong statement?"

Williams nodded.

"The question is," said Crane slowly, "can she prove it?" He shook a finger at Williams. "Proof is ninety points of the law."

"You're thinking of whiskey," objected Williams. "Ninety proof whiskey."

"I know what I'm thinking of." Crane was indignant. "I'm thinking of Verona Vincent Paletta." He liked the sound of the name.

Courtland said. "Well, she's here at the party."

"Verona Vincent Paletta?"

Courtland nodded.

"This is interesting." Crane staggered against the champagne bottle, knocked it over. "Good old Verona here." He bent over and after a time managed to stand the bottle on the rug. "Are we on a yacht," he demanded, "that the floor keeps moving so?" He dusted his hands on his white trousers. "Did Sue say which one old Verona was?"

"She says she doesn't dare tell us."

"So that's what she says? Very well! If that's what she shays, that's what she says. Very well! We'll carry on, however."

Williams asked, "But how're you going to find her?"

"That's not the problem. No, sir. I've found her already. The problem is, how're we going to get her out of here?"

Courtland asked, "You've found her already?"

Crane said, "Frankly, yes, old pal." He added, "Have I thanked you for saving my life, old pal?"

Williams signaled O'Malley.

"Forget about that life stuff," said Courtland.

"No. I do not forget, old pal. Allow me to show my ap're'cion. Allow me to secure you a drink. I know the bartender person'ly."

"Wait a minute," said Williams. "We gotta do something about this Paletta dame."

"Good. I'm glad you realize it. It's about time, too. Let's take her home to Paletta."

"Suppose she don't wanta go there," objected Williams.

"We'll give her a choice." Crane kicked over the champagne bottle again, bent down to pick it up. "She can go back to Paletta, or she can go back to Frankie French, or she can go back to Paletta."

"She won't wanta go back to either," said Williams.

Four men in another corner of the living room were singing "I wish I was in Dixie." Outside it sounded as though someone had fallen in the fountain. The radio was playing "Minnie, the Moocher."

"What we going to do, then?" asked Crane, tossing the bottle so that it fell on the davenport, just missing the head of the man necking the girl there.

"We'll snatch her," said O'Malley.

Bottle in hand, the man came over from the davenport. "Listen," he said, "you can't get away with that sort of stuff." He planted himself in front of Crane. "You almost hit me."

"What if I did?" asked Crane.

O'Malley said, "Yeah, maybe we can do better next time."

"My error," said the man. He took the bottle back to the davenport with him.

"How we going to get her in a cab?" asked Crane. "She'll scream."

"Knock her over the head," said Williams.

"Wait a minute." Courtland crossed to the mantel over the fireplace and picked up a bunch of keys. He thrust them in his pocket, said, "I saw a man put those up there." He crossed to where the men were arguing about politics, addressed one of the men. "The doorman phoned up and said one of the cars parked outside was blocking another. Is yours the Pierce Arrow roadster?"

"No," said the man; "mine's a green Packard convertible."

Courtland returned triumphantly. "We now possess a green Packard convertible."

"Good work, pal." Crane turned to O'Malley. "Let's get the dame."

"You're going to have trouble draggin' her out of here," observed Williams.

"I got an idea," said Crane. He told them the idea. He concluded by saying to Courtland and O'Malley, "You two grab her when she gets downstairs."

Courtland said good-by to Sue Leonard and left with O'Malley, and after a short interval Crane hunted up Miss Renshaw. She had half a glass of gin in her hand. He asked, "Don't you ever drink anything but gin?"

Her expression was friendlier this time. "What's wrong with gin?"

Crane took the glass from her hand, drank some of the gin. "It does taste pretty good," he admitted. He drank the rest of it.

She smiled, said, "You're drunk."

"Me? Me drunk? Madam!"

"I like people drunk."

"I'm drunk. Please consider me drunk."

Williams joined them. "I've some good news for you, Bill," he said.

Crane introduced him to Miss Renshaw.

Williams continued, "Frankie says he'll be able to make it, after all."

"Frankie French!" Crane's voice was pleased, surprised. "That's swell. I haven't seen him for a long time. When's he coming?"

"He said it'd take him ten minutes to get over here."

Miss Renshaw's face was suddenly haggard. Her fingers drew the skin tight around her throat. "I'll see you later," she said. "I have to go . . . I . . . I have a headache."

"Don't go," said Crane. "Maybe another drink . . ."

"No!" She turned and hurried across the terrace into the living room.

"That got her," said Williams.

They watched until she went out the front door, a black cape with a scarlet lining thrown across her bare shoulders, and then they took a bottle of champagne and a bottle of gin from the bartender, a corkscrew from the kitchen, and followed. The green Packard was double parked half a block down the street, and in the back seat was O'Malley with Miss Renshaw. Williams got in beside Courtland at the wheel, and Crane got in beside Miss Renshaw. He couldn't see her face.

"Don't think I'm not your friend," he said, handing her the bottle of Gilbey's gin.

Her voice was almost lost in the noise of the accelerating engine. "What do you want?"

Crane cut the tinfoil off the champagne bottle with his thumbnail. "We want to know where you've been for the last month or so, Mrs. Paletta." He shoved on the cork, but nothing happened.

"Where to, Bray-mer?" called Williams from the front seat.

Miss Renshaw said, "I'm not Mrs. Paletta."

"Drive around Lincoln Park," Crane said.

"Where's Lincoln Park?" Courtland asked.

Williams said, "I'll show you. Turn right here."

"Sure, you're Mrs. Paletta," Crane said.

O'Malley said, "Here, lemme open that bottle."

Miss Renshaw said, "And even supposin' I am Mrs. Paletta; what's it to you?"

The champagne bottle went POP.

Williams said, "Mi Gawd! I am shot."

While the Packard slid effortlessly around the curves of the tree-walled inner drive in Lincoln Park they drank the champagne. Miss Renshaw was politely offered the first drink from the bottle, but she refused. Crane demanded the first drink, but was refused. When he finally did get the bottle there were only a few sips left. "A fine bunch of pals you are," he said sadly.

O'Malley took the bottle of gin from Miss Renshaw and twisted the corkscrew into it.

Crane tried to question Miss Renshaw, but she wouldn't tell him anything. He explained he wanted to establish the fact that Mrs. Paletta was alive to prevent Frankie French and Paletta from doing him further injury. He told her of his experience with French and showed her his eye, his bruises and cuts.

She laughed as though they really amused her.

O'Malley had opened the gin bottle and was holding it behind him so Crane wouldn't see it. "Should I knock her off, Boss?" he demanded gruffly.

"Give her a minute or two more," said Crane.

Miss Renshaw laughed huskily. "If you Boy Scouts get much funnier I'll have hysterics," she stated.

Dead white light from passing street lamps played fitfully on her face. Crane saw she certainly didn't appear frightened. "All right," he declared. "All right. If you won't admit you're Mrs. Paletta, you won't. But I know you are. I know French and Paletta would like to see you. And I'd like to have them see you." He had to stop for a breath. "Which one do you want to go to?"

The road curved to the left, crossed over a stone viaduct and neared the lake. There was a faint odor of fish in the warm air. They were on Lake Shore Drive.

Miss Renshaw said, "I don't want to go to either."

"Come on," said Crane. "Pick one." He made a lunge for the gin bottle, but O'Malley deftly passed it to Williams. "We're being little gentlemen. We're giving you a choice."

"You better let me go," said Miss Renshaw, "or you'll be dead little gentlemen."

"Threats, eh?" Crane sat up straight on the seat. "Very well. We'll take you to Frankie French."

Her fingers tightened around his wrist. It was the first feminine move she had made. "No. Not to French. I'm afraid of him." Her harsh voice had a pleading note.

"O.K. To Paletta, then." He spoke to Williams. "Do you know where the guy lives?"

"Sure. Over on Delaware Place."

It took them only three minutes to reach the co-operative apartment building in which Paletta lived. Crane pulled Miss Renshaw out of the car after him. "You better come along, Doc," he said, starting for the door. Williams followed them through the ornate marble-and-gold lobby and into the elevator. The operator was a bright-looking boy. He closed the door, started the elevator and asked, "What floor, please?"

Crane asked, "What floor's Mike Paletta on?"

"I really couldn't say, sir."

Williams hauled out a .45 automatic, pointed it at the boy's startled eyes. "Listen, punk; what floor's Paletta on?"

"Twenty-third, sir."

"That's better." Williams lowered the pistol, let it dangle from his hand. "Always be polite to your elders."

There was only one door on the twenty-third floor. While Williams watched the elevator boy Crane led Miss Renshaw across the hall and pushed the bell. After a time a man opened the door a crack and peered out at them. It was the Italian who had tried to see the body in the morgue. His eyes goggled at them.

"Call Paletta," said Crane.

Bare feet thumping the carpet, small black eyes squinting in the light, Paletta marched ponderously toward them. He was wearing a tan flannel robe with a peach-colored monogram over purple pajamas. He needed a shave. Crane put his right palm in the small of Miss Renshaw's back, pushed her through the door into Paletta's arms.

"Now quit bothering me, you big Dago," he said.

He slammed the door, jumped into the elevator, rode down to the lobby and hurried out to the Packard. He was well pleased with himself. He climbed into the back seat and said:

"To the graveyard, driver, and flail the horses."

He leaned back in the leather seat and in thirty seconds was fast asleep.

Chapter Eighteen

CRANE SHOOK the hand off his shoulder, said querulously, "Lemme alone. Please lemme alone. I don't feel well." He kept his eyes shut. Then he said, "Graveyard. What graveyard?" With a tremendous effort he sat up, asked, "Am I dead?"

In the citron radiance of the low-hung moon they stood and watched him. Their faces were composed and quite pale.

Light reflected from the chromium fittings of the Packard dazzled his eyes. He rubbed them with the sleeve of his linen coat. "I don't feel well," he repeated. His coat smelled of jasmine.

O'Malley had been shaking him. "Come on," he said. "We got work to do."

Dew on the grass sparkled in the moonlight; the air was laden with the thick odors of graveyard flowers, of tuberoses, carnations, lilies, violets. There was no wind at all.

Cautiously, O'Malley opened the gate of twisted iron, closed it after they had tiptoed through. The night attendant's white stone lodge was at their right. A 25-watt bulb burned from a cord hanging just inside the lodge's single window. O'Malley tried the door, found it was open. They could hear the tick-tick of a Big Ben alarm clock. Williams had his pistol in his hand, and he led the way through the door. The night attendant was lying on the cement floor of the lodge on his side, his head almost touching his knees, his back toward them.

For a broken second they thought he was dead.

Swiftly, Crane knelt beside the man. He was white-haired and frail, and a cord held his thin wrists to his bent knees. Over a tight cloth gag his eyes were terrified. Air rushed in and out of his nose in painful puffs, made a noise like an accelerating locomotive.

"What the hell?" whispered O'Malley.

Crane shook his head. He unfastened the cloth gag. "What happened, old timer?" he asked.

The man had difficulty speaking. "Somebody socked me." He worked his cramped cheek muscles. "I was readin' an' I heard a noise behind me. I looked around, and there was a guy. Next thing I knew was all tied up like this." He pulled at the cord around his wrists. "Get me loose, so I kin call the cops."

147

"Later, maybe." Crane bent down, put the gag in the man's mouth and tied it firmly behind his head. "Keep quiet and you'll be all right, old timer."

"What the hell?" asked O'Malley again.

"I don't know," said Crane, "but I fear the worst."

In the tool shed they found spades and then marched single file to the grave of Miss Agnes Castle. Their feet left black stains on the silver carpet of dew. A small wooden cross marked the grave. Fastened to the cross was a metal disk on which was printed:

AGNES CASTLE

BORN—OCTOBER 2, 1910

DIED—AUGUST 4, 1936

REQUIESCAT IN PACE

(Temporary Marker)

From the lilies strewn ankle-deep over the grave came a cloying scent; heavy, sickeningly sweet. "How do you like 'em?" asked O'Malley proudly.

"They're just dandy," said Crane. "Fit for a gangster's funeral." Williams said, "Forty bucks," in an aggrieved tone.

Courtland asked, "Is this the grave?" His voice was excited. "Do you think . . . ?"

"This is the grave, all right." Crane was lifting the lilies from the mound. "But I don't like the looks of that tied-up attendant."

Courtland bent down to help him. "Don't thieves sometimes steal ornaments from a cemetery?" he asked. "Couldn't it have been something like that?"

"We'll see." Crane tried to tell with his fingers how recently the soil had been dug up, but he couldn't. It felt fairly dry. He reached for his spade. "All right, boys, dig for dear old Johns Hopkins."

The only noise was their labored breathing and the soft plop of earth hitting the grass. The dirt came out easily, and in a few moments the cavity was so deep that only one of them could work in it. O'Malley shoveled, and the others smoked cigarettes, watched from a comfortable seat on a near-by grave.

"I don't feel so good about this," Williams announced. "What if the dame is really Agnes Castle?"

Crane let the smoke from his Camel ooze from a corner of his mouth. "We'll toss the dirt right back on her."

"Yeah." Williams' voice was gloomy. "I know. But I wasn't thinkin' about that. I mean . . . about digging into somebody's grave."

A faint mist rose from the graveyard. It was like gauze in the rays of the moonlight; milky, opalescent, faintly colored with blues, greens

148

and violets. In the shadows of tombstones, willow trees, it was like smoke.

Crane pressed his cigarette stub into the damp earth. "You mean if this turns out to be the wrong grave a big black THING will come and snatch us away?"

"Aw, forget it," said Williams.

Two blocks away, on the elevated tracks, a Michigan Central milk train pounded by with scarlet flames pouring from the firebox, was quickly lost in the distance.

O'Malley crawled out of the grave, tossed his spade on the grass and wiped his face with his handkerchief. "For Christ's sake," he demanded, "am I the only guy who can dig?"

Courtland pushed himself to his feet. "I'll do it for a while." He selected a spade and lowered himself into the grave. O'Malley was completely winded. His shirt stuck to his back, his hands were covered with the damp loam. "What are you going to do with the dame when you uncover her?" he asked, stretching out on the grass.

"It depends upon who she is," said Crane.

Williams tossed his box of matches to O'Malley, said, "I thought you were sure the gal was Kathryn?"

"I was, until that letter came."

O'Malley asked, "Somebody could've imitated her writing, couldn't they?"

"The colonel says she wrote the letter. He saw it when it arrived in New York last Saturday."

O'Malley scratched his neck. "Well, I'll be damned!"

Courtland's voice floated over to them. "I've hit the casket," he announced excitedly.

It took only a few thrusts with the spade to lay the top bare. It was a cheap casket of stained pine. Williams took the hammer and pried the cover loose. He and Courtland took hold of an end and lifted it until it was at right angles to the casket. "What'd'ya see?" he asked.

O'Malley leaned over the grave, blinked his eyes. "She must be out to lunch," he said.

"Empty?" asked Williams.

"Yeah," said Crane.

They rested the cover against a wall of the grave and inspected the coffin. It was absolutely bare. Courtland ran his hand around the interior. "Maybe nobody was ever buried here," he suggested.

"My God!" Crane rubbed his hand on his trouser leg. "Do you suppose that entry in the undertaker's book was made to throw us off the track?"

Williams nodded his head. "They could've made up the name of a girl and buried an empty coffin, pretendin' she was in it."

"A phony funeral!" breathed Crane.

O'Malley lowered the lid on the empty coffin. "What'll we do? Scram out of here?"

"We better fill in the grave." Crane seized Courtland's hand, hoisted him out of the pit. "We don't want the police to know we've been interested in it."

With all four of them throwing dirt into the rectangular opening it was only a matter of seconds until the mound was as they had found it. When Crane bent over to help the others scatter the lilies his head began to ache. He didn't know if the ache came from the liquor or from thinking. He hoped it came from the liquor, because he felt he was going to have a great deal of thinking to do.

O'Malley artistically draped the last lily over the small white cross. "There," he said with satisfaction; "you couldn't want a nicer grave."

"Forty smackers for lilies," Williams mourned, "and there's no body home."

"Maybe we can sell them to somebody else, for their grave," O'Malley suggested.

"No. Let 'em lie there." Crane slapped the dirt from his hands. "We'll find a body to go under them yet." He put on his linen coat. "We better break open a couple of these mausoleums."

Courtland stared at him in surprise. "What for?"

"We want to make the police think we were looking for valuables, not for a lady's corpse."

Courtland led them in breaking open four tombs. In one, above which was inscribed: "Here Lie the Mortal Remains of Benjamin Applegate Griswold," they found two silver birds set on the marble crypt. O'Malley knocked these loose with the hammer and put them in his pocket.

"Atta boy," encouraged Crane. "We may make our expenses out of this."

Williams was mopping his face with his handkerchief. He said, "I don't feel so good about this."

Crane shook his head at him, spoke to O'Malley. "I guess Doc'll never be a first-rate vandal."

"Hell," said O'Malley. "He ain't even a third-class ghoul."

"You guys think you're funny," said Williams.

When Courtland had finished Crane led the way to the lodge by the gate. While O'Malley and Courtland rubbed the fingerprints of the spades and hammer he and Williams went inside. Crane took the gag from the old attendant, loosened his bonds a bit. "There," he said

150

'you'll be able to get free in a couple of minutes or so. By that time we'll be far away."

The attendant's eyes were relieved but still suspicious.

They passed through the iron gate and walked along the street until they reached the Packard. Sparrows in a maple were making a din of peeps and chirps. The sky was milky.

"What are we going to do with this car?" asked Williams.

"That's right. It *is* hot." Crane frowned. "We'll take it around to a garage and park it, and send the ticket to the guy that owns it."

Courtland asked, "How are you going to find out who he is?"

"We'll check on the license number tomorrow." Crane got in the back seat. "We'll take it to a garage now and get a cab to drive us into the Loop."

Courtland climbed into the driver's seat. He pressed the starter, asked, "What are we going to do after we reach the Loop?"

Crane hid his mouth behind his hand, "We're going to bed."

Chapter Nineteen

WILLIAM CRANE impartially examined the toes at the faucet end of the bathtub. They were a trifle large, especially the two big ones, he thought, but on the whole they looked well set as they were, like jewels on the pale-green surface of the water. He wondered how they would look painted cherry red, like Miss Renshaw's toes. He wondered what they thought of his face at the other end of the tub. He wriggled the big toe on his right foot, made circular ripples on the water.

Shaving cautiously with a straight razor in front of the mirror over the washbasin, Doc Williams said, "The colonel called while you were asleep." He wiped the razor on a piece of toilet paper. "He wanted to know what we found."

Crane sank into the warm water until only his mouth, nose and eyes were visible. "What'd you tell him?"

151

"I told him the grave was empty." Williams daubed additional lather on his chin. "He was surprised."

"I bet not any more than we were," said Crane contentedly. He turned on the hot water with his foot. "I wonder if the hotel would serve dinner to me in this tub?"

O'Malley's face, clean-shaven and darkly handsome, appeared in the doorway. "Let's eat in the living room." He had on flannel trousers with a faint blue stripe, a white silk shirt and brown leather slippers. "We been around enough the last two days."

"Boy! We *have* been places," agreed Williams.

Crane said, "A regular Cook's tour."

"You mean a Crooks' tour," corrected O'Malley. "In two days we start a fight in a taxi-dance joint, find a murdered guy and don't tell the police, crash in on Bray-mer and his dope mob, bust in on a party, kidnap a gal, steal a car and rob a graveyard." He paused for breath. "The only thing we ain't done is to park in a no-parking zone."

"If we did that," said Williams, "they'd catch us and send us up for life."

Crane closed the hot-water faucet with his foot. "That reminds me, what about the Packard?"

Williams closed his razor with a snap. "It's all fixed up. While you were pounding your ear I checked on the license number and then had a pal of mine call up and tell the owner where it was. The car belonged to a guy named Brandt, a lawyer."

Crane sat up in the tub, started to soap under his arms. "What time is it, anyway?"

O'Malley looked at his wrist watch. "Eleven past nine. You slept a little better than thirteen hours." He moved squarely into the doorway. "What do you want to eat?"

Through a steaming washcloth Williams said, "Seven dollars' worth of porterhouse steak."

A hand on each porcelain side, Crane hoisted himself from the tub. "You mugs'll have to eat on the run. I got some work for you to do." He jerked a towel off the wall rack.

"Work!" O'Malley's face was pained. "My God! What is there left for us to do?"

"Plenty."

"The hell!" Williams was drying himself with a face towel. "The dame ain't Kathryn Courtland, and she ain't Mrs. Paletta, so why are you interested any more?"

Crane asked, "How do you know it isn't Kathryn Courtland?"

"The letter——" Williams held the towel in his hands. "You don't think it could be her, after all, do you?"

"I don't know." Crane dried a foot, then said, "Yes. I do."

"Well, how do you explain the letter?"

"I don't. I just ignore it."

Williams was completely exasperated. "You're a hell of a fine detective, you are. Any piece of evidence you can't fit in with your theory you just ignore."

"Sure." Crane tossed the towel across the silvered radiator. "I find it makes things much easier." He looked around the floor. "What'd you do with my underwear?"

Williams snorted.

O'Malley grinned at Crane, asked, "What do you want us to do?"

Crane found his underwear under the bathmat. "If Doc isn't too, too disgusted with me, I'd like to have him get hold of a pair of Miss Ross' stockings and her hairbrush at the Princess Hotel. They've probably got her clothes locked away somewhere, and he can bribe the night clerk, or the night bellboy, Edgar, to let him get the stuff." He turned to Williams. "The stockings'll have to be some she's worn; new ones are no good."

Williams' eyes were amazed. "A hairbrush and stockings?"

"A hairbrush and used stockings."

"And me?" asked O'Malley, putting on a blue wash tie.

"You remember that bulldog we saw last night in Brahma's saloon?" O'Malley nodded and Crane continued, "Well, we'll want him for an hour or two." Crane went into his bedroom and picked a roll of bills from the dresser. "Here's four c-notes," he said, handing the money to O'Malley. "Get the dog, if you have to buy or steal him." He saw Williams was putting on his coat. "You both can pick up some food on the way. Come back here as soon as you can."

In the living room Williams asked, "What are you going to do while we're out treasure huntin'?"

"I'm going to call Courtland and ask him to join us."

"And then what?"

"I'm going to look up a guy."

"And then?"

"I'm going to do some thinking."

They paused at the hall door, looked at him respectfully. Finally O'Malley said, "Well, don't strain nothing."

The man Crane wanted to see was named Frankie Thomas and he was a musician in Udoni's band. He played the saxophone, and Crane located him after making a telephone call to the waiter at the Cavern. He was having supper alone in the grill of his hotel, the Bedford. He was perfectly willing to answer Crane's questions.

"Yeah," he said, "Udoni played with us at the Clark-Erie from twelve on both Wednesday and Thursday nights."

"Could he have slipped out for, say, half an hour on Thursday night without your knowing it?" asked Crane.

"Not a chance." Thomas had a long, thin face, and there were pockets under his black eyes. "There are only six of us in the band, and one guy couldn't get away. He was there, all right." He looked at Crane through narrowed eyes. "Are you trying to connect him with that girl who was stolen from the morgue?"

"The hell! How did you know?"

"Well, Udoni told me he knew the girl. We had some coffee together after finishing work the morning she was stolen, and he damn near fainted when he read about it in the paper. That's when he told me he knew her." Thomas thrust a piece of celery in his mouth. "He said 'slightly,' but I figured there was more to it than that."

"Well, it looks as though he couldn't have snatched her body, though."

"Not unless he hired somebody to do it," said Thomas, "and, if he did, why should he have been so surprised to read about it in the papers?"

"I give up," said Crane, "but thanks."

A discreet block from the cemetery entrance they halted the rented Drive-yur-self sedan. O'Malley and Crane, with the white English bulldog, Champion, between them, sat in the rear seat, Williams was driving, and Courtland sat beside him. When the headlights were turned off they found the night was as black as the inside of a closet. Somewhere in the distance a clock was striking, and Crane said in a sepulchral voice:

"It is the witching hour of midnight, when graveyards yawn and . . ."

"What are we doing back here?" Williams interrupted plaintively. "I don't like this place."

The clock hit a last brassy note and there was silence.

Crane climbed out of the car, said to O'Malley, "You stay here with the dog, Tom, until we see if the way is clear." He motioned to the others to follow him.

They found a sheltered place along the wall, and the two of them raised Crane to their shoulders. He found that glass had been imbedded on the wall, and he took off his coat and placed it over a portion of the top. He climbed onto the wall, bent down and hoisted up Courtland, and whispered, "Doc, get O'Malley and the dog."

In five minutes they were all within the cemetery. Crane, carrying

Champion in his arms, led the way to the grave marked with Agnes Castle's name. When he set the dog down Champion licked his hand to show that he was not offended by being carried.

"Are we going to dig this place up again?" asked Williams.

"No," said Crane. "Where are the stockings and the hairbrush?"

Williams pulled the articles out of his coat pocket, handed them to Crane. "It cost me ten bucks to get them."

Champion was sniffing tentatively at the white cross with Agnes Castle marked on it. Crane said, "Hey! none of that." He pulled the dog away from the cross, put the stockings and brush in front of him. "Take a good whiff of those, Champ," he said.

O'Malley said, "Ah-ha! I get the idea."

"What idea?" asked Williams.

"You'll see," said O'Malley.

Heat lightning flickered irritably on the horizon. There was an odor of damp mold about the graveyard. Clouds cloaked the sky, hid the moon. The night was a blindfold on their eyes.

Champion's wheezy sniffing had an interrogative note. Crane felt his harness to make sure the leash was secure and said, "Find her, boy; find her." He held the stockings in front of the dog.

Champion snorted to show he understood, pulled the leash taut. Thrusting the stockings and the hairbrush in his trouser pocket, Crane followed. He pulled out a small flashlight from his hip pocket, trained it on the bulldog. They moved away from the grave at a trot, the others following closely. Champion was delighted with the game. His yellow teeth gleamed in a droll grin; his sailorlike gait was jaunty; he hurried from tomb to tomb. His breath wheezed through his flat nose.

Stumbling over mounds, barking his shins on headstones, sinking ankle-deep in soft earth, Crane flew after him, his right wrist held by the leather leash. His flashlight yellowly illuminated a succession of marble and stone vaults. He caught flashes of inscriptions, dates, names; encountered wreaths and flowers with his shoulders and head. He could hear the others pounding along behind him. He could feel the sweat roll down his back.

Whenever Champion slowed his pace Crane would hold the hairbrush and stockings under his nose and encourage him by saying, "Come on, Champ, let's find her," and Champion would race on with renewed energy. Finally Williams, then O'Malley, and at last Courtland gave up the pursuit and rested on headstones, watching the flashlight circle the graveyard like an eccentric firefly.

The three were seated some distance from one another, and when Crane himself tired he put out the flashlight and led the dog over to

155

where Williams was sitting. In the south thunder muttered. He tapped Williams on the shoulder. Williams leaped to his feet and hollered, "Yow-eee!" Startled, Crane jumped backward, fell over Champion and landed flat on his back. An uncontrollable giggle surged up through his throat; he began to laugh. Champion barked hoarsely at him.

Courtland and O'Malley arrived on the run. "What the hell's the matter?" demanded O'Malley.

"The damn fool came up and tapped my shoulder like a spook," complained Williams. "He scared me silly."

Between gasps of laughter Crane said, "Not half as much as you scared me."

"For the love of God," said O'Malley, "shut up. You'll have an army of cops out here in a minute."

Crane was rubbing soil off the seat of his trousers. "With a mysterious light, a dog barking, a voice going yow-eee! and a laughing spook you aren't going to be troubled with Irish cops out here."

Williams said, "I don't think it's so goddamn funny."

O'Malley said, "You're certainly a daffy sort of detective. I wish old man Pinkerton could see you."

"For all you guys know," said Crane indignantly, "I may be founding a new school of detection tonight. The bulldog school of detection." He flashed the light on Champion, who blinked his beady eyes. "Come on, pal; we'll show 'em."

Courtland asked, "Do you want me to take him for a while?"

"I better do it. I know where we've already been."

As Crane started off O'Malley called, "If you need help send up a flare."

At first Champion didn't go very fast, and Crane was able to keep up for a time by walking. They passed a crypt with white pillars and he read the words, "beloved wife" and "Agnes" and one date, "1874." He let the bulldog smell the hairbrush again. They passed a white cenotaph on which was inscribed "Richard Scott" and "resurgam." Occasionally lightning sheeted a portion of the sky, and he was able to see the immensity of the cemetery. He knew the idea of the bulldog was the most ridiculous he had ever had, but he was determined to give it a fair try. He could at least cover the portion of the cemetery nearest the grave of Agnes Castle. He whispered, "Come on, Champion; where's that girl?"

Champion responded gallantly. They pounded across new grass, circled tombstones, galloped along cinder paths, slid down grassy inclines, broke through hedges, trampled flower beds, tore past countless tombs. Air raced through Crane's throat, water oozed from his body; in his mouth there was a taste of ashes. Suddenly Champion barked, wheeled to the right and began to pull heavily on the leash. Crane pointed the flashlight beam ahead of the dog, gasped, "Atta-boy, Champ."

Champion's whiskey bass sounded again and he came to a frantic stop in front of a small grave. On the top of the headstone, regarding them through scornful yellow eyes, was an orange-colored Persian cat. Champion leered proudly at Crane, wagged his stumpy tail.

"Why, you old lecher, you," said Crane. "You drunken old lecher."

He led the dog away from the cat, back to the others, and sat on a grave. He felt a sudden outflow of energy. He felt very tired. "It's no good," he said. "We're sunk." He wiped his forehead. "The hell with this stuff." He handed the leash to O'Malley. "Let's get out of here."

They walked slowly toward the graveyard wall. Presently Crane became aware that O'Malley was no longer with them. He flashed the light futilely, then turned back alone. He finally encountered O'Malley standing beside a large marble crypt.

"Can I help it," asked O'Malley, "if Champ's gotta see a dog about a man?"

Crane flashed the light on the bulldog and saw that he was indeed busy.

"He don't know a tomb from a tree," said O'Malley apologetically.

The beam from the flashlight moved across a black iron gate at the crypt's entrance, and Crane's heart felt as though it were in his throat, blocking his breath. There was a brand-new padlock on the gate! He pointed the light at the inscription above the entrance. It read:

"IN MEMORY OF THEIR BELOVED MOTHER,
ELIZABETH,
THIS MONUMENT WAS RAISED IN 1923
BY HER FIVE SONS, ROBERT, JAMES . . ."

Crane spoke the date, 1923, aloud exultantly. "Nineteen twenty-three. Hot damn!" The padlock should have rusted by that time. He raced back to the others, whispered loudly, "Come on. I think I've got something."

The padlock broke under the heavy impact of a boulder, the gate opened groaningly and they walked up two steps to the narrow marble door of the vault. Back of them thunder drummed a muffled march for the dead. Under O'Malley's shoulder the marble door gave part way, and a cloying odor of dead flowers clogged their nostrils. Cham-

157

pion whined and Crane said, "Shush!" and followed O'Malley into the vault. The shuffle of their leather soles, the clicking of the bull-dog's toenails on the stone floor, their excited breathing filled the chamber.

As pale as lime juice, the fan-shaped ray from the flashlight illuminated a raised marble sarcophagus in the center of the floor. Below it were artificial wreaths, bright green, and on the lid were withered flowers. Black silk ribbons embraced some of the flowers.

Champion was half sniffing, half whining at something behind the door. Crane swung the light in a slow arc from the sarcophagus to the dog on the floor. Under Champion's ugly muzzle was the face of Miss Ross, cheeks rouged and powdered, lips scarlet, eyes blue-shadowed, dust-colored hair swept back from a pale brow. A gaudy necklace made of pieces of wood lacquered red and green and blue circled her neck. She was lying on her back. Her dress, made of cheap cotton, was too large for her slender body. Her legs were covered by black lisle stockings; her black pumps were too big for her feet. Her face was composed and tragic and inscrutable. . . .

Crane let the flashlight beam rest on her. "Well . . . ?" he asked.

Courtland was bending over the body. "No! No!" he said. "That's not my sister. That's not Kathryn."

His voice sounded like an untuned violin.

Chapter Twenty

HIS CHIN in the palm of his hand, his elbow on his thigh, Crane sat on the stone steps of the tomb. His face, lighted fitfully by lightning, was angry. "I'll be damned if this business hasn't got me," he said. At his feet lay Champion, tongue out, breath wheezing.

Williams, as usual, was practical. "What are you going to do now?" he wanted to know.

The glowing coal on the end of O'Malley's cigarette quivered as he spoke. "Let's bury the dame again and go back to New York. There ain't anything in this for us."

Courtland held his cigarette between his fingers. "It *is* peculiar. Are you certain this is the girl you saw in the morgue, Bill?"

"I'm positive."

A spear-thrust of blue-white lightning split the sky, was followed in eight seconds by a clap of thunder. Champion stirred uneasily. Against their cheeks the air was damp.

"What've you got to gain by going on with this business?" inquired Williams. "You've got the girl, and she isn't Miss Courtland, and that's all you wanted to find out."

Crane gently pulled Champion's ears. "That's all I wanted to find out at first." His voice was low. "Now I'd like to find out who murdered her."

The thunder sounded like a trunk being moved in an attic.

At last O'Malley asked, "You mean she didn't kill herself?"

"Exactly."

Courtland's cigarette was an unwinking red eye in the darkness. "How do you know she was murdered?" he asked.

"A lot of things point to murder." Crane ran his fingers under Champion's collar. "In the first place, a girl isn't apt to climb out of a bath and hang herself without dressing, or at least drying herself. It looks more as though she was disturbed by someone while she was taking a bath and slipped on a bathrobe to open the door." Champion groaned luxuriously. "She must have known the caller, because there were no signs of a struggle, either in the room or on her body."

Crane put a Camel in his mouth and lit it with O'Malley's cigarette, and went on:

"The caller must have twisted a rope around her neck as she turned to go back to the bathroom, and strangled her. Then, to conceal the crime, he fastened the rope over the bathroom door, which was ajar, and strung her up. In the meantime the wrapper had slipped off, and she was naked. He put the wrapper away and completed the suicide picture by taking the scales out of the bathroom and placing them beside the door under her feet." Crane let smoke slide through his nose. "Next problem was to prevent, if possible, the body being identified.

"Well, the caller came prepared to do that very thing. He must have had two large suitcases, and in these he stowed all of Miss Ross' clothes—that is, all her clothes which might provide some clue to her identity. Especially clothes with laundry marks, because a laundry mark is just about the easiest way to identify someone."

Williams objected, "Yeah, but if he took all her clothes there wouldn't have been any in the room."

159

"He brought some with him—brand-new dresses, undergarments and coats without a single mark on them except the name of the store from which they were bought. And in this case the store was Marshall Field's, where you pay cash and where the volume of business is so great that no clerk is going to remember the sale of one cheap dress, or one cheap coat."

A zigzag of brilliant lightning made them all duck, but the thunder was still seconds behind the flash.

"The murderer hung the new clothes in the closet, packed the old clothes except the stockings which, though expensive, offered no clue to anybody but me, and got ready to leave," Crane continued.

"But Udoni . . ." interrupted O'Malley. "He said they were her clothes. I remember you asking him."

"I think Udoni lied." Crane tamped his cigarette on the stone step. "The murderer was ready to leave when he discovered something. He hadn't provided for Miss Ross's shoes. They must have been expensive shoes—if they weren't he wouldn't have bothered to take them. But he was afraid they could be traced, and he hadn't thought to bring cheap shoes (you wouldn't think of shoes in connection with laundry marks), so he packed them, too, and left Miss Ross without any at all."

O'Malley said, "He probably figured she wouldn't be needin' them."

"Shut up," said Williams. "This is interesting."

"That's about all." Crane's voice was weary. "The caller left with the shoes and clothes and any other articles which he thought might help in identifying the girl. He may have even taken her money, if she had more than was found in her purse."

"I follow your reconstruction all right," Courtland's voice was puzzled. "But I still don't see how you can be sure it's murder. Wouldn't it have been possible for the girl herself to dispose of her things, so she could commit suicide without having her identity disclosed?"

"No," Crane said. "It wouldn't. You see her wet heel marks on the door were two feet above the floor. The murderer wanted the police to think she had jumped from the bathroom scales and hung herself. If she had her heel marks would have been below the scales, which is only a foot high. Instead, her heel marks were more than a foot above the scales, an obvious impossibility if she had hung herself."

"Pretty clever." Courtland's voice was awed. "How did you happen to think of it?"

"That's an old gag. I remember a Sûreté case involving a milking stool in much the same way," said Crane. "And there have been others. Criminals seem to have a habit of repeating themselves, or rather, their mistakes."

Williams asked for the second time, "Well, what are you going to do now?"

Crane stood up, stretched his arms. "I'd like to get the body in a place where we could show it to the Udonis and to Paletta and French." He tightened the leash, pulled Champion to his feet. "What time is it?"

"Five minutes of one," said O'Malley.

"Is that all?" exclaimed Williams. "It seems like we've been here all night."

Courtland said, "You'll have to take the body somewhere. You won't be able to bring the gangsters and the Udonis out here very well."

"That's what I'm wondering about." Crane moved toward the place where Williams was sitting. "Doc, you're an old Chicagoan. Do you know any undertakers?"

"Sure. I know one named Barry, over on State Street and Forty-seventh."

Crane asked, "Are you trying to be funny?" Then he said, "Never mind. Do you think he would take the body?"

"For me he would."

"Fine." Crane patted the bulldog. "We'll take her over there and have the others come to look at her."

O'Malley said, "If I know my gangsters you'll have a hell of a time gettin' French and Paletta to come in a strange undertakin' shop to look at some girl. They'd think you were trying to put 'em on the spot."

"That's right," said Crane.

Courtland asked, "Why do you want them to see the body?"

"I want to be sure they don't know her." Champion trotting at his heels, Crane was pacing back and forth along the tomb steps. "I'm not so sure now about that Miss Renshaw. She might not be Mrs. Paletta after all, although I'd bet my shirt on it. She never admitted it, you remember?"

O'Malley said, "She wouldn't have admitted Roosevelt was president."

Now the thunder was louder. They had to raise their voices against it.

Moisture soaked the still air; clung to their skin, their clothes; tickled their nostrils, dampened their hair.

"The only place you could get those guys to come," said Williams, "would be the county morgue. They'd feel safe there."

"Let's get out of here, anyway," yelled O'Malley. "It's going to rain like hell in a couple of minutes."

Crane spoke to Williams. "But I don't want the cops to know I've found the body. If we took it to the morgue again the keeper would notify them."

"Not if the undertaker brought her in." Williams' voice was pitched high. "He could say that somebody left the body with him to be buried and then disappeared, and that he wasn't going to bury it for nothing." He moved closer to Crane. "The night attendant would notify the coroner in the morning."

"That would give us the rest of the night." Crane nodded his head. "All right; let's get going. Doc, you and O'Malley carry the body over to the wall."

Williams said, "If you think I'm going to touch that body . . ."

"She won't hurt you," said Crane.

Courtland said, "I'll help." He led the way inside the tomb. While Crane flashed the light on the floor O'Malley and Courtland raised the body. "Stiff as a statue!" exclaimed O'Malley.

Crane handed the flashlight to Williams. "Lead the way, Doc. Champ and I'll bring up the rear."

Slowly, carefully, they crossed the graveyard. Courtland had the body's feet, one in each hand, like a wheelbarrow, and O'Malley had his hands hooked under the arms, which were folded over her breasts. The woman's face, in the glaring lightning, had the half-human, half-artificial, altogether horrible appearance of a figure in a waxworks. Champion kept close to Crane's heels.

In a moment of silence between bursts of thunder Williams called back, "How we going to get her over the wall?"

"Two of you will have to get up on top," said Crane. "We'll hand her up to you, and then one of you can hold her while the other jumps down on the other side."

They halted at the foot of the wall.

"I bet I could toss her over," said O'Malley.

Thunder pounded their eardrums.

Crane and Williams helped O'Malley onto the wall, while Courtland held the body. When it came Courtland's turn to be helped Crane said, "Lean her up against the wall." Once the two were on top Crane and Williams had no difficulty lifting the corpse up to them. "There," said Crane, "now one of you jump down."

Courtland jumped down, and O'Malley stood there with his arm about the body's waist. "May I have the pleasure of the next waltz, madam?" he asked.

"For God's sake!" said Williams.

162

To Crane the scene looked like one of those horror movies in which mad scientists bring monsters back to life. In the flickering blue-white light O'Malley's face was fish-belly white; the girl's serene, peaceful, terrible. O'Malley held her away from the wall, let her drop. "Good catch," he said, and turning to Crane and Williams, watching bug-eyed, added "Come on, you mugs."

In the space of a dozen major claps of thunder they were beside the rented car. "How're we going t' get her inside?" Williams wanted to know. "You can't bend her."

They finally angled her in the rear door and propped her up in one corner. Crane got in beside her, asked dubiously, "I wonder if she'll act as a conductor for lightning?"

On their way to Forty-seventh Street they halted at an all-night drugstore while Williams telephoned the undertaker, Barry, and gained his reluctant permission to bring him the corpse. They all felt a sensation of relief as Williams climbed back into the driver's seat, meshed the gears, jerked them forward. Crane patted the corpse's shoulder. "I was never so glad to catch up with a dame in my life," he said.

O'Malley was critically examining Miss Castle's face. He said, "She don't seem so damn glad to see you."

"You are glad to see me, though, aren't you, tutz?" asked Crane. He moved the upper portion of the body with the palm of his hand, made it appear as though Miss Castle was nodding, yes.

Williams, watching lollipop-eyed through the mirror, said, "Omigod, don't do that." He gave the gas pedal a convulsive kick.

They skidded around a corner, and it began to rain huge drops like quarter dollars which made wet plops when they hit the windshield. Now the thunder was right on the heels of each lightning flash. Street lights made egg-yolk stains on the gleaming pavement.

O'Malley said, "I like a babe that can hold up her end of the conversation."

"You mean like Aggie here?" Crane asked. "Aggie here is a brilliant conversationalist."

O'Malley leaned over Crane and peered in the corpse's face. "Do you like the weather we're having, Miss Castle?"

Crane made the corpse's head move negatively.

O'Malley asked, "Perhaps you think it is a bit humid, Miss Castle?"

Crane moved the head up and down.

So horribly fascinated was Williams with this conversation that he overlooked a red light at Fifty-first Street and Woodlawn Avenue. There was the scream of a siren behind them, and a Ford squad car cut them to the curb. A crimson-faced officer in uniform stuck his head out into the driving rain, put the spotlight on them. "Where's the fire?" he demanded.

Crane put his arm protectively around Miss Castle's body, let her head rest on his shoulder. Thunder crashed directly over their heads.

"We're sorry, officer," said Courtland. "We didn't see the light because of the rain."

"Oh, yeah," said the officer. He swung the spotlight on the back seat. Crane hunched his shoulder so that Miss Castle's face was in shadow.

"The young lady doesn't feel so well," Courtland explained. "We're hurrying to get her home."

The officer sniffed the air. "Stiff?"

"Yeah," said Crane hurriedly. "Stiff."

The officer was indignant. "A fine bunch of men you are, taking a poor girl out and getting her drunk."

"She's stiff practically all the time," said Crane.

"Well, I'd like to say . . ." began the officer.

"Aw, come on, Jim," said the driver of the squad car. "I'm getting wet sittin' here."

"Be careful you don't get run in for drunken driving," warned the officer. "Yer car smells like a saloon."

Sheets of black rain hid the retreating back of the squad car.

"You see," said Crane. "It pays to smell of liquor. If we hadn't, the cop would have been suspicious of poor Aggie here."

"Hell," said O'Malley; "he smelled the embalming fluid."

Williams started the car with elaborate care and they drove along Forty-seventh Street until they came to a sign, Barry and Son. They turned into an alley beside the establishment and drew up at the rear entrance.

Mr. Barry was a small, brown, elderly man, and his brown eyes were alert. He grinned at them. "So you're up to your old tricks, Doc Williams?" he said. He had on a black suit, a white silk shirt and a bow tie.

Introductions performed, Mr. Barry eyed the corpse. "So that's the girl I've been reading so much about in the papers." His little head, brown-skinned and wrinkled, looked as though South Sea bushmen had started to preserve it and had been called away when the job was half done. "She ain't a bad looker."

Crane explained what they wanted him to do.

"That's going to be tough." Mr. Barry had false teeth and they clicked while he talked. "Undertakers ain't supposed to be able to bring corpses into the morgue after they've embalmed them. Once an undertaker has accepted a party he's responsible for the burial."

164

There was a tremendous flash of lightning and a burst of thunder immediately afterward. "Holy cow! Come inside before they take us all down to the morgue."

In the bare, cement-walled rear room of the building the noise of the thunder diminished. Crane asked, "Then you don't think you can get her into the morgue for us?"

"Oh, I guess I can." Mr. Barry's sparrow eyes were bright. "But it may mean a jam."

Crane said, "Well, we don't want to get you in trouble."

"I been in trouble before." Mr. Barry led the way through a small wooden door into a garage. A battle-ship gray hearse stood with its blunt nose toward a big door hung by wires from the ceiling. Mr. Barry jerked a rope and the big door swung upward. "Stick your girl in here, and we'll be off."

Crane and O'Malley carried the body into the garage, shoved her on the flat stretcher in the hearse, and climbed in beside her. Mr. Barry stepped on the hearse's starter and the engine roared like a tractor. "You guys follow us," shouted Crane to Courtland and Williams. With a jerk the hearse leaped from the garage, raced down the alley. Mr. Barry crouched over the wheel like a monkey. Water made a noise like a falling tree against the four fenders of the hearse. Mr. Barry switched on the siren, the red-and-blue headlights.

The new morgue attendant was a young man with a pale skin, patchy black whiskers and practically no chin. He opened the door to the receiving room, turned on the driveway light and said, "Bring her in." He rolled one of the white-enameled operating tables toward them. "Stick her on this."

They carried Miss Ross's body through a rectangle of rain, through the door, and laid her on the table. The rain had dampened her cheap dress, made it cling to her slender hips, her long legs.

"The hell!" The attendant's voice was outraged. "You can't bring an embalmed body in here."

"The hell I can't." Mr. Barry launched on a long explanation.

The idea was that some dirty so-and-so—Mr. Barry said "so-and-so," not son of a bitch—had brought the body to him and had promised to pay for its burial. But the dirty so-and-so had never showed up again, and when Mr. Barry had looked up the address the dirty so-and-so had given him the fellow didn't live there at all. And did the morgue attendant, or the County of Cook, for that matter, think that he, Mr. Barry, was going to pay out sixty bucks to bury the girl? If they did they had another think coming.

The attendant finally agreed to let them leave the body in the receiving room. He took Mr. Barry's name and address. "I'll have to make a report to the coroner," he said.

"Yeah, get the coroner," Mr. Barry urged. "I'll talk to the coroner." He hopped up and down in front of the attendant's worried face. "Get him right now."

"At two o'clock in the morning?" The attendant was horrified. "Not much, I won't. I want to keep my job. I'll report to him in the morning."

"O. K." Mr. Barry winked at Crane. "Then I'll leave the girl here."

The attendant found a sheet and tossed it over the girl's body, and rolled the operating table away from the alley door. A gust of wind blew rain into the room, but as Crane moved to close the door Williams and Courtland appeared.

"It's about time you got here," said Mr. Barry. He turned to the attendant. "You been pretty good about this girl, so I'm going to do you a favor. These men work for me, that is, all but this one—" he indicated Williams, "—and we may be able to find somebody to take care of the girl tonight. This fellow—" indicating Williams again "—thinks he knows some people who know the girl. I'm going to have him find them tonight and bring them down here to look at the girl. Then, if they do know her, they can claim her."

"Why don't he claim her?" asked the attendant.

"Do you think I'm going to pay out a hundred bucks to bury some dame I think I seen once before?" Williams pulled his mustache. "I ain't that dumb."

"All right." The attendant's eyes were watery. He shrugged his shoulders. "Bring 'em down, and I'll let them take a look at her. That's what this place is for." He started through the door leading to the stairs and the storage vaults where Miss Ross had originally been. "Close the alley door when you leave."

When the attendant had gone Mr. Barry said gleefully, "Well, that's that. I'm going home."

"You did swell," said Crane. "Now, I'll telephone French and Paletta and have them come over here. Doc, you and O'Malley better go and get Udoni and Mrs. Udoni. You can take the dog back to the Cavern and look for Udoni there. Do it as quick as you can."

Courtland asked, "What do you want me to do?"

"You might as well stay here with me. I might need some help." Crane shook Mr. Barry's hand. "We wouldn't have been able to do this without you."

"Aw, hell," said Mr. Barry. "I'm always glad to oblige Doc."

"Yeah," said Williams, "we been buddies ever since we run a load of liquor down from Canada in a hearse and cleaned up five grand."

166

THE ATTENDANT looked at them moodily as they approached the oak rail dividing his office from the waiting room. "You guys still here?" The clock with the cracked glass read 2:12. Outside it continued to rain, lighten, thunder.

"We let the others go for the people to look at the body," said Crane. "We don't want to get our feet wet."

"Well, you needn't think you're going to sit around and bother me," said the attendant. He moved papers about the surface of his desk. "I got work to do."

"Go right ahead," said Crane. He grinned at Courtland. "We wouldn't think of disturbing you." He crossed the marble floor to the public telephone booth and looked up the number of the City News Bureau. It was State 8100. He dropped a coin in the slot and called the number and asked for Johnson. Jerry Johnson. The man at the switchboard said Johnson was covering west police and would probably be at the Canalport Station. He gave Crane the number.

Johnson was at the Canalport Station. He said, hell, yes, he remembered Bill Crane.

"Look," said Crane, "I've got a good story for you, but you'll have to agree not to break it until I give the word."

"What have you done?" Johnson's voice was eager. "Found the girl?"

"How about your word?"

"O.K. I won't bust the story until you give me a nod. What is it?"

"You better come over to the morgue."

"I'll be right over. . . ."

"Wait a minute." Crane was afraid Johnson had hung up. He spoke loudly. "I want you to do me a favor first."

"I can hear you all right," said Johnson. Then he said, "I thought there was a catch in this."

"It isn't much."

"O.K. Shoot."

"Will you see if you can get me Mike Paletta's telephone number?"

"Hell!" Johnson's voice sounded excited. "Is he in this? That's easy. I got his number here, in my little black book." There was a pause. "Good old black book. Mike Paletta, Superior 7736."

"Thanks," said Crane. "I'll be seeing you in a little while."

"In less than that," said Johnson.

Crane called the Superior number and a strange male voice answered. "Who do you want?"

"Tell Mike that William Crane, the private detective, wants to speak to him."

At last Paletta came to the telephone. "I don' care," he said when Crane told him that he had recovered the body of Miss Ross. "I ain't innarested."

Crane said, "But aren't you going to thank me for bringing your wife back to you?"

"Ha, ha, ha." Mike Paletta laughed as though his stomach hurt him. "Thas big joke you pull on Mike las' night."

"What do you mean?"

"Bringin' a dame like that up to my 'partment—a dame I don' even know."

"What! Wasn't that your wife?"

"Naw, she ain't my wife."

Crane blinked his eyes, chewed his lower lip. At last he said, "Well then, don't you want to come down to the morgue and take a look at Miss Ross? She may be your wife."

Mike Paletta repeated, "I ain't innarested," and broke the connection.

Crane rubbed the back of his neck, swore vigorously. He recounted the conversation to Courtland, said, "This is getting cockeyeder and cockeyeder."

Courtland agreed and then said, "Before you make another call I'll telephone Uncle Stuyvesant at the Blackstone. He'll want to know we've found the body."

In two minutes he came out of the booth, his eyes round. "Uncle checked out of the hotel about an hour ago," he announced.

Crane looked at the clock with the cracked glass. It read 2:15. "The hell! Why would he check out at one in the morning? Did he leave any word for you?"

Courtland shook his head. "The clerk says he simply got in a taxi and left."

Frowning thoughtfully, Crane went into the phone booth, called the Liberty Club. Frankie French's voice was unexcited when Crane told him he had Miss Ross's body at the morgue. "I'll be down in a few minutes," the gangster said calmly.

Crane hung up the receiver and said to Courtland, "Well, we got one bite."

It was nearly 3:40 by the cracked clock when Williams and O'Mal-

168

ley returned with Udoni. Water dripped from the clothes of all three, and Udoni's face was milk pale.

"Where's Mrs. Udoni?" asked Crane.

O'Malley said, "She's disappeared. She checked out of the hotel on Wilson Avenue yesterday and left no forwarding address. I don't know how we're going to find her."

Udoni was suspiciously examining Johnson, the *City Press* reporter, and Courtland. "Who are these men?"

"Two of our operatives," said Crane. He took Udoni's arm. "Let's take a look at the girl."

The morgue attendant's name, they had discovered, was Barnes. Dr. Barnes. He was an intern at the County Hospital. He led the way down the winding steel stairs, opened the door to the windowless receiving room and switched on the powerful overhead light.

Udoni screwed up his eyes, stared at the sheet-covered forms on the white-enameled operating tables. "Which one . . . ?" Seven of the twelve tables bore bodies.

The attendant flipped the cover off Miss Ross with a flourish. Udoni moaned, "Oh, my God!" The lipstick on the girl's lips was as bright as fresh paint. Hands suddenly shielding his eyes, Udoni swung around from the corpse, tottered five steps to the calcimined wall, leaned his elbows against it. The attendant replaced the sheet, said in quick alarm, "Is he going to be sick?"

Crane shook his head, waited for a moment, then asked, "Is that her?"

Udoni's voice was cracked. "Yes."

"Well, thank God," said O'Malley. "I was beginning to think she was the sister of the unknown soldier."

The attendant got down to business. "Are you willing to pay the expenses of her burial, Mr. Udoni?"

Udoni took his hands from his face and nodded. His eyes were wild.

"Good," said the attendant. "I'll make a report to the coroner in the morning, and you can have the body as soon as he signs a release." He turned to Crane and said, "I guess that ends it." His voice was friendlier.

"Yeah, except that we've got at least one more person coming down here," Crane said. "He, or they, may be relatives, and you know that relatives have first claim on the body. Mr. Udoni isn't a relative."

"But he'll bury her if they don't claim her, won't he?"

"Sure."

"That's all I wanted to know." The attendant winked humorously at Williams and started for the stairs. He halted to let two men come into the room. One of the men was Frankie French, and the other was the squat driver of the car which had taken Crane and Courtland to the Liberty Club. Johnson, recognition in his eyes, moved forward as though he were going to say something, but Crane caught his arm.

"Good evening," said French. He bowed to Crane, nodded to Courtland. "I have come in response to your telephone call."

There was an alarmed expression on Udoni's face. He moved along the wall to the inside door, said, "I better go now."

O'Malley looked questioningly at Crane.

"Take him upstairs, and see if you can get an idea where Mrs. Udoni could be," Crane said. "Then you can let him leave." As Williams and O'Malley followed Udoni out the door, Crane put a detaining hand on O'Malley's elbow. "Follow the guy. Maybe he'll go to his wife."

French cast a quick, curious glance at the musician as he disappeared up the steel stairs. The attendant asked, "These the relatives you were expecting?" He made a thrusting motion with his thumb at French and his companion.

"They'd like to look at the body," said Crane.

"Okay. The more the merrier." The attendant pulled the sheet off the body for a second time. "Take a good look."

French's handsome, fierce, somber countenance was impassive as he looked down at Miss Ross's delicately tinted face. The overhead light outlined the scar on his right cheekbone, made his green suit bright as spinach cooked with soda. For fully thirty seconds his golden eyes rested on the body. Then he shook his head, said, "I have never before seen this girl."

"You're sure?" asked Crane.

Frankie French nodded.

The attendant put back the sheet and walked to the door. "Turn out the light when you come up. I gotta get back to my work."

Crane waited thirty seconds, then asked, "Does this girl look anything like Verona Vincent?"

"Not a bit." French straightened his maroon tie. "Now let me ask a question." There was red polish on his fingernails. "Is this the girl who was originally in the morgue?"

"It's the same one, all right," Crane replied. "Isn't it, Johnson?"

"You bet." Johnson's food-spotted necktie had become loosened and it no longer hid the fact that his collar had no button. "We both had a good look at her."

"One more question." French's long fingers caressed the edge of the table upon which Miss Ross lay. "How did you manage to bring the body back here without attracting the attention of the police?"

"The attendant doesn't know who the girl is," said Crane. "We told him her name was Anna Temple and that her body had been left with an undertaker by someone who had then disappeared."

"Very clever." French's teeth were white and even. "There will be no discovery until the attendant makes his report to the coroner in the morning." He smiled again. "Very clever, indeed."

The driver seemed to be nervous. "We better be going, Mr. French," he said. His neck bulged over his frayed collar.

French turned to Courtland. "I would like to express my admiration for the manner in which you rescued Crane, Mr. Courtland. Not many wealthy young men would display such courage." He smiled at Crane. "I am sorry you had such an unpleasant experience with us, Mr. Crane. It was purely a matter of business. I wanted to find Miss Vincent, and I believed you had possession of her body. I see now that I was mistaken." He held out a slender hand. "I'm sure you bear me no personal animus. . . ."

"The hell I don't," said Crane. "If I ever catch you out of your own backyard, you greasy Dago, I'll take a good sock at you." He scowled at the gangster.

Warningly, French shook his head at his driver, who was clawing for a pistol under his coat, and smiled at Crane. "I can well believe you would. You have already made an excellent start—the X-ray pictures show you broke three of my ribs." He paused at the door. "I shall try to keep out of your way." His face, suddenly cheerful, was gone.

Johnson said, "Not such a bad guy."

"Yeah?" said Crane, bitterly. "You ought to have him lock you up in his back room sometime."

Courtland yawned. "What's next on the program?"

Crane's face was blank. "I'm damned if I know."

"Then how about letting me break the story that the girl's been found?" asked Johnson.

"Wait till eight o'clock." Crane sighed heavily. "I have a feeling that the solution is only a few inches out of my brain, but I can't get it. I'd like to be able to explain who she is when the story breaks."

"Christ! It'll help you find out who she is if you let the papers have the story," argued Johnson. "Besides, if you hold off until eight the A.M.s won't get the story at all."

"What do you care, as long as you have it exclusive? There's plenty of afternoon papers, anyway." Crane held the inner receiving-room door open for them, and then turned off the light and followed them up the steel stairs. Williams was seated on one of the waiting benches, his eyes half closed. Crane asked him, "Get anything out of Udoni?"

"Naw. He says he don't know where his wife is, and he's got no idea where she might be."

"That's funny." Crane sighed again, added, "Well, O'Malley is tailing him, and if he does go to his wife he'll get her."

"Why do you want to find her?" asked Johnson.

"I don't know," said Crane. "I think she's cute. And I'd like to know why she had that hair tint in her room." He bent over and rubbed a spot off his right sport shoe. "Look! I want to see her very much." He took out a pencil, wrote on the back of an envelope. "Here's a couple of places where you might find some trace of her."

He gave the envelope to Williams, who asked, "Ain't you coming along?"

"Hell, no." Crane máde a fanning, negative motion with his hand. "I'm sticking right here. I had plenty of trouble finding that body downstairs, and I'm taking no chances of losing it again."

Courtland's face was tired. "I don't feel so well. I think I'll go home pretty soon."

Williams handed the envelope on which Crane had written to Johnson. "Where in hell is that last address?" he asked.

The reporter eyed the envelope, his face puzzled. "Which address?" he asked. Then he said, "Oh yeah, Banks Court. That's a little street just off Astor. On the North Side."

"Can you find it, Doc?" asked Crane.

"I guess so."

"You better scram." Crane looked out the windows facing the court of the County Hospital, saw only reflected flashes of lightning. "It's let up a little outside."

"O.K.," said Williams, picking up his hat.

"You mind if I go along?" inquired Johnson. "I might be able to help you find some of those addresses. You'll be back in a couple of hours, won't you?"

"I hope so," said Williams. "Sure, come along."

As they started toward the corridor Courtland said to Crane, "I'll stick around for five or ten minutes and then beat it."

"Sure," said Crane; "stick around. I need company." He called after the others, "Make it as snappy as you can."

The cracked clock over the attendant's head read 4:05. The attendant had apparently worked himself into a state of complete exhaustion. He was sound asleep at his desk, his head pillowed in his arms. Water dripping from the roof of the morgue fell plop-plop-plop into a lake beneath the big windows in the waiting room.

Courtland asked Crane, "What about those gangsters? Have you given up the possibility that the dead girl is Mrs. Paletta?"

"I'm damned if I know." Crane handed Courtland a Lucky Strike, took one himself and lit them both. "If Paletta isn't interested in Miss Ross it proves he knows where his wife really is."

"Yes, that would be true if Paletta *really* wasn't interested."

"You think he might have been lying?" Crane let the smoke roll out of his mouth. "Yes, he could have been." Startled, he whirled around, faced Courtland. "That would mean he is planning to do something about the body—maybe come down here and take it away."

Courtland nodded. "French could have lied, too. It seemed to me he was terribly pleased about something down there in the receiving room."

"My God!" There was horror in Crane's face. "He might be coming back, too."

"Somebody is likely to come back," said Courtland. "Whoever stole the body in the first place proved to be a desperate person, and he still has reasons for wishing to get the body out of the morgue again."

"Christ!" exclaimed Crane. "Maybe I should have kept Williams and O'Malley here."

Courtland blew out a long stream of smoke. "Look," he said suddenly; "why don't we hide down in the receiving room? Then when the fellow comes to get the body, I mean if he comes, we could grab him."

"I don't know," said Crane. "It's pretty dangerous."

"The hell!" Courtland dismissed the danger with a flat, pushing motion of his hand.

"All right." Crane stood up. "I don't mind, if you don't."

He glanced at the attendant, saw that he was still sleeping. He followed Courtland down the stairs and into the receiving room. The powerful overhead light lit the big room brilliantly, made the long sheets over the seven occupied tables white. Miss Ross's body was in the center of the chamber, and past it, near the second door, opening into the driveway, was a vacant table, sheet folded neatly across one end. The room was without furniture, except for a white, instrument-filled cabinet, and there was no place to hide.

"We'll have to lie on a table," said Courtland, "and pull the sheets over us." He indicated the empty table fifteen feet from the driveway door. "You take that one, and I'll lie on the one by this door. In that way we'll be on both sides of the body and have the door guarded, too."

"It'll be good practice for being dead," said Crane, starting for the further table. Halfway across the room he noticed a third door. It opened into the windowless room used by the coroner's physicians for autopsies. He switched on the light, saw there was no other door in this room and switched off the light. As he closed the door Courtland asked, "What's in there?"

Crane told him and added: "Nobody can get in here from that way."

Courtland was spreading the sheet over his table. "I'm right beside the light," he said, "And I'll turn it out. You get fixed."

The sheet was heavy and coarse, like the canvas on a sailboat. Crane spread it out and gingerly climbed on the table, moving carefully so it wouldn't slip away from him on its rubber-tired wheels. He pulled the sheet over his body, over his head, and said in a muffled voice: "O.K. Douse the glim." He wished the county provided the corpses with pillows.

Tarlike darkness followed the click of the switch. From across the room came the swish of cloth being moved. Courtland's voice called, "Sleep tight." Clammy air flowed slowly through the room.

Crane said, "I wish I was tight." His voice echoed hollowly.

He thought how lonely it must be to be dead.

Chapter Twenty-two

THE STORM sounded as though it were moving back over the city. The grumbling of the thunder was louder, more irritable, more often increasing to cymbal-like crashes of noise; it was weird in the windowless room because it was followed by no flashes of lightning. It sounded like stage thunder, like tin being beaten with a hammer and then muffled with cloth.

Crane tried to relax on the metal operating table, but he couldn't loosen his muscles. His stomach felt upset. His skin was covered with goose pimples. This was because of the steady, slow movement of clammy, conditioned air in the room. It couldn't be because he was frightened. There was a curious odor about the air: sweet, musty, sickish; an odor of slow decay. He supposed the odor came from the corpses, from the seven corpses in the room with him. The enameled surface of the operating table was hard on his back; the sheet was rough against his skin. The sheet smelled strongly of disinfectant, and he wondered if it had been washed since it had last been used to cover a body. He hoped so.

A clatter of thunder set his muscles vibrating. His face was damp with sweat; he felt as though the sheet were choking him, choking him.

He waited until the next long roll of thunder, then slipped from the table, toed the cement floor, held his breath in an interval of silence. As the thunder rumbled again he gave the table a tentative push. It moved noiselessly on its rubber-tired wheels. Resting one arm on the table top, he leaned over and pulled off first one shoe and then the other. He put them on the sheet. Next, stockingfooted, he cautiously pushed the empty table toward the wall in movements synchronized with the thunder, pushed it until it touched another table. His searching fingers encountered cold flesh on the new table. Involuntarily he jerked his hand away. He abandoned his table, wheeled the table with the corpse on it to approximately the position on the floor his table had originally held.

Halfway back to his own table an abrupt silence in the sky caused him to pause on tiptoe, his breath imprisoned behind clenched teeth. A reassuring rattle of thunder, like a truck on a wooden bridge, set him moving again. He found his shoes and, after he had folded the sheet on the table, he returned to it with the corpse. He felt under the sheet at one end, and his palm encountered long hair. A woman! He moved to the other end of the table and pulled the sheet off her naked feet. He wondered if she had been young. One of his brown-and-white sport shoes he fitted on her left foot, the other on her right. He adjusted the sheet so that it exposed both shoes, but not the woman's bare ankles, and then he got down on his knees, crawled under her table and stretched out on the floor, his face directed at the point he imagined Miss Ross's table was, some thirty feet away.

Three quarters of an hour later his muscles ached from contact with the cold floor. He changed position several times, but each change brought only new aches. His eyes ached, too, from straining to pierce the chamber's blackness. But particularly his hips and elbows ached, where solid bone had come into contact with solid cement.

Moreover, he was scared.

Several times, now that the storm had moved on southward and the thunder was no louder than the roar of the elevated trains a block and a half away, he thought he had heard a rustle, a movement in the room. Hands clenched until the nails tore the palms, breath held until his lungs throbbed with pain, he had listened. He wondered if it could have been imagination. Neither the driveway door, not more than twenty-five feet away, nor the inside door, close to where Courtland was lying on the table next to Miss Ross, had been opened. He wondered if there *could* be any other entrance to the room. He wished he had asked the attendant.

There was a long roll of thunder, low at first, but increasing in volume until it ended with the detonation of a powder charge. The flash of lightning which followed was faint. The flash of lightning! Crane caught his breath. A door, some opening to the outside, must be open! He jerked his head around toward the driveway door. Was that a diminishing rectangle of grayer darkness? Had someone entered?

Anyway, the rectangle was gone. He wondered if he had really seen the flash of lightning. He rolled over until his chest pressed the floor. The cement was cold on his palms, on his knees, on his stocking-covered toes. He strained every nerve to keep muscles, breath, heart quiet while he listened. Thunder, like an eruption of giant firecrackers, filled the room with sound, abruptly ceased. There was a brief rustling, the sound of a blow, in the center of the chamber, near the body of Miss Ross, near the table on which Courtland was lying! He felt the hair rise on the back of his neck. His heart pounded. Somebody was moving about. The lightning flash had been real; the driveway door had been opened.

Suddenly a pale curtain-rod of light pierced the velvet blackness of the room, swept across the table above his head, paused for a cracked second at the point where his sport shoes stuck out below the sheet, and disappeared. The chamber was as black as licorice again. If he hadn't been completely alert he wouldn't have seen the light at all.

He lay so quiet he could hear the beating of his heart, the ticking of his wrist watch. Each mutter of thunder, he knew, cloaked a movement of the person in the room. He wished he were closer to the light switch, close enough to jump for it, turn on the lights and cover the intruder with Frankie French's pistol. He debated whether he ought to risk crawling around the room to the switch. He knew that if he made a noise the flashlight would catch him, make him a target for the intruder's gun.

Not more than eighteen inches from his ear, from the floor, came a sound of leather being placed on cement. It was the faintest of sounds. A second later it was repeated, twelve inches away this time. The person was standing beside his table!

Like a troop of horsemen passing a house, thunder came, faint at first; reached a noisy climax, faded away.

Crane's eyes caught the reflected glimmer of the flashlight. The beam was on his shoes again. It was extinguished after the smallest fraction of a second. There was a hasty sound of cloth being moved; the person grunted; the table shook under a violent blow. Crane reached out from under the table, seized the person's legs with both arms, gave them a jerk. The movement brought him most of the way out from the table, and the person fell heavily on top of him. The flashlight shattered on the floor. He swung his body so that he rolled on top of the person. His groping hands encountered long hair; thick, sticky fluid ran over his cheek, his neck. There was a strong odor of perfume in the hair. He fastened his knees around the squirming body below him, gave the hair a jerk. It moved in the direction of the jerk, something heavy bumping behind it. Simultaneously, a pair of hands found his throat.

What was happening was as unreasonable, as terrifying as a nightmare. He screamed: "HELP! HELP! HELP!" He tried to fight off the clutching fingers, but the long hair was tangled in his hands, and the object attached to the hair bumped hollowly against his chest. He tried to scream again, but the hands had tightened on his throat. The odor of perfume was strong in his nostrils. Specks of light, red and gold and yellow, danced before his eyes; a vein pounded in his head; his breath came in agonized gasps. He tossed his body from side to side in an effort to break the hold.

Suddenly light flooded the room. Someone shouted, "Hold on, Bill!" A second later there was the thud of a blow, and the hands slid from his throat. His lungs were grateful for air. Vision began to return to his eyes.

Chapter Twenty-three

CRANE'S HAND was still fastened to the hair. He looked down at it and almost screamed again. The hair was soft and blond, and from

177

the other end dangled the head of Miss Ross, neatly severed at the neck. From it dripped a sticky, brownish, bloodlike liquid, staining his trousers, the front of his coat. Embalming fluid!

Their eyes like overcoat buttons, Williams and Johnson watched him struggle to release his hand. Johnson's eyes, from the head, wandered up to the table under which Crane had hidden. "For the love of God!" he exclaimed.

Crane peered up at the table and saw his brown-and-white shoes on the feet of the dead woman. "I stuck those there," he explained.

"No. Not the shoes." Johnson held out his hand, pointed. "The neck."

Under Crane, between his knees, lay young Courtland, face to the light, eyes blank, unconscious. Crane got to his feet, using Courtland's chest as a support for one knee, and stared at the woman's corpse on the table. She wasn't young, after all. Her face was wrinkled, and there was a mole on her chin. A knife was stuck in her throat, its tan bone handle quivering. The blade had entered the neck just above the V formed by the breastbone, had been driven in to the hilt.

"Who's she?" demanded Williams. "What's the idea of the knife?" His mustache trembled.

Crane said, "The knife was meant for me."

"Courtland?" asked Johnson.

"Yeah." Crane looked down at Courtland's unconscious face. "My old pal, Chauncey." Courtland's face was pale, but it was composed. His hair was tousled. "He saw my shoes at one end of the table and figured my neck must be at the other."

Johnson's black eyes were as bright as a fox terrier's. "Then he's the guy?" he asked.

"Well, he tried hard enough to kill me," said Crane, lifting his foot from Courtland's chest.

"The son of a bitch," said Williams. "I wish I'd socked him harder."

Johnson said, "You slugged him hard enough. He's still out."

Crane removed his left shoe from the woman's foot, put it on. "He seems to be pretty handy with a knife," he said, eyeing the head on the cement floor.

"Why did he cut the head off?" asked Johnson. "I don't understand that."

"He wanted to prevent her being identified." Crane reached for his right shoe. "He couldn't carry the body out by himself, but he could get away with the head."

"Why did he try to kill you?" asked Williams. "I thought you and him was pals."

"So did I." Crane fastened the shoelace, straightened his back. "But I guess he figured that he couldn't get away with the head without disposing of me."

Courtland's eyes moved; he moaned softly.

"But why did he murder his sister in the first place?" asked Johnson. "If this is his sister?"

"Listen." Crane shook Courtland's shoulder. "This guy is coming to life. We'll have to do something with him, quick. I think I got this business straightened out, but I need some people to substantiate some of the things I'm going to say. Nobody has identified this body yet, for one thing. I want to get hold of the state's attorney and Captain Grady and spill the business to them." He shook Courtland again. "I'll see that you get the exclusive story then."

Reluctantly, Johnson said, "Okay, if you say so."

"I say so," said Crane. "Doc, you call the state's attorney and Captain Grady and have them come right over here. Also have Grady get you the watchman in the cemetery where we found Miss Ross. Then get Uncle Stuyvesant (if you can find out from the Blackstone where he is) or Mrs. Courtland, and that night club babe, Sue Leonard. Also the stewardess on the eight o'clock plane from New York to Chicago, Thursday night, the night Miss Ross' body was taken from this joint. Have 'em all come over here."

Before Williams left, he pulled off Courtland's belt, fastened his hands behind his back with it. "I'm not going to take any chances with that guy," he announced.

Crane looked solemnly at Courtland. "My pal . . ."

It was exactly 7:45 A.M. and the sunshine, seen through the narrow windows of the room where the inquest into the death of August Liebman had been held, was as bright as egg yolk. State's Attorney Thomas Darrow was there, as was his assistant, Burman. They and Captain Grady, and fat Coroner Hartman, stared at O'Malley as he entered the double door with Udoni and Mrs. Udoni. A breeze off the lake made it cooler.

Mrs. Udoni's face was pale. Her lips were red and her eyes had indigo shadows under them, but Crane couldn't tell whether they were made by mascara or not. He smiled at her. She looked at him in cold anger. She had on a tan camel's-hair sport coat, a brown felt hat with a turkey feather angling from the left side.

On the first of the pewlike benches sat Courtland, his right wrist linked by a steel cuff to a burly plainclothes man. His eyes were closed, his face pained, dazed.

Mrs. Udoni's blue-green eyes lingered over Courtland, then questioned Crane. "Who's this?"

As she spoke Courtland's eyes opened, stared at her blankly, closed again.

"Just a guy," said Crane.

"What'd he do?"

"Among other things, tried to kill me."

Mrs. Udoni's eyes were hard. "Too bad he didn't." She and her husband moved toward one of the windows..

Williams stuck his head in at the door. "Uncle Stuyvesant will be right over."

"Where'd you find him?" asked Crane.

"At the Blackstone. He said he'd been there all night."

Crane said, "The hell!" He moved over to O'Malley, said, "Tom, will you get something for me?" O'Malley nodded, and Crane's voice sank to a whisper. "Get me a big basin from the hospital and have it filled with hydrogen tetra-oxide. Just tell the chemist H_2O_4—he'll know what you want. Bring it right over here."

The breeze fluttered the soot-darkened curtains, set a shade to banging.

Crane leaned against the desk the deputy coroner had used at the Liebman inquest. "While we're waiting for Mr. Stuyvesant Courtland to come over and look at the woman's body," he said, "I might as well tell you some of the things I found out."

Captain Grady was scowling at Crane. "Suppose you tell me what you got on this fellow here." He turned a thumb at Courtland.

"I got plenty," said Crane. "Johnson and Williams have already told you how he cut off the woman's head and tried to kill me."

"Yeah," said the captain, "but I don't know if trying to kill you is a crime or not."

"Let him talk," said State's Attorney Darrow. "Let him talk."

Crane leaned back on the desk, crossed his legs. "To start this we should go back about six months—to the time Miss Kathryn Courtland saw Udoni in an orchestra at the Savoy-Plaza. She fell in love with him and—" he glanced through the corners of his eyes at Mrs. Udoni "—he, let us say, was temporarily infatuated with her.

"So much so, indeed, that she was able to persuade him to leave his job, start an orchestra of his own and sign a contract with the Kat Klub in Chicago. She came to Chicago with him."

Crane took the first letter from Kathryn Courtland from his pocket, handed it to the state's attorney.

"Now to switch to the Courtlands," he said after the officials had read the letter. "Naturally, Mrs. Courtland and Stuyvesant Courtland were worried when they received this letter, especially since Kathryn had been estranged from her family for two years. And when they read of the mysterious suicide in Chicago they called in Colonel Black, my boss. That was Thursday afternoon."

Crane accepted the letter from Captain Grady.

"Now back to the woman downstairs again." Crane grinned at Captain Grady. "It may surprise you to learn that she was murdered."

He explained the impossibility of using a foot-high bathroom scale for a suicide and at the same time leaving heel marks two feet high. He explained why there weren't any shoes in the room, why all the clothes were new, adding: "Udoni will tell you that the clothes he saw in the room weren't those of Miss Ross."

"Yes," Udoni said, "I see they are different. That's how I know it is murder, and that's why I am so scared."

"What's the motive for this murder?" asked Captain Grady.

"The Courtland estate," said Williams.

"I'll come to that in a minute," said Crane. "Now let's go back to Courtland. He attended a conference with Colonel Black, his mother and his uncle in New York Thursday afternoon. They decided he should go to Chicago to look at the body. He pretended to take the sleeper plane at midnight, but actually he caught the last regular plane at eight o'clock." Crane pointed a finger at Williams. "Is that stewardess here?"

Her name was Miss Gardner and she had an uptilted nose and bright brown eyes and a dimple. She weighed ninety-two pounds and she identified Courtland at once.

"He was on the eight o'clock plane Thursday, all right," she said. "I remember him particularly well."

"Why?" asked Crane.

She blushed, said, "Well, I thought he was so clean-looking."

After she had given her name and address to Burman, the assistant state's attorney, and had departed, Crane said:

"That puts Courtland in Chicago at midnight Thursday, not four o'clock Friday morning. And in that four hours he and a friend stole Miss Ross' body from the storage room downstairs. He probably hired somebody to ride on the sleeper plane so as to have an alibi. Now, I'll show you how he happened to know a left-handed, red-haired undertaker." He jerked a thumb at Williams. "Varlet, page Miss Sue Leonard."

In daylight Miss Leonard's blond beauty appeared a trifle faded. She was wearing a Nile-green evening gown with a silver lamé wrap and square-toed silver slippers. She explained, "I was just coming home when Mr. Williams telephoned, and I didn't have time to change." She glanced around the room, exclaimed, "Why, Tom Darrow! What are you doing here?"

A shade of color appeared on Mr. Darrow's cheeks. "I'm sort of a state's attorney," he said.

"Well, imagine that," said Miss Leonard.

Coroner Hartman's fat cheeks quivered. "It's a small world," he said. When the state's attorney glared at him he coughed into a handkerchief.

Crane said, "Some time ago you knew a man named Jackson at the Venice Club in New York, didn't you?"

"Yes. He was one of the assistant managers." She was looking wide-eyed at Courtland, who sat beside the detective, face to the floor.

"Was Jackson particularly friendly with any of the club's patrons?"

"Yes. With Mr. Courtland. They used to go on parties together." She looked inquiringly at Crane. "I remember they . . ."

"I think that's enough right now, Miss Leonard," Crane interrupted. "Thank you very much."

In leaving, Miss Leonard waved a gloved hand, said, "See you later, Tommy."

The coroner giggled, repeated, "It's a small world."

"Too damn small," said State's Attorney Darrow.

"To continue the story," said Crane, "Jackson and Courtland stole the body from the morgue. It would have been an easy job—Jackson, having turned undertaker, knew his way around—if they hadn't run into August Liebman. Liebman tried to stop them, and in the struggle Courtland attempted to stun him. The blow was too hard, though, and Liebman died. I think it was accidental, however. Then they took the body back to the undertaking establishment on Lake Street, and while Jackson was preparing it for burial Courtland returned to the morgue.

"He had to put in an appearance there because both his uncle and Colonel Black would wonder why he hadn't after coming all the way from New York. He didn't want to arouse their suspicion, and he wanted to keep clear of the police, so he took the name of A. N. Brown of San Diego, which he had seen on the passenger list of the sleeper plane. By using a false name he would be able to keep clear of the police, and at the same time satisfy his uncle and Colonel Black that he had done so only to protect the family name."

One of the shades was making a fluttering noise, like the jib on a sailboat, and Crane closed the window behind it.

"The only trouble with this plan was that I happened to be at the morgue when he arrived, and so I recognized him the next day.

"In the meantime, I had figured out that an undertaker must have aided in the removal of the body, that he must be red-haired and left-handed. So we started to look for him. Unfortunately, I wrote Colonel Black that I was searching for such a man, and Courtland saw the letter while I was examining a portrait of his sister in my room at the Hotel Sherman."

Crane swung himself back on the table, crossed his legs again and lit a cigarette.

"Courtland and the undertaker had already arranged to have the body buried in the Edgemoor Cemetery as an Agnes Castle, but with the killing of Liebman, the excitement over the body's theft in the newspapers, and the burial permit he had been forced to forge, I imagine the undertaker was pretty nervous. So he was killed.

"We came along six hours later and found the body. We left a note calling Captain Grady's attention to the red hair and saw the notation of Agnes Castle's burial in the record book, on the very day the body of Miss Ross was stolen from the morgue.

"Our next step was to go to the cemetery early Sunday morning and dig up the grave of Agnes Castle. However, it was empty. This didn't surprise us so much, as we had already found the attendant tied up in his lodge by the gates and knew somebody had been in the cemetery before us. Williams, invite the attendant to join us."

Angus Orr was the attendant's name, and he nodded respectfully to Captain Grady. He said he remembered Crane, remembered his loosening his bonds the night he was tied up.

"Now, Mr. Orr," said Crane, "do you see the man who struck you over the head anywhere in this room?"

Finally the finger of Mr. Orr's right hand pointed at Courtland. "That's the man. I had a good look at him before he struck me."

"You see," continued Crane when Orr had gone, "Courtland had beat us to it, had dug up the body and hidden it. He thought that would end our search, especially since his mother had received a second letter from Miss Courtland, but he didn't know how persistent we were."

Crane gave the second letter to State's Attorney Darrow and continued:

"This letter is in Miss Courtland's handwriting, all right, but the address is typewritten, a fact which caused me considerable thought."

Assistant State's Attorney Burman fingered his glasses, said, "You mean the girl actually wrote the letter, but somebody else typed the address and mailed it."

Crane smiled at him. "As for the empty grave, I finally figured out that whoever took the body wouldn't risk carrying it far. I decided that it must be hidden somewhere in the cemetery. The problem was to determine the hiding place among all the tombs."

Crane halted while O'Malley crossed the room with a large white-enameled basin and a towel, gingerly balanced the basin on the reporters' table. "There's your bath," said O'Malley.

"Thanks," said Crane. "Well, with the help of Lady Luck we found the tomb, broke open the door and found the body. We still didn't know whose body it was, and Courtland, who was with us, said it wasn't his sister's. So we brought the body to the morgue and placed it in the receiving room. We got Udoni to identify it as the Miss Ross he had known. I wanted Stuyvesant Courtland to look at it, but Courtland telephoned the Blackstone and informed me his uncle had mysteriously checked out. This was a lie, as we found out a few minutes ago.

"I thought possibly the body might be that of Mrs. Paletta, but after Mike had refused to come to the morgue and Frankie French had failed to identify it I gave up the idea, though I did have a faint feeling that French might be concealing the identity from me."

One of the homicide men showed Uncle Stuyvesant into the room. He had on an Oxford gray suit, a stiff collar with an ascot tie, a white carnation in his buttonhole. He had evidently heard from the homicide man that Courtland had been arrested. He was angry.

"On what grounds do you charge my nephew with murder?" he demanded.

"He hasn't been charged with anything yet," said Crane. "A lot depends on whether or not you can identify the body we are having brought in here."

"We're sorry to trouble you, Mr. Courtland," said the state's attorney, "but your nephew *won't* identify the body, and we must have somebody who will."

While two detectives were bringing the body upstairs Uncle Stuyvesant tried to talk to Courtland. It wasn't any good. Courtland simply stared at the floor. Mrs. Udoni was seated in such a way on a window sill that her slender legs were exposed above the knees; her face was turned toward the street outside. She had on very sheer silk stockings. Udoni was apprehensively watching the door where Miss Ross's body would appear.

Noiseless, on rubber tires, the operating table glided into the room. One of the detectives pushed, the other pulled. The man who pushed checked the table, flipped off the white sheet. The coroner's physicians had sewn Miss Ross's head onto her neck again, and there were stitch marks on her throat. Her face was still heavily, gaudily painted.

The state's attorney said, "This is the body, Mr. Courtland."

184

Uncle Stuyvesant bent over Miss Ross's face, then jerked around to the state's attorney. "Why, I've never seen this woman before."

"You mean it's not Kathryn Courtland?"

"Of course not."

Crane, still seated on the deputy coroner's table, felt the outraged eyes of everyone upon him.

The state's attorney said, "Well, Mr. Crane, that shoots your case to hell."

Sliding smoothly off the table, Crane crossed to the windows, seized Mrs. Udoni by the waist, the back of the neck. There was a heady odor of perfume about her. He pulled her over to the reporters' table, thrust her face, her head, in the basin of liquid.

"What the hell!" shouted Captain Grady.

His body blocking Udoni's attempts to reach the table, O'Malley said, "No, you don't."

Courtland was struggling with the detective he was handcuffed to, was trying to jerk his arm free.

Mrs. Udoni kicked Crane's ankles with her heels, threw her body from side to side, but he held her head in the oxide rinse.

Udoni shouted, "Let me go, you fool. Let me go."

Crane jerked the woman upright, dried her face and hair with the towel, holding her tight to him with his left arm. With the disappearance of the heavy makeup her face became younger. Her hair was blonde with black streaks of dye in it.

"Jeeze!" exclaimed Williams. "She was a blonde after all."

Uncle Stuyvesant said, "Kathryn!"

Chapter Twenty-four

"NOW YOU get the idea," said Crane. "The dead woman is Mrs. Udoni. She was murdered by her husband because she wouldn't divorce him so he could marry Miss Courtland. And in the murder he was helped by Miss Courtland." Crane was watching Courtland. "That makes her equally guilty."

Udoni, held lovingly by Williams and O'Malley, shouted wildly, "You can't prove I killed anybody."

Courtland, beside the detective, said, "My sister didn't know anything about it. Udoni did the murder by himself."

"Good," said Crane. "I'm glad you're willing to talk."

"I want to save Kathryn," said Courtland. "I don't care about myself." His face was alert now, his eyes bright.

Kathryn Courtland was sobbing in Uncle Stuyvesant's arms. Her hair left black smudges on his stiff collar.

"How do you know Udoni killed his wife?" asked Crane.

"He told me he did."

Udoni spat, "He lies." O'Malley slapped the musician's face, said, "Speak when you're spoken to, Dago."

Crane turned to Captain Grady and the state's attorney. "Courtland's the best witness the state will have." Their faces were bewildered. "I don't think you can pin anything but second degree murder on him, anyway." He looked at Courtland. "Your sister ask you for help in the first place?"

"Yes. She had been living with Udoni, was expecting to marry him. But on Wednesday night, or rather Thursday morning, when Udoni told her his wife, who had been following them, had committed suicide, it frightened her. So she telephoned me to come to Chicago. She didn't suspect it was murder; she was just upset about the death."

Crane asked, "Then you would have come to Chicago anyway, even if Colonel Black and your mother and uncle hadn't had that conference?"

"Yes. But when Kathryn told me over the telephone about the bathroom scales and the footmarks on the door I knew Udoni had murdered his wife. I knew then we had to do something desperate to keep Kathryn out of scandal. I accused Udoni privately of killing his wife, and he admitted it. He seemed to think there wasn't a chance of it being found out.

"But I knew if the body was identified as that of Mrs. Udoni, as was likely with all the newspaper publicity, Udoni would be in trouble and also Kathryn. I remembered an undertaker friend of mine and persuaded him to help me remove the body from the morgue."

Crane asked, "And you accidentally killed Liebman when he tried to stop you?"

"Yes, just as you said. And Jackson had the body buried as Agnes Castle, as you saw in the record book."

"But how did Jackson get killed? Udoni?"

"Yes." Courtland was watching his sister with somber eyes. "I read your report to Colonel Black and later told Udoni that we'd have to

186

send Jackson away to protect ourselves. He told me he'd see to it, and the next thing I heard Jackson was dead." Courtland shook his head angrily. "I should have handed Udoni over to the police, but I was too involved myself. Besides, I still wanted to protect the family. So when you told me—you remember, right after I saved you from Frankie French?—that you knew where the body was I got Udoni, and we dug up the grave and hid the body in the tomb where your persistence later found it."

Crane said, "You didn't know I was really Bulldog Crane, the never-say-die detective, did you?"

Courtland shook his head, managed a weak smile. "I can't imagine how I ever worked myself into trying to kill you."

"The hell!" Crane made a vertical, sweeping motion with the palm of his hand, as though he were polishing a window. "All the best people have tried to kill me at one time or another."

State's Attorney Darrow said, "I'm beginning to get this straightened around, all right, but I'm curious to know how you figured it out, and how you happened to be hiding in the room downstairs."

"It just seemed to work out." Crane returned to the table, sat on it. "I believed the murderer, whoever he was, would still like to get hold of the body, and I wanted to be around in case he tried. I had already sent O'Malley off after Udoni, and I told Williams and Johnson, whom I had asked to help me, I would write down some addresses where they might find Mrs. Udoni.

"While I was giving them the piece of paper Courtland announced that he was tired and was going home in a few minutes. This was for the purpose of establishing an alibi, since as soon as the others had left with my piece of paper he suggested that we try to trap the murderer by hiding in the receiving room with the corpses, each of us on a table under a sheet.

"This was exactly up my alley, so we went downstairs and hid. I got off my table, pushed it to one side and put in its place one carrying a woman's body. I put my shoes on the woman's feet, so it would look as though I were lying on the table, and climbed under the table and waited. After a time I saw the driveway door open, and I thought someone, maybe Udoni, had entered the room. I know now it was Courtland trying the door to make sure it was open for his escape. Next, using the sound of thunder to hide his movements, he cut off Mrs. Udoni's head and then came over to kill me. He knew he couldn't take the head, which would effectively prevent Mrs. Udoni ever being identified, without putting me out of the way. He flashed his light on the table, caught sight of my shoes, then jerked down the

187

sheet at the other end and thrust in his knife at the point where he thought my neck ought to be.

"I suppose, even if at the last minute he saw the woman, he couldn't stop the blow. Anyway, I grabbed his legs and pulled him to the floor, and shouted for help. It was a good thing I did shout, too, because he came within a few seconds of throttling me. Johnson and Williams arrived just in time to save me."

Mr. Darrow frowned. "I get the idea, but how did your friends happen to be on hand? I thought they were looking for Mrs. Udoni."

Crane waved a hand at Williams. "Doc, show him the envelope I wrote the addresses on."

The state's attorney looked at the envelope, then laughed. He read aloud:

"You guys pretend to scram, but stick around under cover."

Crane smiled at O'Malley, beside Udoni, and said, "I had to catch somebody red-handed, as I didn't have enough proof to convict Udoni. Now, with Courtland's testimony, Mr. Darrow, you ought to have an easy job." Crane crossed his legs, found that his left foot was asleep. "The motive, of course, was money. Udoni knew Miss Ross was Miss Courtland and wanted to marry her for her fortune. His wife was in the way, and he killed her. He seems to be a pretty cold-blooded guy.

"On the other hand, Courtland was trying to protect his sister. He killed the morgue keeper accidentally, his only crime."

"How about trying to stab you?" asked Captain Grady. "That's a crime out in Illinois."

Crane said, "It isn't a crime if there isn't any complaint. I figure Courtland and I are all square. He saved my life when Frankie French had me, then he tried to kill me. What could be fairer than that?"

Johnson asked, "Why'd French want Mrs. Paletta's body, anyway?"

"She double-crossed him." Crane lit a cigarette. "I think he was going to have his revenge, dead or alive." He blew out the match. "I wouldn't be surprised if he would have put her through a sausage grinder, or something. Anyway, she's got Mister Paletta to protect her now."

"Then you think it was Mrs. Paletta we found at the penthouse party?" asked Williams.

"Sure. Mike would have come to the morgue in half a minute if it wasn't."

State's Attorney Darrow moved nearer Crane. "One more thing. How did Udoni manage to pass off his dead wife as Miss Ross?"

188

'That was easy. Both Miss Courtland and Mrs. Udoni checked into the Princess Hotel early Wednesday morning. They had rooms next to one another. Both slept until late Wednesday afternoon, and therefore the hotel staff didn't have much of a chance to see them. Both were blondes, and both looked somewhat alike. Moreover, neither of them were ever together, so nobody had a chance to compare them. So, when Udoni killed his wife Wednesday night before going to work with his orchestra, it was an easy matter to move her into Miss Ross' (Miss Courtland's) room, string her up on the bathroom door and leave the unidentifiable Marshall Field's clothes in the room. Naturally, if you find a dead blonde in a room, you think it is the blonde who lived in that room."

Mr. Darrow nodded, asked, "But why was the body wet? Why the filled bathtub?"

"Mrs. Udoni was taking a bath when her husband called on her, murdered her. He strangled her and dragged her wet body from her room through the connecting door into Miss Courtland's room. She was still wet when he hung her on the bathroom door. Then, when he got through the job of exchanging the clothes, he found that her body had made wet marks on the door and that there were water marks where he had pulled her across the carpet. I saw those marks myself, and wondered about them. So he filled the bathtub to explain them."

Captain Grady asked, "But what was Miss Courtland doing all this time?"

Courtland had been looking at her sister. He said, "She wasn't there at all. She'd been working in the Clark-Erie so as to be near Udoni, and when they came home together that morning he told her his wife had killed herself in her room but that he had removed all the clothes so she wouldn't be involved. That's one of the things that frightened Kathryn, made her call me."

Mr. Darrow asked, "How in the devil did you work this all out, Crane?"

"Mostly by just blundering along. But when I found that our two best suspects, Courtland and Udoni, each had perfect alibis for different parts of the business—Courtland was in New York when the murder took place, and Udoni was working when the body was stolen from the morgue, and again Courtland was with his mother when Jackson, the undertaker, was murdered—I wondered if they hadn't been helping each other."

Mr. Darrow rested a hand on Crane's shoulder. "I guess that pretty well ties everything up. You did a remarkable job, even though you sailed pretty close to the law."

"Pretty close." Captain Grady snorted. "I could pinch him on a dozen counts." Strong white teeth gleamed in his turkey-red face. "But I won't." He shook Crane's hand, nearly shattered his knuckles.

Crane said, "I'm glad somebody realizes what a hell of a fine detective I am."

The others were moving out of the room. Two homicide men were half supporting, half dragging Udoni. His face was yellow; his eyes wild; he started to hiss something at Crane, but one of the homicide men jerked him away. Kathryn Courtland watched him disappear through the door with no change in her expression. Crane moved over to Uncle Stuyvesant, said, "I'm sorry to get the Courtland name involved, but I think Udoni will be the only one convicted." Uncle Stuyvesant had his arm around Kathryn's waist. He said, "To hell with the family name."

The anger was gone from Kathryn Courtland's face. "Thank you for being so good about my brother," she said, touching Crane's arm.

On the other side of Crane was young Courtland. "Yes," he said, "I owe a lot to you."

"The hell," said Crane. "I'm sorry I was so bright."

"I don't think you were so bright," said Kathryn Courtland. "You might have seen that I was a blonde the first night you met me."

"You mean—when I was in bed with you?"

"Yes."

"Oh!" Crane pretended to be shocked. "I'm a gentleman. I didn't peek."

Jaw gaping in amazement, Uncle Stuyvesant stared at Crane's departing back. Williams and O'Malley were discussing a plan involving a party with the airline stewardess and friends. Crane tenderly massaged his bruised knuckles, said, "Count me in."

"I don't know as you're clean-lookin' enough," said O'Malley.

"I can wash," said Crane.

LIBRARY OF CRIME CLASSICS®